# OUT COLD

This Large Print Book carries the
Seal of Approval of N.A.V.H.

A BRADY COYNE NOVEL

# OUT COLD

# WILLIAM G. TAPPLY

**THORNDIKE PRESS**

*An imprint of Thomson Gale, a part of The Thomson Corporation*

**THOMSON**
————✦————™
**GALE**

Detroit • New York • San Francisco • New Haven, Conn. • Waterville, Maine • London

**LIBRARY OF CONGRESS CATALOGING-IN-PUBLICATION DATA**

Tapply, William G.
  Out cold : a Brady Coyne novel / by William G.Tapply.
    p. cm.
  ISBN-13: 978-0-7862-9203-5 (alk. paper)
  ISBN-10: 0-7862-9203-2 (alk. paper)
  1. Coyne, Brady (Fictitious character) — Fiction. 2. Teenage girls — Crimes against — Fiction. 3. Boston (Mass.) — Fiction. 4. Large type books. I. Title.
PS3570.A568O98 2007
813'.54—dc22                          2006031015

Published in 2007 by arrangement with St. Martin's Press,LLC.

Printed in the United States of America on permanent paper
10 9 8 7 6 5 4 3 2 1

For Vicki
At last, my actual spouse

# ACKNOWLEDGMENTS

Writing a novel is a solitary, often lonely business, and when it's finished, the writer has nobody to blame but himself.

So blame me.

But insofar as this novel works for you, give credit to all those who, intentionally or inadvertently, helped me to make it the way it turned out. Specifically:

Fred Morris, my agent, who takes such good care of my business that I don't have to worry about it; Keith Kahla, my editor, whose astute editorial comments and suggestions on early drafts made all the difference; Vicki Stiefel, my wife, who, besides propping me up all along the way, helped me to work out this story's plot; my writing students at Clark University, whose enthusiasm and creativity continuously inspire me; my many writing friends, who help me keep it in perspective — the old pros who've been doing it for a living for a long time, the new pros who are just breaking in, and the beginners who are determined to succeed.

And, my readers all across the globe who care enough to write or e-mail me to share their feelings about my books. They remind me that writing novels is all about them.

"It's snowing still," said Eeyore gloomily.
"So it is."
"And freezing."
"Is it?"
"Yes," said Eeyore. "However," he said, brightening up a little, "we haven't had an earthquake lately."
— A. A. Milne, *The House at Pooh Corner*

The public regards lawyers with great distrust. They think lawyers are smarter than the average guy but use their intelligence deviously. Well, they're wrong; usually, they are not smarter.
— F. Lee Bailey

# ONE

The alarm jangling beside my ear failed to rouse Henry, my Brittany spaniel. He remained curled up on the bed beside me, where Evie usually slept. He was a warm body, but otherwise a poor substitute.

Evie had been gone for two days. It seemed like months already. She left on Sunday afternoon for a week-long gathering of hospital administrators at some conference center in Scottsdale, Arizona, with the word "Rancho" in its name. She wouldn't be back until next Sunday night.

She'd been promoted back in the summer. New title, big raise. Her new responsibilities included attending conferences and drinking margaritas with her counterparts from other hospitals. She called it "networking" and claimed it was a key element in her job description.

As near as I could tell, hospital administrators were obsessed with finding ways to save

11

money. Evie had a word for that, too. "Streamlining," she called it.

I told her it looked to me like they were mainly interested in finding ways to justify cutting staff and reducing services to patients.

She said that was unfair. Efficiency, she said. That's what streamlining meant. Finding ways to deliver the same services at lower cost. In fact, she said, the way she saw her job, it was all about finding ways to avoid cutting services in times of skyrocketing medical costs.

I could have gone to Arizona with her. She claimed she wanted me to. Some of her fellow hospital administrators were bringing their spouses, and so what if, technically, I was not Evie's spouse.

"Virtual spouse," we called each other. Close enough.

I told her I didn't like it out there. There was no water in Scottsdale, Arizona. A place without water has no fish, and a place with no fish is not my kind of place.

"You could get away from this horrible winter," she said, and when she put it that way, the idea was tempting. The sun hadn't shone on Boston since the arrival of the new year two weeks earlier, just day after depressing dark day of cold gray grunge, with frequent doses of rain, or sleet, or snow, or some miserable combination of all three.

"What would I do while you're busy conferring?" I said.

"Sit by the pool, drink mai tais, ogle the girls in bikinis," she said. "Play golf."

"I gave up golf and ogling many years ago," I said. "Too stressful."

"You used to ogle me."

"Still do," I said. "That's different."

"Well," she said, "you could just relax and get away from the office for a few days and be with me. We never go anywhere anymore."

I arched my eyebrows. "A conference for hospital administrators? In the middle of the desert?"

She smiled. "Point taken. Maybe this summer we can go somewhere, though, huh?"

I agreed to that and began thinking about Montana and British Columbia and Alaska and other watery, trout-filled destinations that Evie might like.

Meanwhile, though, she was out there in sunny Arizona, and I was here in wintry Boston.

I shut off the alarm, yawned, and stretched. Henry yawned and stretched, too. Then he slithered off the bed and trotted into the hallway. I considered rolling over

13

and going back to sleep. Except I had a job, a Tuesday full of obligations, and a secretary who'd make my life miserable if I was late to the office. So I slid out of bed, pulled on a T-shirt and a pair of sweatpants, and staggered into the bathroom, where I peed and splashed water on my face.

When I came out, Henry was sitting at the top of the stairs with his ears cocked and that particular expectant look on his face that meant he needed to go outside.

So he and I padded downstairs. I opened the back door, and Henry waded out into the three or four inches of last night's new white snow that had fallen on top of the two feet of old grimy snow in our walled-in backyard garden on Beacon Hill.

While Henry did his business and played in the snow out back, I switched on the electric coffeepot in the kitchen and went back upstairs. I showered, shaved, selected the day's office pinstripe, and got dressed except for the necktie and jacket.

Back downstairs, I poured a mug of coffee, made Henry's breakfast, then opened the back door to let him in. In all seasons except winter, Evie and I joined Henry in the garden with our morning coffee. We sat at the picnic table, watched the birds flock at the feeders, and sipped our coffee. We didn't say much. Neither of us was a morning person.

Henry was definitely a morning dog, however, and he liked hanging out in the garden twelve months a year, even in the dark depressing doldrums of midwinter. Usually when I opened the door he'd be standing there on the stoop with his stubby tail all awag in anticipation of breakfast.

On this Tuesday morning in January, though, he wasn't on the stoop. Henry was orange and white, mostly white, and it took me a minute to spot him in the shadows against the snow. He was near the high brick wall that separated our garden from the back alley. He had his butt up in the air, and he was growling and whining and poking at a mound of snow with his nose.

"Hey," I said. "Your food's ready. Come and get it."

I noticed that the gate — the door in the wall that opened out onto the back alley — was half open. The lock was broken, and it must have come unlatched. Last night's wind had blown it open, and the snow had come swirling in and drifted around it.

Henry was ignoring me.

"Henry," I yelled, "for crissake get in the house. Let's go. It's too cold to stand here yelling at you."

He kept whining and growling and poking his nose into the snow. This was odd. Henry was usually pretty obedient.

"If I have to put on my boots and slog out there in the snow and drag you inside," I said, "you can forget about breakfast."

The word "breakfast" got his attention. He lifted his head, turned, and looked at me.

"Come on." I clapped my hands. "Right now, dammit. I'm serious."

Henry pondered his options, then resumed growling and poking around in the snow.

And just about then the snow-covered mound in the shadow of the back wall of my garden began to assume a recognizable shape.

I muttered, "Oh, shit," pulled on my Bean boots, and plowed through the snow to where Henry was nosing around. I grabbed his collar and hauled him away. Then I pressed my nose close to his, stared him in the eyes, and said, "Get in the house. Now. I mean it."

He took a look at me and saw that I did, in fact, mean it. So he shrugged and headed for the back door.

I knelt down and brushed the snow off the mound beside the garden wall. It was, as I'd feared and suspected, a body. A human body.

I couldn't tell if he was old or young, black or white, rich or poor. I couldn't tell whether he was alive or dead. He was curled fetally on his side facing the wall with his knees pulled up to his chest and his arms hugging himself and his hands jammed into his armpits. He wore a black knit hat pulled tight over his head, a dark blue wool topcoat, sneakers, jeans.

I got one arm under his knees the other under his shoulders, hugged him against my chest, and lifted him. He was small and not very heavy. He hung limp in my arms.

When his head lolled back, I saw his face. It was a young face with smooth, unwrinkled skin. Not a man. A young woman. A teenager, I guessed. Just a kid.

Her skin was gray. Her lips were blue. Her eyes were half-lidded, and her mouth was open. I could detect no movement whatsoever in her body or around her mouth and nose that would suggest she was breathing.

I hugged her tight, stood up, and plowed back through the snow to the house. I pushed the back door open with my hip, squeezed in sideways through the doorway, and lugged the girl into the living room. I laid her on the sofa, opened up the crocheted afghan that Evie kept folded over the back, and spread it over her.

Henry was right on my heels. He sat down on the floor next to the sofa, looking at the girl.

I touched her face. It felt cold and clammy, like the skin of a freshly caught trout.

The bottom halves of her eyes under her half-closed lids looked dull.

I pressed my finger under her jawbone. I could find no pulse. No sign of life. No movement. Nothing.

I went to the kitchen for the cordless phone.

I hit 911 on my way back to the living room. When the dispatcher answered, I told her my name and where I lived and said I'd found a young woman in my backyard. I explained that when I found her, she was covered with last night's snow. She had to have been out there for several hours to get covered with snow. I couldn't find a pulse, she didn't seem to be breathing, and her skin was cold and clammy and kind of grayish, and —

"Take it easy," the dispatcher said. "Somebody will be right there."

I said I was afraid the girl was dead, but I wasn't sure.

"Cover her with a blanket."

"I did that already. Is there anything else I can do?"

"No. Just keep her warm. What's the victim's name?"

"I don't know. I never saw her before. She must've come into my backyard in the nighttime, looking for a place to curl up, get out of the cold, and —"

"Right," she said. "You sit tight, Mr. Coyne. Don't do anything. The EMTs will be right along."

Then she disconnected.

I put the phone on the coffee table and stood there, looking down at the girl. She was small, barely over five feet tall. Blond curls stuck out under the edges of her knit cap. She had a little rosebud mouth and a slightly upturned nose. I noticed that she wore a stud with a tiny green stone in the crease alongside her nose. It looked like jade.

I figured she was a runaway. Who besides a runaway would slip into somebody's backyard looking for a place to get out of the weather on a winter night?

Her arm was hanging off the sofa. I picked it up and folded it over her chest. I laid my hand on top of hers. It felt cold and still and lifeless.

I studied her motionless face. She was terribly young. Fifteen or sixteen, I guessed. Just a kid.

I wondered if she'd called for help, knocked at my door in the nighttime wanting to be let in out of the cold.

I would have heard her, wouldn't I? Surely Henry would have gone racing downstairs, barking. Wouldn't he?

Could I have saved this girl's life?

"Who are you?" I said. "What happened to you? Why aren't you home with Mommy and Daddy? Why did you come crawling into my garden?"

And then I said, "Please don't be dead."

Two EMTs came banging on my front door six or eight minutes after I called. One of them had sandy hair. The other was older, Hispanic, with a thin black mustache. They were grumbling about the ice and snow. Mt. Vernon Street hadn't been plowed yet this morning. They said they almost didn't make it up the hill. They seemed to be implying that it was my fault.

I showed them where the girl was lying on my sofa. They bent over her. The Hispanic guy took her pulse and peeled back the afghan and listened to her chest with a stethoscope. The other EMT strapped an oxygen

20

mask over her mouth and nose.

"Oxygen," I said. "She's alive?"

The Hispanic looked up at me. "You didn't tell the dispatcher she was bleeding."

"Bleeding? I didn't know . . ."

"It's dried on her pants," he said. "Coagulated. The cold does that. There was a lot of bleeding."

"Was," I said.

"It's mostly stopped."

"So is she —"

But he'd returned his attention to the girl. They were ignoring me, doing their job.

The Hispanic guy said something, and the blond EMT nodded, straightened up, and went outside. He came hustling back a minute later pushing a collapsible gurney. The two of them slid a board under the girl, strapped her on, stabilized her head, and lifted her onto the gurney. Their movements were efficient and coordinated. They made a good team. They'd done this before. They knew what they were doing. It was comforting.

They wheeled her out the front door, down the steps, and lifted her into the emergency wagon. They moved fast and efficiently, and that gave me hope. I figured, if the girl was dead, the EMTs would have no reason to hurry.

She was still wrapped in Evie's crocheted afghan. I followed behind them and watched from my front steps.

The blond EMT climbed in back with the girl. The Hispanic guy slammed the door shut and sprinted around to the driver's side. The wagon's motor had been left running. He turned on the siren, and a minute later they went skidding and slewing up unplowed Mt. Vernon Street.

I stood there on my front steps until the wagon disappeared over the crest of the hill and the siren faded in the distance. Henry had wandered out, and he sat on the steps beside me.

I kept thinking: She'd been bleeding, and I hadn't noticed. The EMT said it had "mostly" stopped. Meaning not entirely. Meaning, maybe, if I'd noticed she was bleeding when I first found her and had told the 911 dispatcher, there might have been something I could have done.

Instead, I'd assumed she was dead. She seemed lifeless. No pulse that I could detect. No movement. She'd spent a cold January night curled up in the snow in my backyard. How could she not be dead?

I hadn't thought to ask them where they were taking her. I clung to the desperate, probably irrational hope that she'd survive in spite of the fact that I'd screwed up.

I poured myself some coffee and sat at the kitchen table, warming my hands on the mug. It had all happened so fast, and it was so unexpected and shocking, that it didn't quite seem real.

What had made her bleed? Where was the blood coming from? Had she been stabbed? Or shot?

And why was she in the alley out back in the first place? What brought her into my yard? Was my garden door the only one that had blown open? Did she wander into my backyard to find shelter? Was it as simple and random as that?

Maybe somebody dumped her there.

I didn't think I'd ever forget her face. It was a sweet, young, innocent face, the face of a girl, not quite yet a woman, with her whole life still to be lived.

I wondered who she was — whose daughter and granddaughter, whose sister and niece and cousin and best friend and teammate and girlfriend. A runaway, I assumed. There were a lot of runaway teenagers in Boston. But they all had run away from somewhere.

And I couldn't stop wondering . . . if I had found her sooner, if I had noticed that she was bleeding? . . .

I pulled on my boots, went out into my yard, and went over to the place by the back wall where I'd found her. I could see the faint dimples of her footprints in the snow where she'd come in. A couple inches of snow had fallen on them. They were close together, as if she'd been walking slowly and with some difficulty.

In the hollowed-out compressed place where she'd lain, I saw the stain of old blood. There wasn't much of it, just a patch a little smaller than a tea saucer, but it was unmistakable. It was dark brown, almost black where it had seeped into the snow.

If I'd noticed this stain when I'd picked her up, and if I'd recognized it for what it was, I might have been able to save her life.

I tried to tell myself I'd done my best, but I wasn't convinced.

I took another look around the yard, but I noticed nothing that would tell me anything else about the girl. Just those faint snow-covered footprints coming in through the gate and the bloodstained place where she'd huddled for the night, dying in my backyard while I slept.

# Two

I walked to the office, as I do most days regardless of the weather. They hadn't cleaned last night's slush off the sidewalks on Mt. Vernon or Charles or Beacon or Newbury streets on this particular Tuesday in January, and a soft drizzly mixture of snow and freezing rain — one of the annoying Boston TV weather women called it "snizzle" — was sifting down on the city.

Every vibrant young woman I passed on the sidewalk — and Boston, a city of colleges and universities, is filled with vibrant young women — reminded me of the girl in my backyard and made me feel sad and guilty all over again.

Julie sits at the receptionist's desk in my office. When you walk through the doorway, Julie is right there to verify that you're not selling vacuum cleaners or magazine subscriptions. If you have an appointment with me, she'll give you a welcoming smile, suggest you have a seat, assure you that Mr. Coyne will be with you shortly, and offer to bring you coffee. All the things that friendly and efficient receptionists do.

But Julie is way more than the receptionist. She is the spell checker and grammar guardian, the appointment maker and the excuse maker, the timekeeper and the bookkeeper, the ambition and the conscience. She sends out the bills, and she pays the bills. She knows every lawyer and judge and prosecutor in Boston. She remembers their spouses' and children's and grandchildren's and golden retrievers' names.

I defer to Julie. In our office, I'm just the lawyer. She's the CEO and the CFO and the CIO of Brady L. Coyne, Attorney at Law. People sometimes call my practice a one-man business. I correct them. It's a two-person operation, and I'm the secondary person.

When I walked in at 9:45 that Tuesday morning in January, stomping snow off my boots and rubbing my hands together, Julie didn't even look up from her computer. I knew why. I was three-quarters of an hour late, and I hadn't called with an excuse. Even though, for once, I had a good explanation, I felt a pang of guilt anyway. I could have called, at least.

Julie had a talent for making me feel guilty.

I said, "Nasty out there."

She continued pecking at her keyboard.

I hung my coat on the rack beside the door, went over to the coffeepot, and poured myself a mugful.

Julie continued to ignore me.

Damned if I was going to grovel, offer excuses, and apologize. I was too upset to play that game this morning.

So I just took my coffee into my inner office and closed the door behind me.

I sat at my desk and swiveled my chair around so I could look out my big floor-to-ceiling window at the gray slush on Copley Plaza. I sipped my coffee and thought about the girl in my backyard.

Five minutes later, as I knew she would, Julie tapped on my door.

"Come on in," I called.

She pushed the door open. "You ready for a refill?" she said.

I tilted my mug up to my mouth, drained it, then held it out to her.

She came over, took the mug from my hand, frowned at me, then shrugged and left my office.

She was back a minute later with two mugs. She handed mine to me, then pulled

27

my leather client chair up to my desk and sat down. She lifted her mug to her mouth. Her eyes questioned me over the rim.

I sipped my coffee and said nothing.

After a minute she said, "You didn't tell me you were going to be late. All I ask is that you call. I was worried. I was thinking, you're all by yourself. Evie's not there to take care of you. What if something happened? I mean, what if you fell and hit your head, or had a heart attack, or —"

"I'm sorry," I said. "It just didn't occur to me. Something did happen. It was quite upsetting."

She leaned forward. "What's the matter? What happened, Brady?"

I told her about how Henry found the girl under the snow in my backyard, how the EMTs came, how she'd been bleeding. I told her I was afraid the girl was dead. I told her how it felt like my fault.

Julie listened — skeptically at first, but gradually sympathy and tenderness, and then something like fear, spread over her face. I was pretty sure I knew what she was thinking. Julie's daughter, Megan, was about ten. Before you knew it she'd be a teenager like the girl in my backyard.

"We've got to find out if she's okay," said Julie.

I nodded. "I'd like to. But I don't know her name. I don't even know where they took her."

She reached across my desk and patted my hand. "I'll take care of it." She stood up, then pointed at my coffee mug. "Need a warmup?"

"I'll get it," I said.

I followed her back to our reception area and refilled my coffee mug. When I turned to head back into my office, Julie said, "Not so fast, buster."

"Buster?"

She smiled and handed me a manila folder. I knew what it contained. My day's schedule, broken down by the half hour. A list of phone calls to make. The rough drafts of some documents, with Julie's edits and questions, to revise. The polished drafts of letters and memos to sign. Checks to endorse. Three afternoon appointments with clients.

I bowed my head. "Thank you, Miz Legree."

An hour or so later I was on the phone with Barbara Cooper, the divorce lawyer who was representing Howard Finch's estranged wife, Anna, when Julie tapped on my door, then opened it. I crooked my finger at her and pointed at my client chair.

She came in and sat down.

"She gets the black Labs," I was saying to Cooper, "and he keeps the boat. Quid pro quo. Each of them gets what they want. They've both agreed to it."

"Maybe they think they agreed," she said, "and maybe they think that means something. But you know better. My client neglected to consult with me about it. She doesn't have any idea how the numbers work. The quid isn't anywhere near equal to the quo. What's that boat worth?"

"What's a woman's love for her dogs worth?"

"Apples and oranges," she said.

I found myself smiling. "Exactly."

There was a long pause. Then she said, "We'll have to look at the numbers."

"The numbers," I said.

"Sure," Cooper said. "The numbers. It's all about numbers. You know that as well as I do."

"Remind me," I said. "There's the mother Lab and there are the two pups. Siblings. A male and a female. Right?"

"So?"

"So I see three options," I said.

"Three, huh."

"One, she gets the dogs, he gets the boat.

Which is what they both want."

"Okay," she said. "What else?"

"Two, sell the dogs and sell the boat, and neither of them gets anything they want, and they split the money."

"How it usually works," she said. "Or?"

"Or cut the boat in half and cut the three dogs into halves and divvy it all up fifty-fifty."

Barbara Cooper actually chuckled. "Why Brady Coyne. You old Solomon, you."

Julie was watching me with a bemused smile playing around her mouth. Julie knew Attorney Cooper. Cooper represented wives in divorce proceedings. She was a notoriously relentless defender of her clients' interests. Behind her back, those of us who represented the husbands shortened her name — Barbara Cooper — to "Barracuda."

Cooper and I had had many battles over the years. I respected her enormously. When I opposed her, she tended to bring out the best in me. Sometimes I even found myself liking her.

"No way he gets the boat for the dogs," she said. "I know you know better. Let's talk when you're ready to get serious."

She was right, of course. No judge would buy the boat for the black Labs.

We agreed to consult with our clients and

talk again. I hung up and arched my eyebrows at Julie.

"You still got it," she said. "That was pretty good. About cutting the dogs in half."

"Thank you," I said. "It's stupid and futile, of course. But it's kinda fun, yanking the Barracuda's chain. What's up?"

"The Suffolk County Medical Center."

"That's where they took the girl?"

She nodded.

"How is she?"

"I talked to the admissions secretary, woman by the name of Lorna. She wouldn't tell me anything or let me talk to a doctor or a nurse or anybody."

"Is she alive, at least?"

Julie shook her head. "I don't know. This secretary was quite guarded. I had to lie and dissemble just to get her to divulge that the girl was there."

"I can only imagine," I said. "I don't suppose she told you the girl's name."

Julie shook her head. "Maybe they'll tell you," she said. "You being an important lawyer and me being a mere secretary."

"You," I said, "are hardly mere. And I strongly suspect you didn't tell them you were a secretary, mere or otherwise. Who did you pretend to be?"

Julie smiled. "I guess I was the cop at the scene."

"It's illegal to impersonate a police officer," I said. "Jeez. You could get us disbarred."

"I didn't exactly impersonate anybody," she said. "It was the secretary who inferred it."

"Still . . ."

"Anyway," she said, "they can't disbar me. I'm not a lawyer."

"Well," I said, "if she wouldn't divulge any information to the cop at the scene, she surely won't divulge any information to some random lawyer."

"You're hardly random," she said, "any more than I am mere."

"True," I said. "Still . . ."

"You can always lie and dissemble," said Julie.

"Not me," I said. "Unlike you, I have my professional ethics to think about. Anyway, next to you, I am a rank novice at lying and dissembling."

"So what are you going to do?"

"I need to know how she is," I said. "I feel responsible. You should've seen her face. She was too young to be huddling in the snow on a January night. She was bleeding,

and I didn't notice it, and maybe if I had
. . ."

Julie reached across my desk and squeezed my wrist. "I'm sure she'll be all right."

I looked at her. "You are?"

"No," she said. "Of course not. That was a profoundly stupid thing to say. I have no idea whether she'll be all right or not. What do you want me to do?"

"Just hold my calls."

I called the Suffolk County Medical Center and managed to get transferred to the Emergency unit, where I was connected to the admissions desk. The woman who answered confessed that her name was Lorna. She didn't seem particularly impressed with the fact that I knew it.

I told her in my most official-sounding tone that I was a lawyer, and I needed a medical report on the young woman who'd been brought in around eight o'clock that morning from Beacon Hill.

She said that the hospital had strict privacy rules and that if I really was a lawyer I'd know that. She said that I could be the mayor himself for all she cared, and she still wasn't at liberty to tell me anything. She didn't sound the least bit regretful about it.

I tried to convince her to bend her rules,

but Julie was right. Lorna was unimpressed with my charm and utterly lacked a sense of humor.

So I called Sergeant Currier at the Joy Street Precinct, the Boston police station that covered Beacon Hill. Currier was a local cop who I'd had some dealings with even before Evie and I moved into our townhouse on Mt. Vernon Street. I figured that since my 911 call had been made from an address in his precinct, and since the emergency wagon had picked up a victim at that same address, Currier might know something about it.

He didn't.

"Saw the call logged in," he said. "Figured, some homeless person. You know how many homeless people're being brought to emergency rooms these days, all this cold crappy weather we're getting?"

"Lots of young girls being found in backyards on Mt. Vernon Street?" I said.

"How young?"

"Fifteen, sixteen maybe?"

"Runaway, probably. I hate it when that happens." He paused. "Lemme look into it, Mr. Coyne, okay? I'll get back to you."

"She was in bad shape," I said. "Maybe dead. She'd been out in the snow for a long time. Turned out she'd been bleeding, too.

They took her to the Suffolk County Medical Center."

"Right," he said. "I'll check it out."

"I really want to know if she's okay," I said. "I'm very concerned about this."

"I hear you, Mr. Coyne. Protect and serve. You'll hear from me, I promise."

# THREE

I ushered out my last client of the day a little after four that afternoon, and I was standing beside Julie's desk looking over her shoulder at a document on her computer when the door opened and a woman came stomping into our reception area. She was wearing blue jeans and calf-high leather boots. Her hip-length leather jacket was the same shade of brown as the boots. A shapeless canvas hat with the rim turned down all around shaded her face. A black ponytail hung out behind it. She was carrying a slim attaché case, but I didn't take her for a lawyer.

"It's ugly out there," she muttered. She took off her hat and slapped it against her leg.

And that's when I recognized her. Saundra Mendoza. Even in her high-heeled boots, she barely came up to my shoulder. She had a sturdy gymnast's body and big flashing black eyes and a happy, uninhibited smile. You'd never know how tough she was by looking at her.

Saundra Mendoza was a Boston homicide cop.

"I really didn't want to see you," I said to her.

She gave me a sample of that great smile. "I get that all the time," she said. "Nobody wants to see me. I hardly ever bring good news." She looked at Julie and nodded. "Hey."

Julie returned her smile.

"Is this about that girl this morning?" I said.

Mendoza nodded and jerked her head toward my office. "Can we talk?"

"Okay," I said. "Coffee?"

"Coffee would be great." She took off her coat and hung it on the coatrack.

I poured Detective Mendoza a mug of coffee, refilled my own mug, and took them into my office. She followed and closed the door behind her.

She sat on the sofa in my sitting area. I took the leather chair across from her. I put our mugs on the coffee table between us.

Mendoza leaned her attaché case against the side of the sofa, picked up her mug, cradled it in both hands, and tilted it to her mouth. She looked at me over the rim with those big chocolate eyes.

"The girl died, huh?" I said.

She nodded. "I'm sorry."

"Who is she? Did you identify her?"

She shook her head. "No ID on her. It might take a while."

I blew out a breath. "I feel terrible."

"I understand." She put her mug on the table, looked up at me, and nodded. "By the time the EMTs got her to the hospital, it was too late. We don't have an M.E.'s report yet, but there was massive internal bleeding, not to mention a seriously depressed body temperature."

"I figure if I'd realized she was bleeding when I first found her . . ."

I wanted her to tell me that there was nothing I could've done. That the girl was beyond help when I brought her into the house. That I did everything I could. That it wasn't my fault.

She shook her head. Her dark eyes were liquid and sympathetic. "I doubt there was anything you could've done, Mr. Coyne. She was out in the cold all night. She was probably dead when you found her."

"Do they know why she was bleeding?"

"The ER doc who looked at her figures it was a miscarriage," said Mendoza. "All that blood, it was leaking from her vagina."

"Jesus." I blew out a breath. "A miscarriage. Or an abortion, huh?"

She shrugged. "I don't know any more than what I just told you." She hesitated. "A miscarriage is the same thing as a spontaneous abortion, you know. They're synonyms."

I shrugged. "I was thinking of the non-spontaneous kind of abortion."

"Abortions are quite safe, Mr. Coyne."

"Not if they're performed by amateurs."

She nodded. "Good point. We'll see what the M.E. has to say about that."

"When?"

"When? . . ."

"When will we have the M.E.'s report?"

She shook her head. "It depends."

"On?"

"If there is suspicion of a homicide, or —"

"Would an amateur abortion qualify as homicide?"

She nodded. "You bet." She hesitated. "Until her body is identified, it's doubtful that the M.E. will make this a priority case."

"Since she wasn't stabbed or strangled or shot or something?"

"That's how it works."

"It was an unattended death," I said.

"Right. It is a Medical Examiner's case." She shook her head. "Just not a high-priority one. The M.E.'s office has a lot of cases. Nobody's clamoring for action on an unidentified teenager, probably a runaway, some street kid who seems to have died of natural causes."

"What if I clamored for action?" I said.

Mendoza smiled.

"Or you. You could clamor."

"I could. It's not that —"

"An illegal abortion gone bad is not natural."

"True," she said. "But we don't know that's what it was."

"She was just a kid," I said. "A pretty young girl."

"Yes," she said, "I know. Don't get me wrong. I'm with you. I intend to clamor. But you've got to understand how it works. Most likely, besides being pretty and young, this little girl was also a runaway. A stray. Probably a shoplifter or a hooker or a crack addict. All those things, maybe. She got pregnant, no place to go, nobody to take care of her, something went wrong, and she died all alone in the snow. All we can really do is check the missing-children files and look for a match."

"Run her description through your computers, huh?"

Mendoza turned to face me. She was smiling and shaking her head. "You watch way too much television, Mr. Coyne. This isn't *CSI,* you know. *Nowhere* is *CSI* that I know of. Yeah, we got some stuff on our computers. You can get stuff on your computer, too, for that matter. But here in Boston what we've mainly got is old-fashioned steel cabinets crammed with files, and more files piled on desks and tables that haven't gotten put into the cabinets yet. Manila folders with reams of photos of missing people. Babies and teenagers, mothers and fathers, Alzheimer's victims and Gulf War vets. They run away, they wander off and get lost, they get kidnapped. They might end up in California or Mexico. They might end up dead. They often end up dead, actually. Some of them just stay missing. Some of them show up after a while, surprised that anybody was worried about them, and nobody bothers to report that. And I'm not talking only about Massachusetts. We get missing-persons reports from all over the Northeast. They are so out-of-date and incomplete it's a joke. If somebody turns up alive, or if their body is found, in, say Vermont, we might never hear about it."

"It sounds hopeless," I said.

"Yeah, well, we do what we can, we really do," she said. "I want to know about this girl as much as you do. I'm just trying to be straight with you."

"So what *can* you do, then?"

"We'll circulate her picture among the precincts, see if anybody recognizes her or can match her up with a photo or a description. We'll check the FBI databases. If she ran away, or however she disappeared, if it was fairly recently, say a week or two, chances are pretty good that we'll identify her. The longer she's been gone, the worse the odds get."

I looked out my office window. A foggy kind of gray darkness had settled over the city. There were orange haloes around the lamps that lit the plaza. They reflected in the slushy puddles and glowed on the piles of dirty old snow.

When I turned back, I saw that Lt. Mendoza was frowning at me. "You're really upset about this, aren't you?" she said.

I nodded. "I am. It feels personal. My dog found her. I carried her into my living room. I couldn't tell whether she was alive or dead. I can't think of her as some statistic. The place where I found her in the snow, there was a bloodstain. I should have noticed it, figured it out."

"You did all right, Mr. Coyne. Don't blame yourself."

I shrugged.

"So have you thought about why she picked your backyard to . . ."

"To die in, you mean?"

She nodded.

"I've thought about it," I said. "I don't know. I assume it was just that my gate was open so she wandered in."

"Random, you think."

I nodded. "I guess so."

She reached down for her attaché case, set it on her lap, and opened it. She took out a plastic evidence bag and put it on the coffee table in front of me.

I bent to look at it. It contained a small sheet of square notepaper. Printed in childlike block letters on it in dim but readable pencil were the words: "77 Mt. Vernon St."

I looked up at Mendoza. "Why didn't you show this to me before?"

"I wanted to hear what you had to say first."

"You suspect me of something?"

"I suspect everybody of everything."

I frowned at her.

She smiled quickly. "Relax."

I touched the plastic bag with the scrap of paper in it. "Where'd you get this?"

"It was in the girl's pocket."

"It's my address."

"Yes."

"So she didn't just end up in my backyard randomly," I said. "It was her actual destination."

"So it would appear. It would appear that she was looking for you. She went to Mt. Vernon, climbed up your hill, found your place, number seventy-seven, walked around to your back alley, opened the gate, went into your backyard —"

"And died," I said.

Mendoza nodded. "And died. Yes."

"She didn't knock on my door or anything," I said. "I might not have heard her, but my dog would've. He would've barked at the door. I'd've heard him bark."

Mendoza gave me a soft smile. "Sure," she said.

"I don't know why she had my address," I said. "I'm positive I don't know her."

"Suppose you met her, say, four or five years ago."

"You're thinking, she was a child then, a young woman now, and she'd look a lot different."

She nodded.

"I guess it's possible," I said, "but I don't think so. Ever since this morning I've been trying to think of people I know with young teenage daughters, or people I used to know who had daughters who'd be about this girl's age now. I'll keep thinking, but . . ."

Mendoza picked up the evidence bag with the note in it, slid it back into her attaché case, and took out a manila envelope. She opened the envelope, took out a photograph, and put it on the coffee table. She turned it around and pushed it toward me with her forefinger.

It was a five-by-eight color shot of the girl. Her face and bare shoulders. Her skin was grayish. Her lips were blue. Her hair was limp and dull. Her eyes were closed. She looked absolutely still, utterly lifeless.

There was no question that she was dead.

I looked up at Saundra Mendoza. "Yes, that's her," I said. I pushed the photo back to her.

She pushed it back to me. "Keep it. Maybe it'll jog your memory."

I looked at the photo again. "She was pretty, wasn't she?"

Mendoza nodded. "Yes, she was." She glanced at her wristwatch, then pushed herself to her feet. "I've got to get going." She held out her hand. "Thanks for your time, Mr. Coyne."

I took her hand. Her grip was firm. "I

46

should thank you," I said, "for keeping me informed. I half expected never to hear anything more about it."

She smiled. "Sergeant Currier said you were pretty upset."

"I was, yes. Still am. Now you tell me she had my address in her pocket." I shook my head. "I'm more upset, now that it seems I should know her."

"Believe it or not," she said, "I understand. We cops sometimes actually care about our cases, too."

# FOUR

I walked Lt. Saundra Mendoza out to the reception area and helped her on with her coat.

She twisted her hat onto her head. "Thanks for all your help," she said.

"Will you keep me posted?"

"No promises, Mr. Coyne. You, on the other hand . . ."

"I know," I said.

"If you go poking around . . ."

"You can't expect me not to."

"I could order you not to."

"But? . . ."

She smiled and shook her head. "Never mind. Try to stay out of trouble, that's all."

After Saundra Mendoza left, I went into my office, retrieved the morgue portrait of the dead girl, took it back to our reception area, and laid it on Julie's desk. "This is her," I said. "The girl in my garden."

"She," said Julie.

"Huh?"

"This is she. Not, this is her." Julie stared down at the photo. She touched it with her fingertips and traced the outline of the girl's face. When she looked up at me, I saw that her eyes were glittery. "I'm thinking of her parents," she said.

I nodded.

"They don't even know."

"She was pregnant," I told her. "She had a miscarriage or something. Massive internal bleeding. She bled to death in my backyard."

"So what are you going to do?"

I shrugged. "I'm going to try to figure out who she is and why she ended up in my backyard. She had a piece of paper with my address on it."

Julie's head snapped up. "Really?"

I nodded. "I can't figure that out. I'm sure I don't know her." I tapped the photo. "Make some color copies of this for me, would you?"

By the time I left the office and headed home, whatever cruddy mixture of precipitation that had been falling during the day had changed over to soft fluffy snow. Already a thin layer of glistening virgin white powder covered the mounds of old plowed and shoveled snow along the sidewalks. The flakes were as big as nickels, and they drifted weightlessly in the air, in no hurry to reach the ground, and for the first time since the arrival of the new year, the city looked clean and pure and kind of pretty.

Louise was standing on the corner of Dartmouth and Boylston outside the Public Library, as she always was around five o'clock when the offices were letting out. Louise was a gray-haired African-American woman who wore a hand-lettered cardboard sign around her neck that read: "Homeless and Hungry." She held an extra-large Starbucks coffee cup in her hand, and she jiggled it rhythmically so you could hear the quarters clanking in it.

I put a five-dollar bill in her cup, as I always did.

"Bless you, Mr. Coyne," Louise said. "You're a gentleman."

"Is it ever going to stop snowing?"

"The Lord has his ways," she said. "It's not for us to question them."

"You're absolutely right." I reached into my jacket pocket and took out one of the copies of the girl's photo that Julie had made. I showed it to Louise. "Do you recognize her?"

Louise took the photo. She was wearing

red mittens. She squinted at it, then shrugged. "Nope."

"I think she's a runaway," I said.

"A street kid, you think?"

"I don't know. Maybe. She died."

She shook her head. "Lordy lord."

"I'm very anxious to know who she is."

"You want me to ask around?"

"I'd appreciate it," I said.

Louise took another look at the photo, then tucked it into a pocket inside the bulky parka she wore and resumed jiggling her cup, which was her way of suggesting that I move on so somebody else could give her some money.

There were three more homeless people working their regular spots along Boylston and Newbury Streets on my way home. Two of them — Montana John and Big Tony — were Vietnam vets. John was black and Tony was white, and both had snarly beards and empty eyes. The other was a middle-aged Hispanic woman on crutches, named Clara. I gave money to all of them whenever I saw them, and this time I also gave them a copy of the girl's photo. None of them seemed to recognize her, but they all agreed to keep the photo and ask around.

I didn't have much faith that these poor souls, sick and disturbed and preoccupied with survival, would be much help, but I didn't know what else to do. It was something, anyway.

At the end of Newbury Street I took one of the diagonal paths across the Public Garden. Then I crossed Beacon onto Charles Street and climbed halfway up Mt. Vernon to the townhouse Evie and I shared. All along the way were young girls and boys — college kids, I supposed — laughing and throwing snowballs and wrestling and hugging each other. They seemed to be bursting with innocence and energy and boundless possibilities, and seeing them alongside the homeless folks was dramatic and ironic.

I thought of the girl in my garden and was filled with sadness.

Henry was sitting inside the doorway with his head tilted and his ears cocked expectantly, trying to make me believe that he'd been sitting there all day waiting for me.

He followed me through the house to the kitchen. I turned on the floodlights and let him out into the back garden. The day's two inches of snow covered the footprints Henry and I had left in the morning, and it fuzzed over the place where the girl had been lying next to the brick wall. It looked as if nothing had happened.

I stood there in the kitchen, and through

the window over the sink I watched Henry go about his business. He gave the place where he'd found the girl a cursory snuffle, that was all. The new snow had covered the old dark blood stain, and apparently whatever scent Henry had found there in the morning was gone.

After a few minutes, he climbed up onto the back stoop and gave himself a shake.

I opened the door, let him in, made him his dinner, and then went into my home office. I checked my phone for messages and my computer for e-mails and found none of either of any importance.

I thought about calling Evie. The house felt empty without her, and I was missing her. I wanted to tell her about finding the girl, how I couldn't help feeling responsible. Guilty, even.

Evie would understand. She wouldn't tell me I was being ridiculous.

But in Arizona it was only a little after four in the afternoon. Evie would still be conferring. I'd have to wait.

I went upstairs to our bedroom and changed into a pair of blue jeans and a flannel shirt.

Evie had only been gone for two days, and already the place seemed haunted by her absence.

Back downstairs, I took out the girl's morgue photo and propped it up against my desk lamp. I looked at it for a minute, then turned to my computer and Googled "missing children." I found dozens of databases and thousands of other entries — books, articles, Web sites, blogs.

I clicked on some of the databases. In one of them I found a way to enter information on a missing child. It asked for name and date missing (I left those categories blank), state (Massachusetts), height (5'0" to 5'4"), weight (95–115 pounds), age (13–16), sex (female), race (white), hair (blond), eyes (blue). I hit "enter" and came up with . . . no hits. I found this hard to believe, and concluded that many missing children were never entered in this particular database.

I tried it again, entering "all" instead of "Massachusetts," and found photos of half a dozen girls. None looked like my girl.

Other sites showed photos of missing children. None resembled the girl I'd found in the snow.

I stuck to it for more than an hour before I quit. If I were a more dogged person, I could have plowed through all of the sites. It would've taken me all night, at least, but I could have done it.

I figured the police had more expertise

and more resources and better databases. I certainly hoped so.

It occurred to me that a lot of missing people are never officially reported missing, and many of those who are reported do not get entered into computer databases. It also occurred to me that my dead girl might not have been missing at all.

Without Evie around, I'd been opening cans and frying hot dogs and cooking frozen things in the microwave and making sandwiches and generally regressing to my bachelor eating habits.

This evening, I needed to get out of the house.

So I walked down the hill, across the Common, and along State Street to Skeeter's Infield. Back when I was renting the apartment on Lewis Wharf, before I moved into the townhouse on Beacon Hill with Evie, Skeeter's was halfway home from my office in Copley Square, and I used to stop there a couple times a week for a beer and the best cheeseburger in town. Since I moved, Skeeter's was no longer on my way home. I hadn't been there very often lately, and I missed it.

Skeeter Cronin had been a backup infielder, a spare part for seven or eight major league teams. His last team was the Red Sox, and Skeeter instantly became a kind of cult hero among Sox fans. He would do anything to win. He didn't mind turning his ass into an inside pitch to get on base. If a catcher blocked the plate, Skeeter, all 155 pounds of him, would barrel into him to knock the ball loose. He dove into the stands for foul balls and rolled into second basemen to break up double plays. His uniform was always dirty. Red Sox fans loved that.

When he finally, inevitably, blew out his knee, Skeeter bought a dumpy little bar at the end of an alley down in the financial district, fixed it up with leather booths and dark woodwork and several giant television sets, stocked it with about a hundred kinds of beer with an emphasis on New England microbrews, and created a menu offering five or six really good bar meals for reasonable prices.

He was no absentee owner. From noon to midnight seven days a week you'd generally find Skeeter himself behind the bar. His old Red Sox buddies liked to hang out there, and so did the new generation of Sox players when they were in town, and now and then they brought some of their friends from visiting teams. Celtics and Bruins and

Patriots players showed up, too, and they all mingled comfortably with the State Street crowd — the bankers and lawyers and secretaries and account executives and reporters and hookers who worked in the neighborhood.

Skeeter had one rule, which he strictly enforced: Famous athletes are people, so don't gawk at them. There were logical corollaries to the rule. Don't start arguments with the celebrities. Don't ask them for autographs. Don't sit at their booth unless you're invited. Don't offer to buy them a beer.

I hung up my coat on the rack inside the door and found an empty stool at the end of the bar. The guy on the stool beside me was fat and bald and wearing a gray suit, clearly not a celebrated Boston athlete. He nodded at me, then turned back to his conversation with the woman on the other side of him.

*SportsCenter* was playing on both TVs over the bar.

Skeeter was down the other end. When he saw me, he grinned and came over. "Hey, Mr. Coyne. Long time. You get married, you forget your friends, huh?"

"I'm not actually married, Skeets," I said. "Just, um, cohabiting."

"Same thing, ain't it?"

I nodded. "It's pretty much the same thing, I guess."

"So how's Miz Banyon?"

"She's great," I said. "Except she's in Phoenix."

Skeeter smiled. "Great for her, anyway. You ready for a brew?"

"Long Trail Double Bag, if you've got it."

"Course I got it," he said. He reached into a big cooler and came up with a brown bottle. He popped the cap, slid the ale in front of me, and gave me a frosted mug. "You gonna want something to eat?"

I ordered a cheeseburger, medium rare, with a slice of Bermuda onion and a side of home fries, and Skeeter went off to deliver my order to his cook.

I took one of the copies that Julie had made of the dead girl's photo out of my jacket pocket, put it on the bar in front of me, and looked at it.

*Who are you? Who gave you my address? Why did you pick my backyard to die in?*

"What happened to her?"

I turned. The bald guy on the barstool next to mine was frowning at the photograph.

"She died," I said.

He shook his head. "Jesus. Just a kid, isn't she?"

I nodded. "Just a kid."

"She's not? . . ."

"I don't know who she is," I said. "She was — I found her — her body — in my backyard this morning."

"Oh, man."

I nodded.

"So whaddya think?" he said. "Some runaway or something?"

I shrugged. "I guess so. I don't know."

Skeeter came over and craned his neck at the photograph. "Whaddya got there?" he said.

I turned the photo around so he could look at it.

"She looks dead," he said.

I nodded. "She is."

"Did I hear you say she's a runaway?"

I shrugged. "I don't know who she is or where she came from."

He shook his head. "What a world."

I nodded.

"What happened?"

"She bled to death," I said. "She was pregnant, had a miscarriage or something. My dog found her in my backyard this morning. I brought her inside, called 911, but she — she died."

Skeeter shook his head. His eyes brimmed with sympathy. "Hang on a minute," he said. He turned and went back to the kitchen.

A minute later he returned, steering a lanky fortyish woman by her elbow. The woman shuffled along, looking down at her feet. Under her long apron she was wearing baggy overalls, green rubber boots, and a black T-shirt. Her frizzy brownish hair was streaked with gray and cut short all around her head.

"Let's go sit," said Skeeter, and he led the woman and me over to one of the booths against the wall.

I slid in one side. Skeeter gestured for the woman to sit across from me. She frowned at him, then shrugged and sat down.

"This is Mr. Coyne," Skeeter said to her. "Mr. Coyne, meet Sunshine."

"Hello, Mr. Coyne," Sunshine said. She gave me a shy smile.

I smiled at her. "Hi."

"Sunshine lives in the shelter," Skeeter said. "I give her as much work as I can, but it ain't enough for her to get by on her own, you know? She's trying to save up to get her own apartment, get her kids back."

"Which shelter?" I said to Sunshine.

"The Shamrock," she said.

"It's off Summer Street," Skeeter said. "She's been there quite a while. Since they took her kids away from her. Close to a year now, right Sunshine?"

She looked up at Skeeter. "It will have been a year on Groundhog Day," she said. "They came at three-thirty in the afternoon."

Skeeter looked at me. "I was wondering . . ."

I nodded. "Can you give me and Sunshine a few minutes?"

He grinned. "Take your time."

Sunshine frowned at him. "I don't . . ."

"Mr. Coyne's a lawyer," he said.

She looked at me and nodded.

Skeeter ambled away.

"You don't have a lawyer?" I said to Sunshine.

"No," she said. "I don't have any money for a lawyer. I'm saving everything so I can get my kids back. So I can't —"

"Don't worry about that," I said. "Tell me about your kids."

She looked away, and a little smile appeared. It instantly took ten years off her appearance. "Franny, my daughter, she's fifteen. Bobby's twelve. No. Thirteen. He just turned thirteen." The smile faded and died. Sunshine dropped her chin onto her

61

chest and gazed down at the tabletop. "I didn't see him on his birthday. They're in foster homes. I can visit them. I mean, I have permission. Except I can't get there. Franny's in Medford and Bobby, he's with a family in Fitchburg. I haven't seen them in almost a year. How'm I supposed to get there?"

"That can be arranged," I said. "Do you want to tell me what happened?"

"Why they — why I don't have my own kids?"

I nodded.

She let out a long breath. When she looked up at me, her eyes were wet. "I'm sorry," she said. "It makes me sad."

"Of course it does."

"Artie Quinlan — that's my husband — one day he just left. He ran off with some woman. Never said good-bye. Not even to the kids. Just left. This was April three years ago. Next thing I know, my bank account's empty and they won't take my credit cards, and then I lost my job. . . ."

"Why'd you lose your job?" I said. "What happened?"

She flapped her hands. "I just couldn't do it, Mr. Coyne. I was a teacher. I couldn't go." She looked up at me. "Okay. I started drinking again. I'm supposed to say it,

62

admit it, and there it is. I started drinking and not showing up at school, so they suspended me, and then they got rid of me, and next thing happened, the bank foreclosed on my house and my kids were skipping school. . . ."

"I want to make some notes," I said. I flipped over one of Skeeter's paper menus. The back was blank. Then I slapped my pockets, but I hadn't brought a pen with me.

"Here," said Sunshine. She handed me a ballpoint pen. It had red ink. "What do you think you can do?"

"I can see about arranging visits with your kids. If you can't go to them, maybe we can bring them to you. I can check with DSS, see who the caseworker is, figure out exactly what we need to do to get you and them back together. I can track down your husband — Artie Quinlan, you said his name was — and see about getting him declared a deadbeat dad. I can check on that mortgage foreclosure, see if there's anything we can do about that." I was writing notes to myself as I talked to her. "There are other things."

"You can get me my kids back?"

"Not today or tomorrow," I said. "These things take time, and I don't want you to get your hopes up. But I can get the facts and we can decide how to proceed from there." I looked at her. "Are you still drinking?"

She smiled quickly, then dropped her eyes. "Not so much. I'm trying."

"It would be really good if you quit."

She nodded. "I know."

"How can I reach you?"

"At the Shamrock." She gave me a phone number, which I wrote down. "And here. Skeeter's. I work here most nights."

"I'll check back with you, tell you what I've learned."

"You promise?"

I nodded. "Promise," I said. "I wonder if you could do me a favor."

"You kidding?" she said. "Anything."

I took the girl's photograph out of my pocket and put it on the table in front of her. "Tell me," I said, "have you ever seen this girl?"

She picked it up and narrowed her eyes at it, then shook her head. "I don't know," she said.

"You think you might recognize her?"

"I might have seen her. I'm not sure."

"At the Shamrock?" I said.

"I don't think so," she said. "Not there.

There aren't many girls there. On the street, maybe."

"What do you remember?" I said.

She closed her eyes for a minute, then shook her head. "Nothing. I'm sorry. Maybe it will come to me."

"Maybe somebody you know might remember seeing her. Somebody at the shelter, maybe. What do you think?"

She shrugged. "I don't know."

"Sunshine," I said, "would you mind taking this photo and showing it around, see if somebody remembers this girl?"

"All right," she said.

I turned the photo over, wrote my home and office phone numbers on it with her red pen, and pushed it to her. "Those are my phone numbers. Give me a call if you learn something, would you? I'm very anxious to find this girl's family."

Sunshine looked at me. "She's dead, isn't she?"

"Yes. She died just this morning."

She slid the photo into her pants pocket. "My daughter," she said. "Franny. She's about this girl's age. I'll see what I can find out." She tried to smile again. It almost worked. "I think I better get back to the kitchen." She slid out of the booth, then held her hand to me. "Thank you, Mr.

Coyne. You give me hope. I almost forgot what it's like to be able to hope."

I watched her shamble back to the kitchen, and I've got to admit, right about then I liked being a lawyer.

A minute later Skeeter came over with my burger.

"How'd it go?" he said.

"I'm going to try to help her," I said. "I'm afraid I might've gotten her hopes up too high. She'll have to be patient. But there are things we can do. I told her she should try to quit drinking."

Skeeter nodded. "I been working on that, too. Anyway, don't get the wrong idea. Sunshine's pretty sharp. She's just very cautious, very frightened, very depressed. Life has screwed her over pretty bad. She doesn't trust many people."

"Except you," I said.

Skeeter smiled. "Right. She trusts me. I got the feeling she trusts you, now, too." He arched his eyebrows at me.

"I won't let her down," I said. "I promised her I'd do whatever I can."

# FIVE

I was in bed slogging through some whaling lore in my tattered copy of *Moby-Dick,* my customary bedtime reading, when the phone rang. I glanced at the clock. Eleven-thirty.

It had to be Evie. No one else would call me at that time of night, and besides, I hadn't talked to her all day. Evie and I talked every day when one of us was away.

I picked up the phone and said, "Hi, babe."

"Hi, honey." Evie had a low, throaty telephone voice that never failed to make me think about sex, no matter what words she happened to say. "All tucked in?"

"Me and Melville, questing for the white whale."

"Beware of white whales," she said. "They'll take you down with them."

"Why don't you junk that conference and come home," I said.

"It was eighty-seven degrees at the pool today. Not a cloud to be seen. I got in almost an hour of bikini time. How was it there?"

"Cruddy."

"I rest my case, Counselor," she said. "So how was your day, aside from the weather?"

"Could have been a lot better, actually." I told her about finding the girl under the snow, how I carried her inside, and how she was dead. "She couldn't have been much older than fifteen, sixteen," I said. "Just a child."

Evie was silent for a long minute. Then she said, "I don't think I ever want to have children."

"I understand," I said. "You never stop worrying about them." I had two grown boys. Billy, the older, lived in Idaho. He guided fly fishermen in the summer and was on the ski patrol in the winter. He was hard to track down, and sometimes weeks passed between the times we talked. Joey, a couple of years younger, was studying to become a lawyer, of all things, at Stanford. He and I talked and e-mailed regularly. That was the difference between the two of them.

I loved them equally and boundlessly.

"This girl," I said. "She had a scrap of paper with our address on it."

Evie was silent for a moment. Then she said, "As if she was looking for our house?"

"Yes."

"Meaning she was looking for you?"

"I guess so." I hesitated. "Or you."

"Me?"

"Do you know any sixteen-year-old girls?"

"I don't know," she said. "I suppose so. I see lots of people at the hospital. Maybe if I saw her picture . . ."

"When you get home I'll show it to you."

"Did it have one of our names on it? That note she had, I mean?"

"No," I said. "Just our address."

"Maybe she was looking for Walter or Ethan."

Walter and Ethan Duffy had lived in our townhouse. Evie and I bought it from Ethan after Walter, his father, died a couple of years earlier. "Good point," I said. "Maybe the girl's one of Ethan's friends. Though she looked quite a bit younger than him."

"Something to think about," she said.

"Yes," I said. "But I've got to admit, thinking about this whole thing is unpleasant. There are other things I'd rather think about."

"Like what?" said Evie softly. "Do you miss me or something?"

"Oh, yeah."

"Me, too," she said.

"A bikini, huh?"

"That little lime-green job," she said. "Wait'll you see my tan."

"It's your tan lines that I'm thinking about."

"I've got to admit," she said, "they're quite dramatic."

The next morning, Wednesday, when I woke up, sunlight was streaming in through my bedroom window and Henry was sitting in the doorway whining. The clock on the bedside table read 7:36. I'd overslept by about an hour, not unexpectedly. I'd lain awake for a long time after hanging up with Evie. I was thinking about the dead girl, picturing her face, trying to convince myself that nothing I could've done would have saved her life.

When I finally fell asleep, I had weird, depressing dreams that kept waking me up. They didn't make any sense, and the specific images and events dissipated instantly, but the vague feelings of dread and horror lingered, and I'd stared up into the darkness for a long time, reluctant to go back to sleep where I feared the dreams were waiting for me.

Now, with sunlight filling the bedroom, it

all seemed long ago and far away. I couldn't remember any of those dreams. I couldn't picture the dead girl's face. I was convinced that what happened to her was not my fault. It had nothing to do with me. I'd done everything I could for her, I really had.

It had been two weeks since the last time I'd seen the sun. Amazing, what it did for my spirit.

It was one of those crispy cloudless winter days — bitter cold and dust dry, with a sky so blue it was almost purple. When I walked to the office, the sunlight glittered and ricocheted off the fluffy new snow as if each flake was a tiny gemstone. I smiled at the people I passed on the sidewalk on Boylston Street, and some of them actually smiled back at me.

It was that kind of day.

I spent the morning meeting with clients and the afternoon talking on the telephone. Julie, as usual, had scheduled the whole day, but I did find time to talk with DSS. I found out who Sunshine's kids' caseworker was and left her a message to call me. I also talked with an ADA in the Attorney General's office about investigating Artie Quinlan and getting a warrant out on him for nonsupport. He promised to look into it.

It wasn't much, but it was progress, and I

71

felt good about it.

The next day was Thursday. I spent most of it at the district court in Concord, where I managed to accrue a day's worth of billable hours, to Julie's delight. Between no-shows and delays and continuances and recesses, I accomplished very little for any of my clients, which bothered me more than it seemed to bother them. Nobody expects much out of lawyers.

When I got back to the office, Julie reported that neither the DSS caseworker nor the ADA had gotten back to me on Sunshine's case. Bureaucracy.

I called both of them again and left messages.

One my way home that afternoon I talked with Louise outside the Public Library, and Montana John and Big Tony and Clara at their spots along Boylston and Newbury Streets. They all claimed to have shown the girl's picture around. I wasn't sure I believed them. Homeless people, I've learned, develop the ability to lie convincingly. It's a survival skill on the street.

I gave each of them five bucks, as I always did, and asked them to keep trying.

I got home from work a little after five. I let Henry out, checked my messages, changed out of my lawyer suit, let Henry back inside, fed him, and told him to guard the house.

Then, under a star-filled winter sky, I walked down the hill and across the Common to Skeeter's.

I sat at the bar between a blond portfolio manager wearing a very short skirt and a young guy with an earring who never took his eyes off the television. When Skeeter came over to take my order, I asked him if Sunshine was there.

He shrugged, said, "Nope," and shook his head. "Not tonight. You got any news for her?"

I shook my head. "Not really. I wanted to tell her that I've made some phone calls and expect to hear from her kids' social worker and a prosecutor who might be able to get some money out of her husband. I was hoping she'd be here."

"Sunshine's a troubled lady, Mr. Coyne," he said. "Life keeps beating the shit out of her, you know? Sometimes she gets ahold of some wine, or she just gets so depressed she can't do anything, and then I don't see her for a few days. I don't depend on her. When she shows up, I always have work for her. She's a good worker, when she's here. Sweeping, washing dishes, stocking the shelves, bussing the booths, like that. She says she wants to cook, says she's a good cook, and I tell her, I say, I've got to be able to rely on you, Sunshine. You gotta be able to promise you'll show up on time every day, sober and ready to get to work, I tell her. You'd think she'd say, Oh, you can rely on me. I'll be here. I promise. But she don't. She just says she'll do her best, and she gives you that look that says she knows that even her best ain't that good."

"I was hoping she'd stop drinking," I said. "It would help her cause."

Skeeter smiled. "She knows that. She just ain't there yet."

I got home a little after ten-thirty. Evie called around midnight. She told me a funny story about a hospital CFO from Cedar Rapids who Evie was quite sure had been hitting on her. The CFO was a fifty-year-old woman who actually had a great body, Evie said, and was I jealous yet?

I assured her that I was.

I read half a chapter of *Moby-Dick,* and this time Melville did his job. It was all about ambergris, and I had no trouble falling asleep.

A little before noontime the next day, Friday, I was on the phone with Howard

Finch, trying to explain to him that his forty-three-foot Viking Sport Cruiser with its twin 375-horse Volvo engines and custom mahogany woodwork was simply not an acceptable swap for three black Labrador retrievers, no matter how impeccable their AKC papers were and regardless of how much Anna, Howard's wife, loved them.

"But," Howard was saying, "she *agreed* to it."

"We'd never get it past the judge," I said. "What'd we say that boat was worth?"

"I paid a little over four hundred for it three years ago."

"Almost half a million dollars," I said. "How about the Labs?"

"Apples and oranges," said Howard. "Jeez. I mean, she agreed."

"Your wife's lawyer used the same fruit analogy," I said. "It works both ways."

"Those dogs were damn expensive," he said.

"I've explained this to you a hundred times," I said. "So stop being stupid and listen to your lawyer."

I heard his quick exhale of breath. "You calling me stupid?"

"You want to keep a half-million-dollar boat," I said, "you better think about what you're willing to give up. It should be worth about half a million. That's how it works."

*"Give up?"* His voice went up half an octave. "Are you shitting me? I'm not willing to give up anything except the fucking dogs. And if I liked the dogs, I'd expect you to get them for me, too."

"You've got to work with me here, Howard."

"The hell I do. You work for me."

"Half a mil worth of your blue chips might do it," I said. "Or here's an idea. How about the Winnipesaukee cottage?" Just then Julie knocked on my office door. "Hang on a minute, Howard." I held the receiver against my chest. "Come on in," I called to Julie.

She pushed my office door open. Julie never interrupted me when I was conferring with a client, either in person or on the phone, unless it was some kind of emergency.

She held up one finger, which meant she needed to talk to me for a minute and it was important.

I put the phone to my mouth. "Howard," I said, "I'm going to put you on hold for a minute. Don't go away. Okay?"

"You trying to tell me you want me to buy my own damn boat all over again?" he said. "And what the hell are you talking about, the Winnipesaukee cottage?"

"Sit tight," I told him. I hit the hold button, then looked at Julie and said, "What is it?"

"Detective Mendoza is here," said Julie. "She says it can't wait."

"Is it about? . . ."

She shook her head. "She didn't tell me anything. Nobody ever divulges anything to the secretary."

"I do," I said. I hit the hold button and said, "Howard? You still there?"

"Bet your ass I'm still here," he said.

"I'm going to have to get back to you."

"Make it snappy. I want to get this done."

I hung up the phone. "Okay," I said to Julie. "Send her in."

I stood up when Saundra Mendoza came into my office. She was wearing black pants and a red sweater and big silver hoops in her ears. Her black hair hung halfway down her back in a braid.

Right behind her was a skinny guy, mid-forties. He had straw-colored hair and a receding hairline. He was wearing a brown suit and a green necktie. Mendoza's partner, I guessed.

"Sergeant Hunter," she said. "Mr. Coyne."

He reached out and we shook hands.

Mendoza plopped her attaché case on my desk and sat in one of the client chairs.

Hunter sat in the one beside her.

I sat across the desk from them. "You're probably not collecting for the Police Athletic League today," I said.

Hunter frowned. He didn't know me well enough to figure out when I was joking.

I shrugged. "Have you got some news on my dead girl?"

Mendoza shook her head. "Do you know a woman named Maureen Quinlan?"

"Sunshine," I said. "Yes. She's a client. What about her?"

# SIX

Saundra Mendoza looked down at her lap and shook her head.

"Don't tell me," I said.

She shrugged. She didn't have to tell me. Mendoza was a homicide detective.

"They called her Sunshine because she never smiled," I said. "Because she was so gloomy all the time. Like calling a tall guy Shorty, you know?"

Mendoza looked up at me and nodded.

"Jesus," I muttered.

She nodded again.

Sgt. Hunter nodded also. He looked at me with his eyebrows lifted, as if he were about to speak.

I waited. Hunter shrugged and said nothing, so I said, "What happened?"

"No," said Mendoza. "I'm gonna ask the questions. Skeeter Cronin said Mrs. Quinlan talked to you a couple nights ago. Said you agreed to be her lawyer. Tell me what you talked about with her."

I told her about meeting Sunshine — Maureen Quinlan — at Skeeter's on Tuesday evening, how she'd told me her sad story, how I'd been making some phone calls for her. And I told her how Sunshine had agreed to ask around about the dead girl. "I had Julie make a bunch of three-by-five copies of that morgue shot you gave me," I said. "I gave copies to some homeless people I know, hoping maybe they could help me figure out who she was."

Saundra Mendoza had a little notebook opened on her knee. She was taking notes in it with a ballpoint pen. Sgt. Hunter just watched my face. I couldn't read his expression. Boredom, maybe.

Mendoza looked up at me. "You gave Mrs. Quinlan a photo?"

"I figured, if the girl was a runaway, maybe —"

"I get it," she said. "She didn't have any photo on her when we found her. Nor was there one in her stuff at the Shamrock."

"Maybe she lost it," I said. "Or just threw it away."

"Maybe," she said. "Still, seems like a coincidence."

"Between Sunshine and the girl in my backyard? Between me asking her to see what she could find out, giving her that photo, and . . . and what happened to her?"

"Maybe it is a coincidence," said Mendoza. "Or maybe there's a connection." She shrugged. "I don't really believe in coincidences. I believe in cause and effect. I always go on the assumption that for every effect, there's a logical cause." She looked up at me and shook her head. "But sometimes there just isn't. Sometimes things just . . . happen. Things without causes. Coincidences. They happen all the time. Especially to homeless people. Homeless people get killed all the time."

"Murdered," I said.

She shrugged.

"All the time?"

"You know what I mean. Too much. Homeless people are instant victims."

"You don't hear much about those cases," I said.

"Sometimes we can't even identify the victims," said Mendoza. "Even when we do, it's often a person without anybody who cares about them anymore. We take every single one of them seriously, believe me. Murder is murder. But when homeless people get murdered, it's generally they're killing each other, no particular motive, and nobody ever knows anything. The six o'clock

81

news, they aren't much interested in stories about homeless, nameless people. We do our best, but we're not proud of our solve rate."

"Are you going to tell me what happened to Sunshine?"

She nodded. "Last night — this morning, actually, around two a.m.— they found her — her body — her dead body — in an alley behind a Chinese restaurant down off Beach Street, few blocks from the Shamrock, where she was staying. Old Chinese guy was closing up, emptying the night's trash, saw her lying there beside the Dumpster. Her throat had been ripped open. Not what you'd call sliced. Not neat and clean like you'd get with a nice sharp razor or knife. More like somebody had taken the neck of a broken bottle and rammed in into her throat, twisted it around." She looked up at me.

I blew out a breath. "Okay," I said. "You're trying to upset me."

She shrugged. "It's upsetting. What do you want?"

"A broken bottle?" I said. "The kind of weapon some homeless person would use, you think?"

"A spur-of-the-moment weapon," said Hunter. It was the first thing he'd said. His voice was deeper and raspier than I'd expected. "A weapon of opportunity."

"Or maybe somebody trying to make it look like a spur-of-the-moment thing."

He gave a little cynical shrug.

I looked at him. "You think this was an argument or something random like that?"

"Sure, like that," Hunter said. "We seen it before. Homeless people, you know?"

"The people we talked to," said Mendoza, "said everybody knew that Mrs. Quinlan had a job and was saving her money. There wasn't any money on her when they found her body this morning. That's what we've got for a motive, such as it is. They took her money. Emptied her pockets, probably."

"They killed her for a few bucks?"

She shrugged. "They kill each other for less."

"They took the photo, too," I said.

She shrugged "Whatever. It's the usual violent bullshit that goes on among marginal people, and we're trying to get a handle on it. Who her allies and enemies and sexual partners were. Who was jealous of her, whose feelings she'd hurt, who wanted something she had. Homeless people are always on the edge of disaster. Just about all of them have serious psychological problems. They have diseases, but they don't have the medication they need. AIDS is rampant. So is hepatitis. You name it. They're extremely possessive and jealous and territorial. Paranoia is the norm. And violence. Homeless people tend to get murdered, Mr. Coyne. They'll kill each other over a pair of boots or a crust of yesterday's pizza or the last swallow in a wine jug, and they sincerely believe they're justified." Saundra Mendoza blew out a breath. "I apologize. I get wound up. Everybody would just as soon homeless people disappeared. Nobody wants to think about them, think about who's responsible for them. It's a terrible thing, a social tragedy, and I hate it."

"You don't need to apologize," I said.

She smiled without warmth. "It wasn't a sincere apology." She shrugged. "So anyway, what we've got here is most likely one of those random, senseless murders. Just some homeless person, murdered by some other homeless person."

"Except," I said, "I gave her that photo."

She nodded. "Maybe whoever killed her was reacting to the photo. Grabbed it from her. Killed her for it. It's a possibility."

Hunter nodded, too.

"Maybe not the photo per se," I said.

"Okay," said Mendoza. "Maybe the dead girl herself. What happened to her. We'll

84

have to go back now, start all over again, see if Maureen Quinlan was showing the photograph around." She looked up at me. "When was it you gave it to her?"

"Um, three days ago. Tuesday. The same day I found the girl. That evening. I had supper at Skeeter's. Sunshine worked there. Skeeter introduced me to her."

"You were doing some work for her, Skeeter said."

I nodded. "I made some phone calls, got the ball rolling. DSS, the AG's office. You know how that goes."

She smiled. "Bureaucracy. Hate it."

"So you don't have any suspects, huh?"

"Besides you, you mean?" said Hunter.

I gave him a quick smile, then looked at Mendoza.

"Nobody," she said, "will admit to having seen or heard anything." She shut her notebook, slid it into her briefcase, stood up, and reached her hand across my desk. "Thanks for your time."

I stood up and shook her hand, then shook Hunter's, too. "I'd appreciate it if —"

"If we need you," she said, "you'll hear from us. That's all I can promise."

"I'm feeling kind of responsible," I said. "First the girl, now Sunshine. . . ."

"You should," said Hunter.

Mendoza narrowed her eyes at him, then shrugged and turned to me. "Don't you worry about it," she said. "They're just homeless people. Not your problem."

"That's not how I think about it," I said.

"Yeah, I know," she said. "Me, neither. But most people do."

"I can't help feeling that what happened to Sunshine was connected to the girl in my backyard."

"The photo," she said.

I nodded.

"So you are going to worry about it."

I shrugged. "Don't see how I can help it."

"You're thinking it *is* your problem."

I nodded. "I guess I am."

"Blaming yourself," she said.

"Yes."

Saundra Mendoza peered at me for a minute. Then she reached into her pocket and took out a business card. She handed it to me. "I'd rather you just kept your nose out of it," she said. "But I don't expect you're going to do that. If you learn anything or come up with any brilliant ideas, your obligation is to let me know immediately, me being the cop and you just being some lawyer. My cell phone number's there. I'm not inviting you to call me for idle conversation, you understand."

Sgt. Hunter, standing beside her, touched her elbow, as if he was in a hurry to get going.

I tucked Saundra Mendoza's card into the corner of the blotter on my desk. "If I call you," I said, "I promise it'll be because I have something to say."

I actually tried to do what Detective Mendoza recommended. I tried not to worry about it.

I believed that I shared a collective cultural guilt for the plight of the homeless in America. But what happened specifically to the girl and to Sunshine, I told myself, weren't my problems.

It didn't work. I couldn't stop thinking about them. Even aside from the fact that she was my newest client, if Sunshine was murdered because she was showing the dead girl's picture around — because I'd asked her to — it was definitely my problem.

My fault.

It all came down to the girl. Who was she? Why did she have directions to my house? Why did she pick my backyard to die in? Why did she have to die in the first place?

And — an equally interesting question — why would somebody kill a homeless woman who had this girl's photo?

Finally at three o'clock I said the hell with it. I looked up Ethan Duffy's cell-phone number on the file on my computer and dialed it. When his voice mail came on, I said, "Ethan, it's Brady Coyne, calling around three on Friday afternoon. I'd like to buy you dinner tonight. It would be good to see you, but I admit, I do have an agenda. I need to ask you a couple questions. If you get this message and can do it, meet me at Skeeter's around six. No need to call me back. I'll be there anyway. Hope to see you."

Ethan Duffy had lived in our townhouse on Mt. Vernon Street before Evie and me. We bought it from Ethan when Walter, his father, was killed two-and-a-half years ago. Henry, our dog, came with the place.

I was thinking the dead girl might have known Ethan and Walter and come into my backyard thinking the Duffys still lived there. Worth a try.

Ethan was a junior drama major at Emerson College, doing okay, as far as I could tell, despite the murder of his father. The last I heard he was living in an apartment on Marlborough Street. When Evie and I first moved into our townhouse, Ethan used to come around now and then, mostly to visit with Henry, though we always made a point of cooking a big dinner for him. We hadn't seen him in about a year.

I was staring out my office window at the grimy January cityscape feeling gloomy and guilty when my phone buzzed.

I picked it up. It was Julie. "It's Mr. Finch," she said. "He sounds none too happy."

"That's tough," I said. I hit the blinking button on the console. "Howard," I said.

"You said you'd get right back to me."

"So I did."

"Well, you didn't."

"Believe it or not, Howard, I've got other clients."

"I don't care about them. I care about me. I care about my boat."

"Give Anna half a million in stocks or something. It's got to be equal or the judge won't buy it. Massachusetts is a community-property state. I've explained that to you."

"I'm not going to buy my boat from her. I already bought the boat from a guy named Mel. It's my fucking boat. Anna wouldn't even go out on it."

I sighed. "Give her the Winnipesaukee cottage and the dogs, then. I think her lawyer would go for that, and I think the judge would buy it."

Howard was silent for a moment. Then he said, "Whose side are you on, anyway?"

"Yours."

He blew out a breath. "I worked my ass off all those years," he said, "making money. And I made a shitload of money. And Anna, all those years, what she did was, she spent my money. I love that Winnipesaukee cottage, and I love my boat, and I love my money, and I'm getting screwed here, and you're the one who's screwing me."

"Me," I said. "Screwing you."

"Damn right. My own fucking lawyer."

"That's how you see it, huh?"

"I do," he said.

I didn't say anything for a moment. Then I said, "I know how to solve all your problems."

"Well, good," said Howard. "That's more like it. What've you got in mind?"

"Get yourself another lawyer."

"Huh?"

"Fire me."

"What? No. No fucking way. You're my lawyer. Do your job."

"My job is to advise you. I'm advising you to fire me."

He laughed quickly. "Jesus. You're being ridiculous."

"I'm not doing a good job for you," I said.

"So do a better job, for Christ sake."

"I can't. I'm doing my best."

"Well —"

"Okay," I said. "Never mind. I quit."

"Huh?"

"You won't fire me," I said, "so I'm firing you."

He hesitated. "You can't do that."

"I just did."

"I'll fucking sue your ass."

"Okay," I said. "Good luck finding a lawyer to take that case. I'll see you in court. Look forward to it. Meanwhile, when you find another divorce lawyer, have him give Julie a call and she'll ship all our files to him. Good luck, Howard."

As I put the phone down, I heard Howard Finch's voice, but I couldn't tell what he was saying.

I leaned back in my chair, laced my fingers behind my head, and smiled.

After a few minutes, I turned off my computer, went out into our reception area, and told Julie to go home and have a nice weekend.

"You're grinning like a goofball," she said. "What's up?"

"I just fired Howard Finch."

She frowned. "Can you do that?"

I shrugged. "Probably not. The hell with it. Life's too short. Howard's a pain in the ass."

"He was paying us a lot of money," said Julie, doing her job, worrying about money.

"He wasn't worth it," I said.

Julie nodded. "He'll come crawling back to you, all contrite and cooperative, right? That your strategy?"

"No," I said. "I don't have any strategy except I don't like him and don't want to work with him anymore." I shrugged. "It felt good to fire him, I know that. We'll see what happens."

We left the office together. Outside in Copley Square, Julie headed over to the parking garage, and I took my usual walking route.

I was happy to see that Louise and all my other homeless friends were still at their corners asking for money. I gave them some, as I always did. They all looked me in the eye and said they'd been showing the photo of the dead girl around but had learned nothing. I hoped they were lying. The last thing I needed was another dead homeless person on my conscience.

I told them I was all set now and asked to have the photos back. They didn't ask why, and I didn't tell them.

# SEVEN

When I got to the Common, I didn't turn onto Charles Street and climb the hill to my house like I habitually did. I continued down Boylston, crossed Tremont, and went looking for the Shamrock.

I found it on the corner of a shadowy one-way street and Summer Street, a few blocks from Chinatown. It looked like it had been a warehouse in some previous incarnation. It was narrow and deep, four stories high, with tall windows showing cheerful pink-and-yellow curtains.

A wooden sign over the front door sported a picture of a green shamrock. It read: "The Shamrock Inn for Women, Founded 1997."

I tried the door. It was locked. I rang the bell.

A minute later the door opened. A hefty fiftyish woman with long blondish-gray hair and a half-glasses perched low on her nose stood there with her eyebrows arched. She was wearing an ankle-length blue dress and a bulky orange sweater, and she had a cordless telephone in her hand. She looked me up and down for a minute, then said, "May I help you, sir?"

"I'm a friend of Maureen Quinlan," I said. "Sunshine?"

The woman blinked. "You didn't hear?"

"I heard," I said. "Do you work here? I need to talk to somebody about it."

"Are you with the police?"

"No," I said. "I'm Sunshine's lawyer."

She cocked her head and frowned at me, then put the telephone to her ear, said something into it, hesitated, then clicked it off. "I work here," she said to me. "I run the place." She held out her hand. "I'm Patricia. Patricia McAfee."

I shook her hand. "Brady Coyne."

She stepped away from the door. "Come on in, if you want."

I stepped into a big open rectangular room. In the front corner beside the doorway, some sofas and upholstered chairs were clustered in front of a big clunky console television set. The furniture was colorful but threadbare, and the TV looked like a ten-year-old model.

A dozen or so women of varying ages and ethnicities, along with three or four toddling children, were watching what sounded like an afternoon talk show. The women weren't talking with each other. They all appeared to be thoroughly immersed in the TV show, or in their own private worries.

The children were sitting on the rug on the floor. They were unnaturally still and quiet, as if they expected to be punished if they made any noise or sudden movement.

The rear of the room was apparently devoted to dining. There were eight long wooden tables with folding chairs lined up around them. I counted the chairs around one table, multiplied by eight, and estimated that they could feed sixty-four souls in this place.

One wall was lined with tables. At one end were several stacks of dishes and some plastic tubs that I guessed held silverware. At the other end was a big coffee urn. I figured they served meals buffet style.

I assumed there was a kitchen area behind the doors at the back of the room.

"This," said Patricia McAfee, sweeping her hand at the sofas and chairs, "is our common area. That, as you can see, is the dining room back there. The dormitory is upstairs." She shrugged. "Well, it is what it is, which isn't much. We provide breakfast and dinner for up to sixty-four women, and we can sleep about fifty. Weather like we've been having, some nights we squeeze in a few more than the fire regulations allow. Anyway, you said you wanted to talk. My office is over here."

I followed her across the room, and she opened a door off the dining area. "Here we are," she said. "Come on in. Have a seat."

Her office was small and crowded, cheerless and Spartan. One small square window with wire mesh over it looked out onto a side alley. The room was lit by harsh fluorescent bulbs in the ceiling. It held a metal desk, several head-high file cabinets, a couple of bookcases stacked with manila folders and three-ring binders, a table bearing a computer and a photocopier, and three or four straight-backed chairs. Everything was industrial gray. There were no pictures on the walls or on the desktop. No decorations whatsoever.

Patricia McAfee sat behind her desk. I pulled up one of the other chairs.

"Sunshine told me she'd found a lawyer to help her," she said. "That's you, huh?"

"Yes."

"Were you making any progress?"

"I made some phone calls, got the ball rolling. I only met her a few days ago. And then . . . then this happened."

"At first she was very elated," said Patricia McAfee. "That was, um, Wednesday morning. Right after she met with you, I guess."

"Yes," I said. "What do you mean, at first?"

"Next thing I know, she's depressed again. She wouldn't talk about it. I think she was just being pessimistic. She'd been yanked around so much, I guess she didn't dare get her hopes up again."

"I wasn't yanking her around. I was going to help her."

"Well," she said, "now she's dead. What a world, huh?"

I nodded. "I want to know who killed Sunshine."

"Me, too." She picked up a manila folder that had been lying on her desk. She held it in both hands and tapped the bottom of it on her desktop to square the papers that were inside. "This is her folder," she said. "I made copies of everything for the police. You can look at it if you want. Everything I know about her is in here."

I thumbed through the folder. There were three or four sheets of paper in it. I skimmed through them and found nothing I didn't already know. "Do you have any idea who might've killed her?" I said to Patricia McAfee. "And why?"

"Sorry," she said. "That information isn't in her folder, I guess."

"Do you have any thoughts?"

"Me?" she said.

"The police seem to think it was some other homeless person," I said, "wanting something she had."

"They got that idea from me," she said. "I told them that's probably what it was. That's what it usually is. Somebody wanted her hat or some worthless trinket she had. Something trivial. Something stupid. Not that I have any specific knowledge of anything. Just that our guests — well, let's say they're not exactly one great big happy family. These are not calm, peace-loving, well-integrated members of society. These people are mentally and physically ill. They are economically and intellectually deprived. They are social misfits. Their lives are in chaos. They survive one day at a time. They are depressed and defeated and desperate. Sunshine was actually in better shape than most of them, and as you know, she was pretty bad off. You want a motive for murder, you've got to understand who these people are, where they're coming from. The police wanted me to name names. I would've been happy to, but I couldn't."

"Surely they're all not like that," I said.

She shrugged. "Most of them are."

"Sunshine worked at Skeeter's," I said. "She had money. Is that what her killer wanted, do you think?"

"Sunshine didn't carry very much money with her. Most of our people knew that."

"What did she do with what she earned?"

"Actually," said Patricia, "she gave it to me. I put it in the bank for her. She had a little over five hundred dollars saved up."

"Did some of her money go to" — I waved my hand around her little office — "to your operation here?"

Patricia dismissed that idea with a flap of her hand. "Wouldn't take it if it were offered," she said. "If our guests are able to earn some money, and if they're actually trying to save some of it, we figure they're that much closer to regaining their lives. That's what we want for all of them. That's our whole purpose. It would be counterproductive for us to take their money."

"If she wanted some money? . . ."

"I gave it to her. It's her money."

"What did she do with it?"

She shrugged as if the answer was self-evident. "Booze."

"But you gave it to her anyway, even knowing how she was going to spend it?"

Patricia McAfee leaned across her desk

and looked at me. "Do you give money to homeless people, Mr. Coyne?"

I nodded. "There are four regulars between my home and my office. I always give them something."

"What do they do with your money?"

"I used to tell them I hoped they'd buy a nice hot meal or a pair of warm gloves or something like that, something I approved of, you know, and they always said, Oh, yes, sir, that's exactly what I aim to do. A pair of gloves. A bowl of soup. Yes, sir, Mr. Coyne." I smiled. "I figured they were bullshitting me, but I liked the illusion. Now that I've gotten to know them a little better, and they understand that I don't intend to judge them, sometimes they'll talk to me a little. They tell me that getting some booze is number one on their list of priorities. After that they might buy a sandwich and a cup of coffee." I shrugged. "I still give them money. I don't ask. It makes me feel good, and I think it makes them a little happier than they'd otherwise be."

Patricia was smiling at me.

"Okay," I said. "Same thing. You gave Sunshine money even though you knew she was going to buy herself some wine."

"It was her money."

"But she didn't carry it around with her."

"If I gave her any, it would only be a few dollars, and she'd spend it immediately."

"So you're saying that whoever killed her wasn't after her money."

She shook her head. "I'm not really saying that. These people readily kill each other for a few dollars, or even just in the hope they might get a few dollars. I'm only saying that most people who knew Sunshine and knew she earned some money also knew she didn't carry much of it around with her. They might've been after her change, just like they'd kill anybody for whatever they happened to have in their pockets. But anybody who might know that Sunshine worked and brought home a pay check, they'd also probably know that she turned it over to me."

"She had had a locker here, the police told me."

"Yes," she said. "The police took everything. I don't think there was much there. A few paperback books. A couple pair of socks. A spare sweater. A picture of her kids. Like that."

I nodded. "Do you know if Sunshine was showing a photo of a girl around before she died?"

"A photo?"

I took one of the dead girl's photos from

my pocket and put it on her desk.

She frowned at it, then looked up at me. "Is this girl dead? She looks dead."

"She is," I said. "She died a few days ago. This is a morgue shot."

Patricia shook her head. "I didn't see Sunshine showing any photo around. She didn't show it to me. What's going on? Who is this girl?"

I tapped the photo. "Look at it, please," I said. "Maybe you've seen her around?"

She narrowed her eyes and looked at the photo. Then she looked up at me. "No, I don't think so." She shook her head. "This is a young girl. A teenager, I'd say. We do get the occasional teen here now and then. The word on the street is that they can come here. The Shamrock is funded entirely by private donations. No government money, which means way less bureaucracy, way fewer forms to fill out, way fewer constraints and restraints on what we can and can't do. If we were government-funded, teenage runaways would never come here. The paperwork, the bureaucrats, the idea of being sent back home — it's all very threatening to them. As it is, compared to the number of them out there, relatively few teenagers come to shelters, even one as unthreatening as ours. There are predators out there who get to them first. Oh, now and then, yes, we'll get a young girl off the street. We take her in, we feed her, we give her a safe place to stay."

"Do you work with them?"

"You mean counsel them?" She nodded. "Of course. I try to find out where they're from. I try to get their permission to phone their parents or somebody. I try to get them to go to the clinic. But there's no obligation. I figure, every day they eat a good meal, every night they have a warm bed to sleep in, that's progress, whether they let me help them or not."

"You probably get pregnant girls now and then."

She smiled. "A lot of homeless women get pregnant."

"You mentioned a clinic."

"Dr. Rossi comes Saturday afternoon, and Monday and Thursday mornings."

"Comes here?"

Patricia nodded. "Noon to four every Saturday, nine to eleven on Mondays and Thursdays. She sets up in the dining room. She'll be here tomorrow."

"Can anybody go to her?"

"It's entirely free. Dr. Rossi accepts no payment, asks no questions. People want to give a fake name, they can. She doesn't

103

care. She just wants to look after these people's health. Street girls, teenage runaways, yes, she examines them, no obligation."

"What about pregnant girls?"

"What do you mean?"

"Well," I said, "would she just examine a pregnant girl, then let her go back onto the streets?"

"I'm sure she tries to counsel them," said Patricia, "but Dr. Rossi is like me. She figures something is better than nothing. Girls get the word that Dr. Rossi is cool, won't pressure them, won't ask too many questions, and so they feel that they can go to her."

"What about Sunshine," I said. "Did Dr. Rossi see her?"

"I don't keep track of who sees Dr. Rossi. That's entirely separate from what we do here. We just provide space for her clinic. I would imagine at one time or another Sunshine saw her."

"Is this the only place Dr. Rossi conducts her clinics?"

"Not hardly. She does clinics all over the city. She's got some kind of grant."

"Government money?"

She smiled. "I'm pretty sure it's a private grant. Dr. Rossi feels the same way I do about the government." Patricia McAfee glanced at her watch. "Was there anything else, Mr. Coyne?"

I touched the photo of the girl that still lay on her desk. "I'm trying to figure out who she was."

She picked it up, glanced at it again, then frowned at me. "May I ask why?"

"She died in my backyard," I said. "I feel kind of responsible."

Patricia McAfee shook her head. "Oh, dear."

"I don't like the idea of her falling through the cracks," I said.

She nodded. "Do you want me to keep this photo, show it around?"

I picked it up and put it in my pocket. "No, that's all right." I gave her one of my business cards. "If you hear anything about a young pregnant girl, fifteen or sixteen, who might've looked like this girl, though, maybe you'll give me a call?"

"Sure," she said. "Absolutely."

Back out in the open room, the number of women in the television area had about doubled. It was approaching dinnertime. I showed the photo of the girl to each of the women. None of them admitted that Sunshine had showed them the photo. None of them admitted to having seen the girl. None of them even reacted when they looked at her picture.

They just nodded and shrugged and looked at it with flat, empty eyes. I couldn't tell whether they didn't care, or if they didn't trust this lawyer in an expensive suit, or if they were hiding secrets from me, or if they just didn't have any emotion left in their souls to squander on somebody they didn't know.

Maybe they saw themselves, or their own future, in the dead girl's photo.

# EIGHT

We were less than a month past the shortest day of the year, and when I walked out the front door of the Shamrock Inn for Women, darkness had already seeped into the narrow city street. A day of what the television weatherpeople call "radiational cooling" had left the evening air so dry and cold it hurt to take a deep breath.

I took several deep breaths anyway. The cold, sharp air cleansed my lungs.

A dozen or so women were hanging around on the sidewalk outside the Shamrock. They were smoking and shifting their weight from one hip to the other and talking among themselves in low, lifeless voices. I guessed that after they'd stomped out their cigarettes, they'd all file inside for dinner.

It was close to suppertime, so I headed for Skeeter's. A block up the street from the Shamrock, I spotted three women talking to the driver of a dark panel truck that was pulled over to the curb puffing clouds of exhaust into the frigid air. As I got closer, I saw that the women were quite young. Late teens, early twenties at the oldest. They were wearing short skirts and high-heeled boots and fake-fur jackets and a lot of makeup.

Streetwalkers, no doubt. Hookers. Once upon a time everybody called the Washington Street part of Boston between Tremont and Chinatown the Combat Zone. It was sprinkled with peep shows and dirty-book stores and strip joints and nudie bars, and it was populated by prostitutes and pimps, coke dealers and crackheads, muggers and scammers and runaways.

The Zone was a good place for a suburban adventurer to get a knife in the ribs or a dose of the clap.

In recent years the pickup bars and adult-entertainment establishments had been pretty much shut down. Those who cared about such things were trying to revive the area's old name: The Ladder District. If you looked down at it from a helicopter, you'd see Tremont and Washington streets running parallel to each other and a dozen or so short narrow one-way streets linking them like . . . well, like the rungs of a ladder.

Nobody I knew actually called it the Ladder District, and a new name would never change the area's history or culture anyway. It was, and would forever be, the Combat Zone to all but the politically correct and those with a public-relations agenda. Besides, nobody was claiming that crime and vice had ceased to be a thriving enterprise in the area no matter what you called it.

I approached the women and said, "Hey, ladies. Can I talk to you for a minute?"

They turned their heads and looked at me. A blonde and two brunettes. One of the dark-haired women looked Asian. The blonde said something to the guy in the truck, and then the three of them started to walk away.

The truck pulled away from the curb and headed up the one-way street. A logo was painted on the side panel. It looked like a stylized silhouette of a couple of bears, a big one and a little one, mother and cub, maybe, with a few pine trees in the background and scrolled lettering under it that I couldn't read. The truck had New Hampshire license plates. Live Free or Die. Some contractor or plumber or car salesman — or lawyer or pediatrician or politician, for that matter — venturing south to the Big City from Portsmouth or Nashua or Manchester at the end of a long week, hoping to buy a Friday-night hookup.

"Please," I called to the women. "I just want to talk to you for a minute."

Two of them crossed the street. The third one hesitated, then turned and came back to where I was standing.

Up close, I saw that she was younger than she dressed. She didn't look much older than my dead girl.

"You wanna party, mister?" she said. She was smoking a cigarette. She had black hair and pale skin. She was wearing a red beret and a fake-ermine jacket and a narrow black skirt that stopped at mid thigh. She wore bright red lipstick and a lot of makeup around her eyes and big hoopy earrings.

"Tempting," I said. "But no thanks. I just want to ask you a couple questions."

"Fuck you, then." She turned and started to walk away.

"Please talk to me," I said. "I'll pay you."

She stopped. "Pay me for what?"

"For answers to some questions."

"What kind of questions?"

"Nothing personal," I said. "About somebody you might know. I'm just looking for some information."

She narrowed her eyes at me. "You're not a cop. Are you some kind of cop?"

I shook my head.

"You don't look like a cop."

"I'll take that as a compliment," I said.

"So what are you? Truant officer? Social worker? Reporter? Preacher?"

I smiled. "None of those things. Not even close. I'm a lawyer."

She laughed. "A horny lawyer?"

"No. Just a lawyer." I took out one of my cards and held it out to her.

She stepped closer, took the card, looked at it, then tucked it into her jacket pocket. She looked up at me. "Fifty bucks," she said. "We just talk."

"How do I know you'll tell me the truth?" I said.

She shrugged. "Why should I lie to you?"

"Why shouldn't you?"

"Because," she said, "whatever you want to ask me, I probably just don't give a shit one way or the other."

I smiled. "Let's give it a shot." I took out my wallet and gave her a twenty-dollar bill.

She took it, looked at it, and kept her hand extended. "I said fifty."

"You get the rest after we talk."

She shrugged and shoved the twenty into her jacket pocket. "Okay. What the hell. Go ahead. Ask away. I'll give you twenty dollars worth of answers."

I took out a picture of the dead girl and

held it up for her. "Do you know her?"

She squinted at the photo, then frowned at me. "What's the matter with her? She looks . . ."

"She's dead."

"Oh, shit," she mumbled. "What happened?"

"Do you recognize her?"

"I don't know. Yeah, maybe. Lemme see." She reached for the photo. I gave it to her. She frowned at it. When she looked up at me, I saw that some of the hardness had gone out of her eyes. "She was sick," she said.

"You *do* recognize her, then."

She took a drag off her cigarette, then dropped it on the sidewalk and ground it out with the toe of her boot. "I saw her just one time," she said. "She's not like a regular around here or anything. It was a few days ago. I only remember her because she was throwing up. I was gonna see if there was anything I could do, but . . ." She shrugged.

"You didn't?"

"I started to, I really did. I felt bad for her. But when she saw me, she walked away."

"Where did this happen?"

She pointed down the street in the direction the panel truck had gone. "Few blocks that way. Over on Kneeland Street, down in Chinatown. It looked like she was hurting pretty bad. She was leaning against the side of a restaurant, just gagging and puking, and when she walked, she was like all hunched over, holding her belly, kind of limping, you know?"

"Was she pregnant, did you notice?"

"You think because she was sick . . ."

I shrugged.

She shook her head. "She was wearing a long coat. I didn't notice her belly." She cocked her head and looked at me. "Funny thing, though."

"What?"

"The guy in that truck?"

"That guy you were just talking to?"

She nodded.

"What about him?"

"Just now. He was looking for a girl. That's all."

"What do you mean?"

"We're just hanging on the street, you know? Me and Zooey and Kayla? So this guy, he pulls up beside us, rolls down his window, gives us a wave, tells us to come over. We ask him if he's looking to have some fun. He looks us over and shakes his head. Not with you, he says. We go, Come on, mister. What's wrong with us? I mean,

Zooey's Asian. Most guys go ga-ga over her. But this guy, he goes, You are not what I'm seeking. Talked like that, very educated, or maybe a phony, you know what I'm saying? It sounded pretty weird, this guy in a truck trying to hook up, talking like he's some creepy college professor or something. I mean, *seeking?*"

"As if he was looking for a specific girl?"

"Well, yeah," she said. "Maybe. It kinda sounded that way."

"This girl, do you think?" I pointed at the photo she was holding.

"I don't know." She shrugged. "I didn't get the idea he was interested in some dead girl. He said he was *seeking* somebody younger than us. Blond, he said. She had to be blond. Young and blond. Some guys, they know exactly what they want. They gotta have a girl reminds them of their daughter or their niece or something." She tapped the photo she was holding. "This chick was young and blond, right?"

"How old would you say she was?" I said. "The girl you saw throwing up."

"I don't know. Fifteen or sixteen. Just a kid."

"How old are you?"

She looked sideways at me. "Nineteen."

I smiled. "Really?"

"Sure. Old enough to know better, right?"

"You'd think so," I said. "So this guy in the truck, did it seem like he was looking for some particular girl, or just any blond girl who was young? Did it seem as if he knew the girl he was looking for?"

She shook her head. "I don't know. I told you what he said. Kayla's a blonde these days, but I guess she's too old for him. She's a year older than me. You think he was looking for that girl in your picture?"

"The idea occurs to me." I hesitated. "What about that panel truck. Ever see it before?"

"I don't think I ever saw that truck before. I think I'd remember it." She narrowed her eyes. "The guy, though, he looked kind of familiar. I think he's been around before, talking to the girls, hooking up."

"But not with you."

"Not me or Zooey or Kayla, no."

"Just now, when you talked with him, did he mention his name?"

"Of course not." She smiled. "If he had, it wouldn't've been the right one anyway."

"What did he look like?"

She shrugged. "Kind of geeky looking. Not handsome, not repulsive. No beard or anything. Round glasses, the kind with wire rims. Short hair. He was wearing a necktie."

"Old? Young?"

"I don't know," she said. "About your age, I guess. I'm sorry. I didn't exactly study his face."

"That's okay," I said. "Did this guy say anything else about the girl he was looking for?"

She shook her head. "No, that was it. Kayla, she started giving him a bunch of shit, and that's when you came along. The guy rolled up his window and drove away."

"His truck," I said. "There was some writing on it. Under the logo. A company name, maybe. Did you catch it?"

She shook her head. "I didn't notice."

I pointed at the photo again. "And you never saw this girl before the other night, right?"

She shook her head.

"Which night was it?"

She frowned for a minute. "Today's Friday? It must've been Monday. Yeah. Monday night."

Monday night was when the girl came into my yard. I'd found her Tuesday morning. "About what time?"

"I don't know. Not late. Nine, maybe?"

"Did you notice where she went?"

She pointed off in the direction of Beacon Hill, where I lived. "You know," she said,

116

"you want an awful lot of answers for fifty dollars."

"Easy money," I said. "What else can you tell me about the girl?"

She shrugged. "That's all I know. I just saw her that one time, puking on the sidewalk."

I pulled out my wallet, slid out two twenties, and gave them to the girl.

She glanced at them. "We said fifty. I don't have any change."

"Don't worry about it," I said.

She shrugged and jammed the bills into her jacket pocket. Then she held up the photo. "You want me to keep this, ask around, see if anybody else saw her?"

"No," I said. "I need it."

"I'll show it to Kayla and Zooey, some other people, if you want."

"That's okay," I said. "Don't worry about it."

She shrugged and gave me the photo.

"You've got my card," I said.

"You want that back, too?"

"No," I said. "Keep it. Call me if you think of anything you forgot to tell me. Or if you hear anything about that girl. Whatever. Even if you're not sure it's relevant, just give me a call."

"You'll make it worth my while?"

"Absolutely. And if you see that truck again, try to get the license numbers and give me a call, okay?"

"Sure," she said. "Why not."

"What's your name?" I said.

"My name?"

I smiled. "Yes."

She cocked her head. "Misty. What's yours?"

"Brady," I said. "So where are you from, Misty?"

"I'm —" She shook her head. "Fuck you. You're gonna tell me to go home to Mommy and Daddy, right?"

I nodded. "Yes."

"Not if you knew my daddy, you wouldn't." She lifted her hand. "See ya." She turned and started to cross the street.

"Wait," I said.

She stopped and looked back at me.

"I'd like to talk to your two friends for a minute."

"You gonna give them money?"

"If that's what it takes."

She shrugged. "Hang on."

I watched her head to the other side of the street. She had the walk. You couldn't miss the message in that walk.

The other two girls — Kayla and Zooey — were standing there on the corner, apparently waiting for Misty. When she got to them, they lit cigarettes and huddled. I could hear them talking and giggling. They sounded like a bunch of high-school girls gossiping about some cute boy, and they kept looking at me.

After a minute, the three of them crossed the street and came over to where I was waiting. Up close, I saw that the other two girls were about the same age as Misty, who I guessed was younger than the nineteen she claimed.

"This is Kayla," said Misty, putting her hand on the blonde's arm, "and this is sexy Zooey."

I held my hand to each of them. "I'm Brady."

They both shook my hand. Kayla might have been a high-school cheerleader. She had a shy smile and blue eyes and dimples in her cheeks. Zooey, who was Asian, didn't smile. She just looked at me without expression. She wore her hair in a long braid. Her eyes looked black.

"You want to tell them what you want?" said Misty to me.

I held out the picture of my dead girl. "Does either of you recognize her?"

Kayla took it from my hand. She squinted

at it, then looked at Misty. "Isn't this the girl? . . ."

"She's the one that was sick the other night," said Misty. "He wants to know if you ever saw her before that."

Kayla shook her head and handed the photo to Zooey, who looked at it and shrugged.

I said, "Misty thought maybe that man you were just talking to in the truck was looking for this girl."

"He said he was looking for a blonde," said Kayla. "But not me. I was too old." She looked at me and laughed. "Me? Too old? Not pretty enough is more like it."

"You're wicked pretty, Kay," said Zooey. "The guy was just a perv. He wanted a child, not a woman."

"Does either of you remember seeing that man or his truck before?"

"I saw the truck once, I think," said Kayla. "Maybe in the fall?" She looked at Zooey.

Zooey shrugged. "I never saw the guy or his stupid truck before." She turned to Misty. "Look, we gotta . . ."

"Kayla," I said, "you think you might've seen it?"

"I remember noticing the cute bears on the side, that's all."

"Was it around here?"

She nodded. "It was just that once. A long time ago. I wouldn't even have remembered it if I didn't see it tonight." She spread out her hands. "That's all I got for you. We really have to get going."

"I told them you'd give them money," said Misty.

I shrugged. "I would think you'd all want to help. This girl died. If she was . . ." I waved my hand.

"If she was hooking," said Kayla. "That what you were gonna say?"

I nodded. "I guess I was." I opened my wallet. "I'll pay you." I took out two twenties.

Kayla put her hand on my arm. "Don't worry about it, Mister. We didn't do anything to earn it. Unless you want to party?"

I smiled. "No, thank you." I held a bill out to Zooey, who looked at it, then waved it away with the back of her hand.

"If you think of anything else," I said, "I'd appreciate it if you called me. Misty has my card. I'll pay you for anything useful, I promise."

They smiled and nodded and waved goodbye, then linked arms and strolled across the street. When they got to the other side, they stopped and lit cigarettes. They looked back to where I was standing, and all three of them waved again. Then they started down the sidewalk, heading in the direction of Chinatown, three pretty girls who could have been on the high-school swim team, heading off to work.

# NINE

I walked into Skeeter's at five minutes of six. I hung my coat on a hook beside the door and looked around. The bar was two-deep with men and women in business attire. I looked them over and failed to spot a college-aged kid with long purple hair and multiple face piercings.

Ethan Duffy might've cut his hair and let it grow natural since the last time I'd seen him. I'd recognize him anyway.

Skeeter was hustling around behind the bar. I tried to catch his eye, but he shouldered his way through the swinging door and lugged a rack of glasses into the kitchen.

Busy Friday night, understaffed. I'd catch up with Skeeter later, when things quieted down.

The bar was mobbed, but only a couple of the booths were occupied. Ethan Duffy wasn't sitting in a booth, either.

I slid into an empty booth where I could

keep an eye on the door. I realized the odds were good that Ethan hadn't gotten my message, or that he had something else going on and wouldn't be able to meet me. I hadn't left him a number to call, and I hadn't asked him to return my call.

He'd be here or not. Either way, I'd have a beer and a burger and some coffee, talk to Skeeter, and then go home.

Tonight Mary-Kate was the waitress. Mary-Kate O'Leary was a bulky fortyish divorcée from Southie with a deadbeat husband somewhere in Canada and three teenagers at home. She came over to my booth, swiped at it with her rag, then pulled her notebook from her apron pocket, plucked her pencil from behind her ear, and said, "So what do you want, Mr. Coyne? You gonna have something to eat tonight, or you planning to wear me out bringing you beers, leave a crappy tip?"

I smiled. "Cheeseburger, fries, bottle of Hibernator. Big tip. How're the kids?"

"Nothing but trouble. Better off in jail. Medium-rare on the burger?"

"Please. And extra Bermuda onion."

"Salad or something?"

I shook my head. "Did anybody come in earlier looking for me?"

"Some broad, you mean?"

I shook my head. "No. Young guy, early twenties."

"Nope." She shoved her pad into her apron pocket and stuck her pencil behind her ear. "You hear about Sunshine?"

I nodded.

"Skeeter's pretty shook up," she said.

"So am I," I said.

Mary-Kate shrugged, as if she wasn't particularly shook up and didn't really understand it, and wandered away.

She came back a minute later with my bottle of Hibernator and a chilled mug.

I was halfway through the ale when Ethan came in. I didn't recognize him at first. Not only was his hair no longer purple, but the ponytail was gone and so was the eyebrow stud. He looked more like a young attorney or stockbroker than a college kid majoring in the performing arts.

I waved at him.

He looked my way, waved and smiled, came over, and slid in across from me.

We shook hands across the table.

"You're looking good," I said.

He smiled and touched his head. "The hair, you mean?"

"Nope. The purple was fine by me. Just, in general. You look healthy and happy. Are you?"

"Yes. Both of those things. I'm doing fine. How 'bout you? How's Evie?"

"Evie's in Scottsdale conferring with hospital administrators and sitting around the pool in her bikini. She tells me she's excellent, and why shouldn't she be, soaking up the Arizona sunshine by the pool?"

"You miss her," said Ethan.

"Sure I do. She'll be home Sunday." I waved the subject of absentee girlfriends away with the back of my hand. "Listen. Thanks for coming. I need to talk to you about something. You get a burger and a beer out of it."

"No need for that," he said. "You saved my life, remember?"

I shrugged. I remembered, all right. It was hard to forget. It happened a couple of years earlier. Ethan had disappeared, and when I finally tracked him down, I found him doused with gasoline, semi-conscious, and imprisoned in a steel storage shed that was about to explode. I managed to get him out with seconds to spare. We both survived by a whisker.

On the basis of that, he kept insisting that I'd saved his life.

The thing that Ethan kept ignoring was the fact that if it hadn't been for me, he wouldn't have been locked in that shed in the first place.

I waved at Mary-Kate, and she came over. Ethan asked for the Ceasar salad, garlic bread, and a Coke. I kept forgetting he was a vegetarian and still too young to drink alcohol legally.

Mary-Kate called him Honey.

When she left, Ethan turned to me. "So what's up, Brady? What did you want to talk about?"

I took out the picture of the dead girl and put it on the table in front of him. "Do you know her?"

He frowned. "This a morgue photo?"

"That's exactly what it is."

"She looks young." He squinted at the photo, then looked up at me. "I'm pretty sure I've never seen her before."

I shrugged. "I just thought —"

"I'm gay, remember?"

"Sure." I smiled. "I didn't necessarily think you had a relationship with her. Just that you might know her. You do know girls, right?"

He smiled. "Some of my best friends are girls. So what's the story? Who is she?"

"She showed up at the house the other night. I don't know why. I never saw her before. But she had a scrap of paper with my address on it. It occurred to me that

127

maybe it was you she was looking for. You or your father. Maybe she knew you from when you were living there."

I told Ethan about finding the girl's body in the backyard.

I didn't tell him about what had happened to Sunshine.

Ethan was shaking his head. When I finished telling him about it, he said, "That's a terrible story. I wish I could help. I mean, if she was looking for me, thinking I still lived there on Mt. Vernon Street, it would've been over two years ago that I knew her. How old is she? I should say, how old was she when she died?"

"Fifteen or sixteen, I'd guess."

"So if I knew her from when I lived there," Ethan said, "she would've been thirteen or fourteen at the most." He shook his head. "I don't think I knew any girls that age then."

"My other thought," I said, "was Walter."

"I suppose she could've been looking for my father," he said, "though I can't imagine why. But even if she was . . . ."

Walter was dead. He couldn't help. That's what Ethan was thinking.

"She had your address written down, you said?" said Ethan.

I nodded.

"If she knew where you lived — or where my dad and I lived — she wouldn't need to write it down, right?"

"Good point," I said. "But maybe she knew one of us from someplace else, had never been to the house, so had to look up the address."

"You're right," he said. "Listen, I'm sorry, man. That's a huge bummer. Wish I could help you. You still gonna pay for my supper?"

"I can't talk you into some good red meat?"

"Couldn't get it past my lips."

"I don't know how you do it," I said. "No steak? No burgers? No lamb chops?"

"You develop a taste for tofu," he said.

Ethan and I had finished eating. He was telling me how he'd switched majors from drama to communications, and we were sipping coffee and talking about Internet advertising when Skeeter came over to our booth. He wasn't smiling, which was unusual for Skeeter.

He gripped the edge of our booth with both hands, put his face close to mine, fixed me with his spit-colored eyes, and said, "You heard about Sunshine, right?"

I nodded.

"I blame you," he said.

"I do, too."

"I mean," he said, as if I hadn't spoken, "you come in here, you tell her you're going to help her, and then you give her this picture, ask her to show it around, and I can tell you, Mr. Coyne, she was hell-bent on doing it. She felt like she owed you something. For helping her. The rest of the night, she kept taking that picture out of her pocket and looking at it and mumbling about it." He narrowed his eyes at me. "After she left that night, I never saw her again. She ends up in an alley behind a Dumpster with her throat ripped open. So you tell me."

"I agree with you," I said. "I think what happened to Sunshine had something to do with that girl in the photo. I think if I hadn't involved her, given her that photo, asked her to show it around . . . if I hadn't come in here that night, Sunshine wouldn't have gotten killed. I feel awful about it. I blame myself."

Skeeter was staring at me. "You saying you agree with me?"

"Yes. It's pretty obvious. She died because of me."

He touched Ethan's shoulder. "Shove in, kid."

Ethan slid over in the booth, and Skeeter folded himself onto the bench beside him, put his forearms on the table, and leaned toward me. "Listen, Mr. Coyne," he said. "I'm pretty upset about this, you know? I mean, I really liked Sunshine. She was making a lot of progress, getting her shit back together. She was a good kid. She had plenty of problems, but she had a lot going for her, too. Best thing that ever happened to her, you taking on her case. That could've turned her whole life around, you know? So it pisses me off. Her getting murdered, I mean. But I guess it probably ain't fair, blaming you for what happened. You didn't kill her. You were trying to help her."

"No," I said. "It's fair."

Skeeter waved his hand in the air. "It ain't your fault, Mr. Coyne. I was outa line. Anyways, I was the one who brought her out to talk to you. As much my fault as yours."

"Blaming ourselves doesn't do any good," I said.

"That good-looking police officer," he said, "whats-her-name, Mendoza, the detective, she came by this morning, talked to me about Sunshine. She seems pretty sharp."

"Detective Mendoza is extremely sharp," I said.

"So what about you, Mr. Coyne? I figured
. . ."

"I feel sad and guilty about Sunshine," I
said, "but Detective Mendoza is working on
her case. It's the girl who died in my
backyard that I'm trying to focus on. Nobody's working on her case. The police will
do their best to find whoever killed Sunshine, but I don't think anybody's trying
very hard to figure out what happened to
the girl. I want to know who she was and
why she came into my backyard to die."

"They gotta be connected," said Skeeter.
"Sunshine and the girl."

"So it seems," I said. "Sunshine, showing
the girl's picture around and then getting
murdered. Seems like more than a coincidence to me."

"Whoever killed Sunshine did it because
of the girl? Is that what you think?"

"I do," I said. "But what the hell do I
know?"

# Ten

I woke up all of a sudden. Henry was curled against my hip, and flickering colored lights were dancing on the bedroom ceiling. I hitched myself into a semisitting position and looked down at the television set at the foot of the bed. A red-and-blue racing car was skidding across the track. It caromed off the wall and went spinning back toward the infield, spewing smoke and gravel. Other cars swerved and skidded around it. One of them smashed into another car's rear end, flipped, and went tumbling end-over-end down the track.

It all happened in eerie silence. Somewhere along the way I'd muted the TV.

Then the phone rang, and my mind registered the memory that it had also rung a moment earlier.

I groped for the phone beside the bed, pressed it against my ear, and mumbled, "H'lo?"

"I'm sorry," said Evie. "I woke you up."

"No you didn't."

"Yes I did. Why lie about it? Nothing to be ashamed of, being asleep at . . . what is it there? A little after midnight? Oh, hell. No. It's like one-thirty in the morning, right?"

"I don't know," I said. "It doesn't matter. I was watching car racing on ESPN."

"You were sleeping," she said. "You never watch car racing."

"It's *SportsCenter.* All kinds of news. There was this awesome accident."

"Sports scores are not news," she said.

"You usually call earlier."

"I always call, though, don't I?"

"I meant to stay awake for your call," I said.

"Long day?"

"Friday, you know?"

"I just got back to my room," said Evie. "It's not even midnight here."

"Out drinking," I said.

"Sure. With some underwriters from Salt Lake City. Mormons."

"Men," I said.

"There's no such thing as a female Mormon underwriter," she said. "We talked about insurance. They drank Diet Dr Pepper. Not me. I had Margaritas. Yum-yum."

"You're a little drunk," I said.

"A little. Makes me horny. I love you."

"I love you, too."

"I'll be home day after tomorrow. No, wait. Tomorrow, where you are. I'll be home tomorrow. It's Saturday already in Massachusetts, right?"

"You're pretty blasted, huh?"

"Kinda. See, it's still Friday in Arizona. So I'll see you, like I said. Day after tomorrow."

"Right," I said. "Sunday afternoon. Fourfifty. American West number eight-twenty. Nonstop, Phoenix to Boston. Expensive."

"The hospital's paying," she said.

"I'll pick you up at the airport."

"That would be dumb," she said. "I'll get a cab. Just be there when I get home, please. You and Henry."

"Dumb?"

"Sweet," she said. "But dumb."

After I hung up with Evie, I lay there for quite a while watching the muted television. I pictured Evie, sitting in some bar surrounded by men in white shirts and black suits and dark blue neckties, Evie laughing and drinking Margaritas, the men shorthaired and smooth-faced, not smiling, sipping Diet Dr Pepper, watching her out of hooded eyes.

She'd been gone for nearly a week. I'd

almost gotten used to living alone again.

Henry was pressing hard against my hip. He grumbled and twitched when he slept. I reached down and scratched his forehead. I didn't think I could get used to living without a dog.

I spent Saturday morning tidying up our house. We have a cleaning lady who comes in every other week. Her name is Sammie. She takes the T over from Dorchester on alternate Tuesdays. She has her own key. Usually Evie and I are at work when she comes. We leave her a check for eighty dollars, made out to cash, on the kitchen counter. When we get home, the check is gone. That's how we know she's been there.

Sammie vacuums the rugs and washes the floors and cleans the toilets, and she seems to do a decent job of it, although neither Evie nor I is the sort of person who notices a little dust or grime — or its absence. When Sammie unplugs something so she can plug in her vacuum cleaner, she never remembers to plug it back in when she's done. So when we go to turn on a light or toast a bagel, it doesn't work. That's another way we know for sure that Sammie's been there.

We told her when we hired her that we didn't want her moving anything, organizing anything, putting anything away, or throwing anything out. Evie, for example, hoards catalogs. I save old fly-fishing magazines. Any sensible cleaning lady would throw away last year's Crate and Barrel catalog or some 1998 issue of *American Angler.* We didn't trust Sammie's judgment. We were worried that she'd be sensible.

On the day Sammie's due to appear, Evie suddenly becomes a whirlwind of house-cleaning energy. Gotta get the place tidied up. Can't have the cleaning lady go back to Dorchester and tell her friends that the white folks in the Beacon Hill townhouse are messy and sloppy and tolerant of filth, even though, basically, we are.

That, I keep telling Evie, is why we need a cleaning lady.

I wasn't cleaning up for Sammie on this Saturday. It was for Evie. She'd be home tomorrow, and I'd been living like a bachelor. So I collected six days of newspapers from the coffee table and the bathroom and the floor beside the bed and piled them in their special box in the storage room behind the kitchen. I loaded the dishwasher with coffee mugs and frying pans and cereal bowls. I changed the sheets on the bed and the towels in the bathroom. I ran a load of laundry.

While I was getting the house ready for Evie's return, my mind kept swirling with thoughts about the dead girl in my backyard, bled out and frozen, and Sunshine, dead behind a Dumpster in Chinatown, her throat ripped out by a broken bottle. I was wishing that somebody would call me and tell me they'd figured it all out.

I thought about the street girl, Misty, which I doubted was her real name, seeing my dead girl throwing up on the sidewalk the same night she came into in my backyard. That reminded me of the panel truck with the New Hampshire plates. Misty said the guy behind the wheel was looking for a young blonde. Most likely he was just another predator, hung up on young blond girls.

But it was possible that he was looking specifically for my dead girl. Maybe he knew her. Maybe he was her father. Or maybe he was her high-school chemistry teacher, or her minister, or her soccer coach, or her uncle. Maybe he was the man who got her pregnant. Maybe she'd been running away from him.

I closed my eyes and conjured up the logo on the side of the guy's truck. In my memory it looked like two cartoon bears, with a couple of pine trees spiking up in the background. It could have been intended to represent some other animals, but to me, they looked like a mother — or father — and a baby bear.

I sketched my mental image of the bears on a piece of scrap paper. There had been writing under the logo. It was in a fancy script, and I hadn't been able to read it, and squeezing my eyes shut and seeing the truck in my mind didn't make it any clearer.

I tried to see the license plate. No numbers appeared in my mental picture. Just the green-and-white New Hampshire plate.

I went on the Internet and Googled "New Hampshire business logo." That produced the web addresses for half a dozen logo designers and an endless list of sites with "New Hampshire" or "logo" in their names or text.

I tried "New Hampshire trademark" and got a long list of Granite State trademark attorneys, several sites at the Secretary of State's office, consulting firms on incorporation, information about intellectual property . . .

I typed in everything I could think of that might convince Google to show me what I'd seen on the side of that panel truck, with no hits. After an hour, I gave up.

I ate a ham-and-Swiss-cheese sandwich

on pumpernickel, with a dill pickle and a handful of potato chips, standing at the sink to catch the crumbs and save a clean dish. I gave Henry a corner of my sandwich and a couple of chips. He turned up his nose at the pickle.

Then I leashed him up and we strolled down to the Common, where I let him off his leash. He hooked up with a yellow Lab and a springer spaniel, and the three of them raced around in the snow chasing squirrels and pigeons and each other while I stood on the plowed path with the elderly couple who owned the Lab and the springer. Their names were Gladys and Irv. Late seventies, I guessed. Spry and happy and in love with each other. They lived in a townhouse on Beacon Street, convenient to restaurants and theaters and the T and the Common. They especially loved theater.

They'd lived in Massachusetts all their lives, they told me, but they were starting to get a little sick of New England winters. They said they were thinking of selling the townhouse and moving down to Asheville, North Carolina. Their daughter lived in Asheville. They weren't ready for Florida. They still enjoyed the change of seasons. The Carolina hills seemed like a good compromise, although they weren't sure if there was any decent theater in Asheville.

I glanced at my watch. It was almost three-thirty. I called in Henry, leashed him up, said good-bye to Gladys and Irv and their two dogs, and with Henry at heel, I headed for the Shamrock homeless shelter.

I rang the bell, and a minute later Patricia McAfee opened the door. Today she was wearing denim overalls and a green plaid flannel shirt and red sneakers. Her gray-blond hair was pinned up on top of her head.

She smiled and held open the door. "Mr. Coyne. You're back. How nice. Come on in." She looked down and saw Henry. "Oh, is this your doggie? Is he friendly?"

"His name is Henry," I said. "He's a veritable pussycat. Can he come in, too?"

"Of course. Animals are welcome here." She scootched down and patted Henry's head. He tolerated it. Then she straightened up and said, "The children always love animals. The women do, too, actually, most of them. But especially the children. We used to have a cat, but it ran off. I want to get another one. Come on. Let's sit."

She led me over to the television nook, and we sat on the sofa. Henry lay down and plopped his chin on my instep.

At the rear of the dining area, a dark-haired woman in a white smock was talking with a beefy black woman and a little girl of four or five with lots of pink plastic clips in her hair. The black woman's daughter, I guessed.

Otherwise, the place was empty.

"Where is everybody?" I said.

"A few women are upstairs," she said. "Most of them have places to go during the day. I don't encourage them to hang around. Our whole mission is for them to get their lives back. They have jobs, they take classes, they attend meetings, they go for interviews, things like that."

I jerked my head in the direction of the back of the room. "Is that Dr. Rossi?"

Patricia nodded. "She's just finishing up. Is that what brings you here today? Did you want to talk to her?"

"Yes. I've got a question for you, too."

She put her elbows on her knees and her chin on her fists and leaned toward me. "Fire away."

"After I left here yesterday," I said, "I noticed a panel truck outside. It had a picture of bears on its side. Looked like a logo of some kind. I wondered if you might've seen it before?"

She frowned. "Bears? What kind of bears?"

I shrugged. "Sort of stylized bears. A

mother and a cub, maybe. A line drawing, with what looked like pine trees in the background. I think they were supposed to be bears. There was some writing, but I couldn't read it. Why? Does it ring a bell?"

"I don't know." She shook her head. "I don't think so. Maybe if I saw it . . ."

I had the sketch I'd drawn in the morning folded in my shirt pocket. I took it out, opened it up, and showed it to her. "I'm no artist, obviously," I said. "It looked something like this."

She narrowed her eyes at it, then looked up at me. "Sorry, no. Why are you interested in this truck?"

"The driver was talking to some girls. They told me he was asking about a young blond girl."

"Your dead girl?"

"I don't know. Could be."

"You think he knows her?"

"I'd like to ask him."

"Some of the shelters," she said, "have vans that drive around the city looking for folks without any place to go at night. But I don't know any that have a picture of bears on them."

"This truck had New Hampshire plates."

She shook her head. "That doesn't make any sense. Maybe Dr. Rossi can help you."

The black woman and her daughter were talking to the doctor. Then Dr. Rossi stood up and gave them each a hug, and the mother and daughter turned and headed for the door.

Patricia stood up and went over to talk to them.

Henry was lying on the carpet with his chin on his paws. I told him to stay, then went to the back of the room, where Dr. Rossi was sitting at a table with half-glasses perched down toward the tip of her nose, writing on some note cards.

I stood there for a moment. She kept writing. I cleared my throat. "Uh, Dr. Rossi?"

She looked up at me over the tops of her glasses. She was somewhere in her forties, I guessed. Up close I saw streaks of gray in her short black hair. Creases bracketed her mouth and squint lines wrinkled the corners of her eyes. "Hello?" she said, making it a question.

"I wonder if I could talk with you for a minute."

She nodded. "For just about a minute. I've gotta be someplace in half an hour."

I pulled a chair up to the table where she was sitting. "My name is Brady Coyne. I'm a lawyer."

She smiled. "Oh, dear. A lawyer."

"Not intimidated, huh?"

"Should I be?"

"No. This has nothing to do with being a lawyer." I took the photo of the dead girl out of my pocket and put it on the table in front of her. "I wonder if you ever saw this girl."

She poked her glasses up onto the bridge of her nose, peered at the photo, then looked up at me. "She's dead?"

"Yes."

"What happened to her?"

"She came into my backyard the other night. She was pregnant. Had a miscarriage. Curled up in the snow and bled to death. Or froze to death. Or both. They haven't done an autopsy yet. They're waiting to ID her, I guess."

"How absolutely awful." She touched the girl's face with her fingertip. "I do see street girls now and then, and sometimes they're pregnant, but I don't remember this one."

"*Would* you remember?" I said.

She looked up at me. "Excuse me?"

"You must see a lot of people," I said. "You might not remember every face."

She smiled quickly. "Every face? Of course I don't remember them all. I see hundreds of faces every week. Different faces every day, and the next week, a different hundred faces. The faces come and go. Do you have any idea what I do?"

"I'm sorry," I said. "Of course."

"I work from grant to grant," she said, "with the occasional charitable donation gratefully accepted. These people have no insurance. Some of them, they want to pay me. They have a lot of pride. I let them. I take five dollars from those who have it. It makes them feel better. Do you understand?"

"Yes," I said. "I didn't mean anything. I was hoping you might be able to help me out. I need to know who this girl is. Was."

Dr. Rossi picked up the morgue photo of the girl and looked at it again. Then she shrugged and shook her head. "I wish I could help you," she said.

"She died last Monday night. I found her body in the snow when I got up on Tuesday morning. I was thinking that you have your clinic here on Mondays, and this girl was seen in the neighborhood that evening, and she was sick, throwing up, so I just thought —"

"That I might have seen her that afternoon."

I nodded.

"I'd remember her. Pregnant and sick?

Having a miscarriage? I'd've gotten her to a hospital."

"Right," I said. "Sorry." I hesitated. "What about a woman named Maureen Quinlan?"

She looked at me blankly.

"They called her Sunshine. She was staying here at the Shamrock."

"I don't remember that name. You should ask Patricia about her."

I nodded. "She was murdered the other night."

"Oh," said Dr. Rossi. "Yes. I heard about that. A terrible thing. But, you know, just not that shocking to me anymore. Violence is commonplace among the homeless. Anyway, no, if I ever saw this person, I don't remember it. I could look her up in my records. . . ."

"No, that's all right. I was thinking of the other day you were here. Thursday. She was killed Thursday night."

"I didn't see her then. I'd remember that." She started organizing the note cards and prescription pads and pamphlets that were scattered across the table. "It must have been a terrible shock for you," she said, "finding this girl's body in your yard."

"My dog found her. I brought her inside and called 911. It's not clear whether she was already dead or she died on my sofa."

Dr. Rossi smiled softly. "I'm sorry."

I cleared my throat. "So where do pregnant street kids go in this city?"

"There is no particular place. When they come to me, I talk to them about diet and lifestyle and responsibility. I try to scare them about drugs. I try to convince them to get off the streets. I offer to intervene with their parents, talk to their boyfriends. I give them the addresses of Planned Parenthood clinics and adoption agencies. I urge them to talk with a priest or minister. I give them pamphlets." She waved her hand at the stacks of pamphlets on the table. "A lot of them are abused. Incest is rampant. A lot of these girls don't like to hear what I have to say."

"It sounds frustrating."

"It's tragic, is what it is. But now and then you save somebody, you know?" She picked up her note cards, tapped them into a deck, put a rubber band around them, and reached down and put them in a black satchel that sat beside her chair. She did the same with the pamphlets. Then she pushed herself back from the table. "I've really got to go."

"One more question, please," I said.

"Make it quick. I'm running late."

"I wonder if you've noticed a panel truck

148

in the neighborhood, perhaps cruising, looking to pick up girls. It has New Hampshire plates and a picture of bears on the side. A company logo, most likely. The driver would be a middle-aged man, round wire-rimmed glasses, well groomed, probably well educated."

"I'm not the kind of person who notices trucks." She stood up, reached down for her satchel, put it on the table, and snapped it shut.

I took my sketch of the logo out of my pocket and put it in front of her. "It looks something like this."

She glanced at it, shrugged, and shook her head. "Sorry," she said.

"You don't recognize it?"

"No."

"It could be important," I said.

"I understand," she said. "I still don't recognize it." She shrugged on her coat, which had been hanging on the back of her chair, picked up her satchel, and held out her hand. "It was nice meeting you."

I shook her hand. It was square and strong and rough, as if she did a lot of hammering and digging. "Please," I said. "If you remember anything about the girl, or if you see that truck, will you call me?"

"Of course I'll call you. Do you have a card?"

I took a business card from my wallet and handed it to her. "Call me any time," I said. "My home and office and cell numbers are all there."

She ran the ball of her thumb over the raised print, then stuck the card in her pocket. "I will. I'm sorry to be impatient with you. There's never enough time in the day, you know?"

I smiled. "I know. Thank you."

She nodded. "Good luck, Mr. Coyne. I hope you get some answers. No girl that age should die. Somebody's responsible."

Dr. Rossi waved at Patricia McAfee, who was sitting in the television area talking on a cordless phone, and left.

I said, "Hey," to Henry, who was still lying where I'd told him to lie. He scrambled to his feet and trotted over. I snapped on his leash and mouthed "thank you" to Patricia.

She wiggled her fingers at me.

Henry and I went outside. The late-afternoon gloom had already begun to seep into the city streets. The snowbanks that lined the narrow streets were dirty. The puddles were sheeted with ice. The January air was cold and damp and depressing.

Unless I was mistaken, we were in for some more snow.

I hunched my shoulders in my topcoat. "Somebody's responsible," Dr. Rossi had said.

I couldn't stop thinking it was me.

# ELEVEN

I took a cab to the airport and got to the arrival gate at 4:25 Sunday afternoon. America West flight 820 was on time, according to the monitor.

I found a pillar to lean against and watched the people go by. I spotted Evie the moment she appeared at the top of the escalator that would bring her down to my level in the baggage-claim area. She was wearing her standard air-travel outfit — baggy blue jeans, loose-fitting men's Oxford shirt with the tails hanging out, Boston Celtics jacket, dirty canvas sneakers, Red Sox cap. A long braid of auburn hair hung out of the opening in the back of the cap. Evie went for comfort, not style, when she knew she was going to be wedged into a window seat for five or six hours.

Still, she looked pretty stylish to me.

I watched her descend. She wasn't expecting me, wasn't looking for me, didn't see me. She looked tired and grouchy. Some people walk up and down escalators, as if they didn't go fast enough. Not Evie. She just rode it down.

She was about five steps from the bottom when her eyes landed on me. At first she frowned. Then she blinked. Then she smiled.

She hopped off the last step, threw her arms around my neck, and kissed me hard on the mouth.

I hugged her against me.

She broke the kiss, rubbed her cheek against mine, and said, "I missed you."

"Me, too," I said.

She stepped back and shook her head. "I told you not to come meet me. What a hassle."

"I couldn't wait."

"Dumb," she said.

"But sweet," I said.

"Dumb but sweet. That's my man." She grabbed my hand. "Let's fetch my bag and get the hell out of here."

In late-Sunday-afternoon traffic in the middle of the winter it's about a twenty-minute cab ride from Logan International Airport to Mt. Vernon Street on Beacon Hill. Evie spent the entire time with her

153

cheek resting on my shoulder and her hand absentmindedly moving along the inside of my thigh.

Or maybe not so absentmindedly. Purposefully, maybe. If so, surely effective.

I told her I intended to make shrimp scampi with risotto, lima beans, and a greens-and-mushroom salad for our dinner. A nice white wine was chilling in the snowbank on the back porch. White linen tablecloth. Evie's grandmother's silver. Miles Davis and Stevie Ray Vaughan, her favorites, were all cued up on the CD player.

She murmured that it sounded perfect . . . she was looking forward to a long steamy shower . . . get into something comfortable . . . maybe I'd mix us a pitcher of martinis . . . all the time, her fingernails scratching little circles on the inside of my leg.

Otherwise, we didn't say much. We didn't need to. We were both comfortable with silence. That was one of the things I loved about Evie. Silences didn't bother her, and she didn't feel compelled to fill them with chatter the way a lot of people — men as much as women — did.

Henry greeted us at the door with his stubby tail wagging, his entire hind end a blur. He barked and jumped at her, and she went down on her knees so he could lick her face. She told him how much she'd missed him. He made it pretty clear that the feeling was mutual.

I carried her bags up to the bedroom. Evie and Henry followed along behind me. I sat on the edge of the bed. Henry sat guard in the doorway, lest we attempt to elude him again. Evie stood in front of me, her eyes on my face. She pried off her sneakers with her toes, kicked them into the corner, and began to unbutton her shirt.

I took off my shoes and unbuttoned my shirt.

She dropped her shirt onto the floor.

So did I.

She unbuckled her belt, unzipped, wiggled out of her jeans.

I lay back, arched my hips, and shucked off my pants.

She unsnapped her bra and let it fall off her arms.

I smiled.

Evie arched her eyebrows.

I curled my forefinger at her.

She leapt upon me.

An hour later, Evie was in the shower and I was downstairs in the kitchen dicing garlic cloves and sipping a martini. I'd left Evie's martini sitting on the edge of the bathroom sink upstairs, right there for her emergence from the shower. Miles Davis was tooting mournfully from the speakers. Henry was lying under the kitchen table, his chin on his paws, his eyes alert for errant morsels.

I was dicing and sipping and humming, and it took me a minute to register Evie's presence behind me.

She was standing in the doorway, barefoot, in her white terrycloth robe, with a pale blue towel wrapped around her hair. She was pressing something against her chest with both of her hands. Her eyes were big and shiny.

"What's the matter?" I said.

She showed me what she was holding. It was one of the photocopies of the morgue shot of the dead girl. I'd left it on top of my dresser in the bedroom.

"It's hard to look at," I said. "I'm sorry. I didn't mean to leave it out. That's the girl I told you about. The girl who was —"

"Right." She blinked. A single tear squeezed out of each eye and rolled down her cheek. "I know her."

I put down the knife I'd been using on the garlic and went to her. I opened my arms. She stepped into my hug and wrapped her arms around my waist.

"You know this girl?" I said.

I felt her nodding against my chest. "Her name is Dana. Dana Wetherbee."

I tilted my head back so I could look into Evie's face. "How do you know her, honey?"

"The hospital," she said. "When I was at Emerson. I haven't seen her for almost three years. She was twelve or thirteen then. She's changed, but . . ."

I brushed a tear off her check with the knuckle of my forefinger. "Are you sure?"

She looked at the photo again, then nodded. "It's Dana." Tears were leaking from her eyes. She let me take her hand and lead her to the kitchen table. I held a chair for her. She sat down, put the photo on the table in front of her, and stared at it. Then she looked up at me. "It's not just her features. I mean, her hair, her nose, her chin, they look right. Three years older, but the same. But that's not what I mean. It's her . . . her look. Do you understand?"

I nodded.

Evie touched Dana's face with the tip of her finger. "This jade nose stud? I remember when she got it. She kept touching it, as if it embarrassed her."

I sat across from her. "Tell me about Dana," I said.

"She came here looking for me," she said. "That's why she was here that night you found her in the snow. She came to see me. She needed me. She was in trouble, and I could have helped her, except I wasn't here for her, to help her, so she died."

"Honey —"

Evie shook her head. "Don't you dare try to tell me this isn't my fault."

"I understand," I said. "I feel the same way. Did you see the martini I left on the bathroom sink for you?"

She nodded. "I drank it. I'm ready for another one. Don't change the subject."

I went to the counter, found another martini glass, poured it three-quarters full, dropped in two olives. I put the glass in front of Evie. "Just sip it," I said.

She looked up at me. "You think I'm drunk?"

"No," I said. "I think you're upset."

"You said she was pregnant?"

I nodded. "She had a miscarriage."

"That makes no sense."

I shrugged. "She was a teenage girl. Those things seem to keep happening."

"Not Dana," said Evie. "I don't believe it. It's totally out of character."

"You knew her how long ago?"

She shrugged. "About three years."

"Big difference," I said, "thirteen and sixteen."

"I know what you're saying," she said. "Still, if you knew Dana . . ."

"Well," I said, "according to the medical people who examined her, this girl was definitely pregnant. No question about it."

"She had a miscarriage? That's why she died?"

"Yes. She bled to death."

"So Dana was in trouble. She needed help. She came here looking for me. And I wasn't here for her." Evie took a gulp of her martini.

"Sip it, honey," I said.

"I am." She took another gulp.

"Tell me about Dana," I said.

She reached across the table and grabbed my hand. "The thing is, I abandoned her. I took my new job, my better pay, my more prestige, my week in Arizona, my moving on up the ladder of success, my chasing the good old American Dream. When I left Emerson Hospital, I left Dana behind. Do you see?"

I gave her hand a squeeze and said nothing.

"There were five or six of them," said Evie. "Girls. Early teens. It just sort of evolved from one day in the cafeteria. It was a weekend afternoon. A Sunday. The place was practically empty. It was in the fall, I remember. October sometime. The sun was coming in through the windows, that beautiful orangey it can be on a late fall afternoon, and outside, the maple trees were all crimson and golden in the sun. I went in to clean up some desk work. Figured I'd get a lot done with nobody around, no phones ringing. So I took a break, went down to get something to eat, and this bunch of girls were sitting at one of the tables. They were eating and talking, and I asked if they'd mind if I sat with them. They sort of shrugged, the way teenagers will, like, okay, whatever. So I joined them. Turned out they all had sick mothers, and they'd kind of found each other. Had their own little support group going, mostly pretending to be strong and brave, but usually one of them wasn't doing so well, and then the others would hug her and tell her how much it sucked and how everything was going to be all right. They asked me a few questions, and I answered them as honestly as I could, and they had a few questions I couldn't answer, and I told them I'd try to get answers for them. Questions about diseases and medications, about prognoses and predictions. Doctors don't say much anyway, and they're even worse with the children of terminal parents. Anyway, the girls, they seemed to appreciate the fact that I was trying to be candid, not holding anything back."

"So you met with them again," I said.

"It wasn't anything formal," she said. "Not like a scheduled meeting. Not a commitment. It sort of evolved. Sunday afternoons some of the girls, at least, would be there, in the cafeteria. I made it a point to be there, that's all. To sit with them, talk with them, and if they had questions, to try to get answers for them. That's all it was."

"These girls all had terminal parents?"

"Mothers," said Evie. "Not necessarily terminal, but seriously ill. Dana's mother, for example, she was in renal failure. She was a severe diabetic. She'd been sick for as long as Dana could remember, in and out of hospitals, dialysis, on the transplant list, the whole sad deal." Evie sighed. "When I left Emerson and took the job at Beth Israel, Verna Wetherbee was still alive. I asked one of the nurses to keep an eye on Dana and the other girls." She shook her head. "I don't know if she did. If she did, I don't know if the girls responded to her. I meant to keep in touch with them, see how they were doing, offer them my support, you know? But . . ." She looked at me. "But I didn't." She was crying silently.

"You can't blame yourself for this," I said.

"Of course I can." She wiped her eyes with the back of her wrist. "Dana had a little brother. I can't remember his name. I just have this picture of him sitting in a chair in the corner of Verna's room, reading a book, ignoring everything around him. He was always reading a book. I don't remember ever hearing him say a word. Dana took care of him. Like she was his mother. Dana was like that, you know?"

I didn't know, of course, but I nodded.

"I heard Verna died a few months after I left," Evie said. "I tried to call Dana, but I couldn't reach her. I left a message, said if she wanted to talk just give me a call, but she never called back. I sent her a card, told her I was there for her, gave her my office and home numbers, our new address." She shook her head. "I never heard from her."

"You tried, then."

She shook her head. "I didn't try very hard."

"You gave her our address?"

She nodded. "Why?"

"I told you the other night. She had a scrap of paper in her pocket with our address on it."

Evie nodded. Her eyes were brimming. "See? She needed me." She pushed her empty martini glass across the table to me. "Refill."

"You sure?"

"I was up this morning at six-thirty," Evie said. "I started my day in Scottsdale, Arizona, where it was seventy-seven degrees at nine o'clock in the morning. I ended up the day in Boston, Massachusetts, two time zones away, where it was twenty-two degrees at five-thirty in the afternoon. A little girl I used to love bled to death in the snow in my backyard while I was gone. It's been a long fucking day, and, yes, I want another martini. You got a problem with that?"

I smiled. "No problem. You gonna be good for shrimp scampi and risotto?"

"I am going to take this martini upstairs," she said, "and I am going to finish drying my hair, and I will get dressed, and by then I will be starved, I promise."

I took her glass to the counter where the pitcher of martinis sat. "Do you remember the names of Dana Wetherbee's parents?" I said as I refilled her glass.

"Her mother was Verna," she said. "It means springtime. Her father . . . he was a truck driver. I remember Dana saying how he was on the road for long periods of time. Wait a minute." She squeezed her eyes shut, then opened them. "Ben was his name. Ben

Wetherbee. I only met him a couple times. A nice man, from what I could see, but fairly clueless. He just seemed baffled by all of it. His wife's illness, his daughter's . . . her girl-ness."

"Where'd they live?"

"The town, you mean?"

"Yes."

Evie was frowning at me from the kitchen table, where she was still sitting in her white terrycloth robe with a blue towel wrapped around her hair. "I don't know," she said. "I did send her that note, but now I don't remember where. Maybe I've got it written down someplace. I'll look. It was someplace fairly near the hospital, I think. Dana used to come and visit Verna after school."

I put Evie's third martini on the table. She picked it up, took a sip, then stood up. "I want to see her."

"Dana?"

"Yes. Her body."

"Why?"

"To be sure. Do you understand?"

I nodded. "I guess I do. I'll see if I can arrange it."

She put her hand on my shoulder and peered into my eyes. "My sweet man," she murmured. She went up on tiptoes, stuck out her tongue, and gave the side of my face a long wet lick.

Then she turned and headed for the stairs.

Evie was a little drunk. She was entitled.

I went into my office, found Saundra Mendoza's cell-phone number, and tried it.

Her voice mail answered, asked me to leave a message.

"It's Brady Coyne," I said after the beep. "I think I have an ID on our dead girl."

I went back to the kitchen, got the risotto started, poured myself another martini, and sliced up some portabella mushrooms for the salad.

It took Saundra Mendoza about ten minutes to get back to me. "What've you got?" she said when I answered.

"Her name was Dana Wetherbee. She'd be about sixteen now. Father's name Ben. Benjamin, I guess. Mother, name of Verna, now deceased, was a patient at Emerson Hospital in Concord about three years ago."

"You got an address for me?"

"No," I said, "but the hospital records should help you."

"Yeah," she said, "thanks. Never would've thought of that."

I didn't say anything.

"What else've you got for me, Mr. Coyne?"

"That's it," I said. "Evie identified her

from the photo. Evie knew her when she worked at Emerson."

"Evie being your girlfriend."

"She's way more than a girlfriend."

"She lives with you."

"Right."

"So the girl . . ."

"We assume Dana came here that night looking for Evie. She was away at a conference in Scottsdale, Arizona."

"And Evie's blaming herself, I bet."

"We're both blaming ourselves."

"She okay?"

"I made martinis."

"Good idea," said Mendoza. "How definite is she?"

"Quite definite." I hesitated. "She wants to see the body."

There was a pause. Then Saundra said, "Sure. Good idea. I can arrange that. How's tomorrow morning, say ten?"

"I'll check with Evie," I said, "but if I don't get back to you, let's call it a date."

"At the Medical Examiner's office. Know where it is?"

"Albany Street," I said.

"I'll meet you there at ten."

"Okay," I said. "So have you learned anything?"

"Not a thing, Mr. Coyne. I'm doing my

best. Don't forget, this isn't a homicide. It's an unidentified body."

"A young girl's unidentified body," I said.

"Yes," she said. "You don't need to keep reminding me."

"Any news on Sunshine?"

"No," she said. "Not a thing. Gotta run. Thanks for calling. See you tomorrow." And she disconnected.

# TWELVE

Monday morning was sunny and, for the first time in the new year, there was a hint of January thaw in the air. When we left for our appointment at the Medical Examiner's office, we let Henry stay outside in our walled-in backyard. Henry always wanted to be outdoors. In the winter, he loved to lie on the back stoop where the morning sun warmed the wood.

Evie and I debated walking over to Albany Street, but in the end we took my car. She'd been away from her desk for a week and was feeling anxious about all the paperwork and phone messages she'd find waiting for her.

OCME — the Office of the Chief Medical Examiner — is an unimposing three-story brick building on Albany Street, surrounded by the more imposing campuses of Boston City Hospital, the Boston University Medical Center, and the B. U. schools of

Medicine, Dentistry, and Public Health. OCME is where victims of homicide and unattended and suspicious deaths go to be autopsied.

We got there a little before ten. When we walked into the lobby, we spotted Detective Saundra Mendoza leaning against the wall on the other side of the room talking on her cell phone.

When she saw us, she waved us over. By the time we got there, she was stuffing the phone into her pocket.

I introduced her to Evie.

She shook Evie's hand and said, "I really appreciate this. I know it's hard."

"I want to be sure," said Evie.

Mendoza nodded. "They're waiting for us. This way."

We followed her down a corridor and then into a small room. The back wall of the room was dominated by a big window with a white curtain drawn over it from the other side. Four wooden chairs were lined up facing the window.

Mendoza gestured at the chairs. Evie and I sat. Mendoza remained standing behind us. "Ready?" she said.

Evie groped for my hand and gripped it hard. "I'm ready," she said.

Mendoza, apparently speaking into a

microphone, said, "Okay. We're all set here."

A moment later the curtain slid away from the window. A gurney had been wheeled up to the other side of the glass. A pale blue body bag lay on it. A young Asian man in a green lab coat stood there looking solemn. He peered at us through the window for a moment, then partially unzipped the bag and pulled it open, revealing the girl's face and bare shoulders.

She looked smaller and paler and more lifeless than I remembered from when I'd last seen her lying on my living room sofa. More lifeless, even, than she looked in the photo I'd been carrying around. She was absolutely still.

I noticed that they hadn't removed the jade stud from her nose.

Evie's hand was squeezing mine so hard it hurt. "It's Dana," she said.

"You're positive, Ms. Banyon?" said Saundra Mendoza.

"Yes," said Evie. "I'm sure." She let go of my hand and stood up. "I want to leave now."

Back out in the lobby, Mendoza touched Evie's arm and said, "Thank you. It was a big help."

"Now what happens?"

"I'll pass the information along to the

Medical Examiner. What happens is up to him."

"That's it?" said Evie.

Mendoza nodded. "How it works."

We got into my car and headed over to Evie's office at Beth Israel Hospital. She sat there huddled against the door, staring out at the window. She told me she didn't want to talk about it, and I didn't argue with her. I could only imagine what she was feeling.

After I dropped Evie off, I swung around to our house on Mt. Vernon Street to let Henry in. It was a warm, almost springlike day, but you could never be sure what the New England weather would decide to do, and as much as he'd like it, I didn't want him staying outside all day.

I left the car parked on the street, went in the front door, checked the kitchen phone for messages, then opened the back door. Henry was curled on the deck. When he saw me, he pushed himself to his feet, yawned, and came sauntering inside.

He sat and looked at me expectantly. I always gave him a miniature Milk-Bone when he came inside, to reinforce his good behavior. That's when I noticed that something had gotten stuck under his collar.

It was a plastic sandwich bag. When I tried

to take it off, I saw that it had been stapled around his collar. I yanked it off. There was something in the bag. Through the transparent plastic, I saw that it was a photo.

It was the morgue photo of Dana Wetherbee.

On the back, in red ink and in my handwriting, were my name and phone numbers.

I had to think for a minute. I always used a pen with black ink. This was red. Then I remembered. I'd borrowed a red pen from Sunshine that night at Skeeter's.

This was the photo that I'd given to Sunshine. The photo that disappeared the night she was murdered. The photo that her killer had taken from her.

And now it was stapled onto Henry's collar. This was a message, and neither a subtle nor a friendly one. A message to me from whoever had ripped Sunshine's throat open.

His message was: "I killed Sunshine because I don't want you snooping around trying to figure out what happened to Dana Wetherbee."

His other plain message was: "I could have killed your dog. I can kill anybody. I can kill you."

My legs suddenly felt weak, and my hands, I noticed, were trembling.

Anger. Well, okay. A little fear, too.

I sat on one of the kitchen chairs. My pulse was pounding behind my eyes. I wasn't thinking about me. I was thinking about Evie. And Henry.

Bastard!

Henry came over, put his chin on my leg, and rolled up his eyes, looking into mine, checking to see how I was feeling.

I patted his head and told him not to worry about me.

I took a few deep breaths, then went to the phone and called Saundra Mendoza.

When she answered, I said, "I just got a message from Maureen Quinlan's murderer."

"What did you say?"

I repeated what I'd said.

"Explain," she said.

I explained.

Mendoza was quiet for a minute. Then she said, "Okay, good. This is good."

"Good? This murderer comes into my backyard and sticks a message on my dog's collar, and you're saying this is good? You'll have to excuse me if I don't see it the same way."

"It's a stupid, desperate thing to do," she said. "He's panicking. Something you've done has scared him. He'll do something else stupid and we'll nail him. So, yeah. It's good."

"Jesus. He could've killed Henry."

"Point is, he didn't. He could have and he didn't. He wants you to back off. Which, as a matter of fact, is a good idea. It's what I want, too. You back off. Okay?"

"This sonofabitch comes into my backyard, lays his hands on my dog, and you expect me to back off?"

Saundra Mendoza sighed. "Last thing I want is your girlfriend or your dog finding you bleeding in the snow in your backyard, Mr. Coyne."

"Well, me neither."

"Or you finding one of them."

"Jesus, Saundra."

"So just leave the detecting up to us detectives from now on, okay? Do you hear me?"

"I hear you," I said. "So do you want this photo?"

"Did you take it out of the plastic bag?"

"No."

"Yeah. Maybe we can lift some prints off it. Where are you now?"

"In my kitchen."

"On a cordless phone?"

"Yes."

"Take me out back and tell me if you see any boot prints in the snow."

I went out onto the deck. "It's pretty much trampled down out here," I told her. "Between Henry and me. Plus the snow settled a lot under the sun today. If this guy came into the yard, there aren't any good prints that I can see."

"How could he not have come into your yard?"

"He might've just opened the gate and given Henry a whistle. The lock's broken. I've been meaning to get it fixed. If he had a Milk-Bone, called him a nice pooch, my stupid, trusting dog would've gone right to him with his tail wagging."

"If we were CSI," said Mendoza, "we'd probably send a team over anyway. But we're not, so we won't. You going to be at your office this afternoon?"

"Yes. I'm late already."

"Bring that photo with you. I don't have to tell you not to touch it. Leave it right there in its baggie."

"Okay." I hesitated. "Will you do me a favor?"

"Maybe. What?"

"If you talk to Evie, don't mention this. It would freak her out."

"It should freak you out," she said.

"It does, believe me. Just don't tell her, okay?"

"Fair enough. As long as you promise to behave yourself."

I crossed my fingers. "I promise."

"You understand what this means, don't you, Mr. Coyne?"

"What?"

"Now we've got a definite connection between Maureen Quinlan's murder and what happened to Dana Wetherbee. It's no coincidence that Sunshine was killed. She was killed because of what happened to Dana."

"I do understand that," I said. "I've assumed it all along."

"Well," said Mendoza, "me, too. But now we know."

After I hung up with Mendoza, I patted Henry some more and told him that I was sorry, but he wouldn't be spending any unattended time in the backyard until further notice.

I had a padlock in my desk drawer. I took it out back and locked the gate in the wall that opened into the back alley. Obviously, if anybody really wanted to get into our yard, he could climb over the wall. But there was no sense in making it easy for him.

Back inside, I put the plastic baggie containing Sunshine's copy of Dana Wetherbee's morgue photo into my briefcase.

Then I said good-bye to Henry, told him I wish he'd bite strangers instead of sniffing their crotches, and went to work.

Outside my office window, the streetlights had come on and the late-afternoon pedestrians were swarming over the Copley Square sidewalks. I'd managed to make some phone calls and clean up some paperwork, but the image of some killer patting Henry and stapling that plastic bag onto his collar was never far from my mind.

I was thinking about heading home to hug my dog and kiss my girlfriend, or kiss my dog and hug my girlfriend, when Julie tapped on my door and stuck her head inside. "Detective Mendoza's here for you," she said.

"Good," I said.

She pushed the door open and Mendoza came in. I started to stand up, but she waved me back in my chair and sat across from me. "So how you doing?" she said.

"Okay," I said. "I'm angry. But I'm not scared."

"You promised," she said.

"Sure. I won't do anything stupid. I promise. You promised, too."

"I won't say anything to Evie," she said, "as long as you keep your promise."

I reached into my briefcase, took out the plastic bag with Dana's photo in it, and put it on my desk. "Here it is."

She picked up the baggie by its corner and looked at the front and back of the photo. Then she fished a plastic evidence bag from her jacket pocket, put the baggie with the photo into it, wrote on it with a black Sharpie, and put it into her attaché case. "Good," she said. "Thanks."

Then, instead of getting up to leave, she put a manila folder on my desk.

"What've you got?" I said.

"Ms. Banyon giving us an ID on that girl's body this morning cleared away the log jam. Now we've got two autopsy reports. Figured you'd be interested. Figured I owed you. You and Ms. Banyon."

"You do owe us," I said, "and I am interested."

She opened the folder and glanced at what was inside. Then she looked at me. "Maureen Quinlan," she said. "Sunshine. No surprises. Unequivocally a homicide. She drowned in her own blood from a lacerated trachea. Basically, her throat was ripped open, wounds consistent with a broken bottle. Slivers of green glass recovered from the wound. She was damn near decapitated. Layman's terms. I'm summarizing here. She had a BAL of point-oh-seven."

"BAL," I said.

"Blood alcohol level. Point-oh-seven, a woman her size, about one-twenty, is certainly buzzed, but not what you'd call falling-down drunk. A few highballs, three or four glasses of wine in an hour, hour and a half. She was probably just getting started when it happened."

"She told me she was fighting it," I said. "The drinking."

"She was fighting a losing battle that night."

"Sunshine," I said. "A sad person. Big black cloud over her. Irony."

"Yeah." Mendoza puffed her cheeks and blew out a breath. Then she flipped through the sheets of paper in the folder. "Anyway, we got autopsy results on the girl, too."

"Dana," I said.

"Yes. Dana Wetherbee. The M.E. hasn't verified her identification, but . . ." Mendoza smiled quickly, then cleared her throat. "He estimates she was between fourteen and seventeen years old. She had a miscarriage. Died from blood loss due to a ruptured uterus. The M.E. noted an anomaly of sorts. Blood tests, or however they do it, hormone tests, maybe . . . anyway, they indicated the girl was two or three months pregnant when she died. But it appeared that the fetus had, well, outgrown her uterus, and that's what the M.E. thinks caused the miscarriage."

"What do you mean, outgrown?"

"The fetus was too big," she said. "It was like a five-or six-month fetus in a two-or three-month uterus, is how the M.E. described it when I talked to him. The girl's insides couldn't keep up with the growth of her fetus."

"How does he explain that?" I said.

"He didn't have a theory," she said, "and I certainly don't. Miscarriages aren't uncommon, and they happen for many reasons."

"Maybe it's just, she was so young, an immature body, narrow hips or something. . . ."

"Yeah," said Mendoza, "maybe. Except there was something else." She hesitated. "This girl, Dana, she was taking clomiphene."

"What's that?"

"It's a fertility drug," she said. "It stimulates hormones so the brain sends messages to the ovaries, instructing them to produce eggs." She cleared her throat. "That's what I got from the M.E. I might not've explained it right, but you get the picture."

"Would this stuff, this . . . what was it?"

"Clomiphene."

"Right. Clomiphene. Would the fact that she was taking clomiphene account for the size of the fetus?"

"The M.E. didn't think so," said Mendoza. "He said it shouldn't have any effect on the growth rate of the fetus. It might produce multiple fetuses, but that apparently wasn't the case here."

"Okay, wait a minute," I said. "If she was taking a fertility drug —"

"Bingo, Mr. Coyne," said Saundra Mendoza. "She was pregnant all right, but she wasn't exactly knocked up. If she was taking clomiphene, it's pretty compelling evidence that this little girl was trying to get pregnant."

I got home before Evie that evening. I figured, after a week in Arizona, her office would be a zoo, not even to mention the turmoil she had to be feeling after viewing Dana Wetherbee's body.

So I had a pitcher of martinis waiting for her, and as soon as she'd changed out of her school clothes, as she put it, and was comfortable in some baggy sweatpants and a ratty sweatshirt with the sleeves cut off at the shoulders — on Evie, a very sexy outfit — I led her into the living room and poured her a drink.

We sat on the sofa. She turned sideways and put her bare feet in my lap.

I kneaded and massaged her feet, which usually made her moan and mumble as if she was about to have an orgasm. But tonight she didn't react very much except to say, "That's nice. Don't stop."

It was hard not to tell her about finding Dana's photo — the one I'd given to Sunshine — stapled on Henry's collar. Evie and I don't have many secrets. We generally share, whether it's good or bad, happy or sad, triumphant or embarrassing. But I couldn't think of a single good reason to share this with her.

"Lieutenant Mendoza dropped by this afternoon," I said instead. "The M.E. finally did the autopsy. Dana was taking something called clomiphene."

"That's a fertility drug," said Evie.

"Yes."

"Hm," she said. She took a sip of martini.

"My sentiment exactly," I said.

"Makes no sense," she said. "Why would she be taking fertility medication?"

"I guess she wanted to get pregnant."

"Is that what they think caused her miscarriage?" she said. "The clomiphene?"

"According to the M.E., no."

Evie was shaking her head. "Dana was just this sweet, virginal child. An innocent. A serious student, went to church, took care of her little brother, very scared about her mother, wouldn't say boo to anybody."

"People change," I said. "After her mother died . . ."

Evie shrugged. "Yeah, but still." She drained her martini glass, reached for the pitcher on the coffee table, refilled it, and took a sip. She looked at me over the rim over her glass. "I made a few calls today."

"What calls?"

"Some old friends at Emerson."

"About Dana?"

She nodded.

"And?"

"I talked to Barbara," she said, "who was one of Verna Wetherbee's nurses at the time she died, and I talked to Ginny in records. I got Ben Wetherbee's old address in Westford, but it turns out he doesn't live there anymore. Searched the Massachusetts White Pages on the Internet, couldn't find any listing for Benjamin Wetherbee. Barbara told me that Verna's parents used to visit sometimes. Ginny looked up their names for me. Richard and Shirley Arsenault. Dana's grandparents. They were living in Edson, Rhode Island. Tiny little town halfway between Woonsocket and Providence. I checked. They still live there." She took another sip of martini.

"So did you call them?"

"No. I'm . . . I haven't quite figured out what to say to them."

"Just do it, honey."

"You mean now?"

"Well," I said, "I suppose you could just give the information to Saundra Mendoza, let her do the dirty work."

"I can't do that. It wouldn't be right. It should be me telling them. A friend. Not the police."

"So why wait?"

She hugged herself. "I've got to think it through."

"You're probably better off just playing it by ear," I said. "Thinking things through is overrated."

Evie was nodding. "I looked up their number," she said. "I picked up the phone to call them half a dozen times today. But I kept thinking, what do I say? I mean, how do you tell them that their granddaughter is dead?"

"You want me to do it?"

She slapped my leg. "I most certainly do not." She unfolded herself from the sofa, stood up, drained her martini glass, and headed for the kitchen.

I heard the mumble of her voice from two rooms away.

Five minutes later she came back into the living room.

I arched my eyebrows.

She shook her head.

"What happened?"

"Mrs. Arsenault was . . . cagey."

"Cagey how?"

"I can't put my finger on it. Evasive. Distant. Mistrustful. I didn't want to just come out and tell her Dana was dead. I mean, what was she doing here in Boston, in our backyard? Why was she pregnant? I didn't know what she knew. So I told her who I was, from Emerson Hospital, and Shirley — Mrs. Arsenault — she said she remembered Dana mentioning me. I said I heard about Verna, Mrs. Arsenault's daughter, how sorry I was, and I'd been meaning to check in with Dana, see how she was doing. And Mrs. Arsenault, she interrupts me right there and says, Well, Dana's not here right now."

"Right now?"

She nodded.

"So Dana was living with her grandparents?"

Evie nodded.

185

"Sounds like she was expecting Dana to return."

"I don't know," said Evie.

"So did you tell her Dana was dead?"

She shook her head. "No. I chickened out. It just didn't seem right, over the telephone, you know?"

"But don't you think — ?"

"God *damn* it, Brady."

"What?"

"I know you would've done it better." Evie was glaring at me, clenching and unclenching her fists as if it was taking all of her will power not to slug me.

"I didn't mean that, honey."

"Sure you did. You always know what to do. Sometimes you're such a . . . a fucking *lawyer.*"

"Ow," I said. "That hurts."

"Tough."

I patted my lap. "Come on. Relax."

She folded her arms across her chest. "I don't want to relax. And don't you dare patronize me."

"I wasn't patronizing you."

"Second-guessing me," she said.

"I wasn't second-guessing you, either, honey."

"Yeah, you were." She blew out a long breath. "Okay, maybe you're right. Maybe I

186

should've just flat-out told her. If I'd told her that Dana was dead, I might've gotten somewhere with her. Maybe she'd've explained it. You're right. But I didn't. I was a wimp, okay? I crapped out. It seemed as if she didn't trust me, and I felt like, if I pushed her, she'd just hang up on me and then I'd never be able to talk to her again. So I let it go."

"You played it by ear," I said.

"That's right." She was still scowling at me.

"Sounds like you handled it perfectly."

"You think?"

"This way," I said, "she'll be comfortable talking to you again. You always know when to push, when to pull back. That's what makes you so good at your work. You've got excellent instincts."

"I do," she said, "don't I?"

"Absolutely." I opened my arms. "Come here."

"No. I'm mad at you. You're such a damned know-it-all."

"I don't blame you," I said. "I'm a truly bad person. But I really think you need to sit on my lap."

"Do I have to?"

"Of course not. You can do anything you want to do. You are the architect of your own future. You are the captain of your own ship. You are the mother of your own invention. You are the sunshine of your own life."

Evie rolled her eyes. She was trying not to smile.

"You are the tears of your own clown," I said.

Then she did smile.

I patted my lap. "Please?"

"That's more like it," she said.

# THIRTEEN

I spent most of Tuesday morning and half of the afternoon in the courthouse in Concord, mostly waiting around in the lobby, but eventually trying to convince Judge Kolb that just because Bob Perry, my client, had gotten a hard-earned raise and an overdue promotion at the bank, it didn't entitle Nancy Perry, from whom Bob had been divorced for eleven years, to more alimony.

After all that, the judge ended up sending us home to work it out, and by the time I left my car in the Copley Square parking garage and strolled across the plaza to my office, it was approaching five o'clock in the afternoon. The rush-hour cars and taxis on Boylston Street were puffing thin clouds of exhaust into the chilly air, and the streetlights were winking on, and the slush on the sidewalks was beginning to freeze.

Julie was talking on the telephone when I

walked in. I gave her a wave, and she wiggled some fingers at me. I hung up my coat, poured myself a mug of coffee, slouched on the waiting-room sofa, and began thumbing through the November issue of *Gray's Sporting Journal.*

After a few minutes, Julie hung up. "So how'd it go?" she said.

I shrugged. "I accrued a whole bunch of billable hours, if that's what you mean."

"Judge Kolb sent you home, told you to go back to the drawing board, huh?"

I smiled. "Right as usual. How about you?"

"Without you hanging around pestering me all day, I got a lot done. Your messages and your mail are on your desk." She jerked her head in the direction of my office. "You ought to take a look at them before you leave."

"That," I said, "is exactly why I'm here. I could've gone straight home, patted Henry, kissed Evie, changed my clothes, poured myself a drink, put my feet up and relaxed, basking in the certain knowledge that I'd earned it. But even after a full and exhausting day in court, a dedicated attorney's work is never done."

Julie rolled her eyes.

I took my coffee into my office and sat at

my desk. In her usual fastidious fashion, Julie had printed out a log of the day's calls, annotating each entry with the phone number, the caller's name, the time of the call, and the message, plus Julie's own commentary: "Ignore this one;" "I took care of it;" "He'll get back to you;" "Beware: This one's a nutcase;" "She sounds neurotic;" "Can't afford us." Like that.

I'd learned to heed Julie's instincts. In the years we'd been together, she'd proved to be an uncanny judge of potential clients and the merits of their cases.

As I ran my finger down the list, I stopped at a 617-area-code number with no name beside it. The call had come at 10:35 in the morning. Julie's comment: "Cell phone. Wouldn't leave her name. Wants you to call."

At 2:57, the same number. This time Julie noted: "Accused me of not delivering her message. Tried to question her and she hung up."

At 3:41, again the same number. "Sounds somewhat stressed," Julie wrote. "You better call her."

I took the list out to her desk. "What can you tell me about this call?" I said, pointing at the number.

She shrugged. "Not much more than I wrote down. She insisted on talking to you.

Wouldn't tell me her name, wouldn't say what she wanted. She's never called us before. Sounded . . . young. Not a child, exactly. A young adult. I didn't recognize her voice. She called those three times, and each time she sounded more anxious than the previous one."

"How did you know she was using a cell phone?"

"It came from the same number, but there were different background noises each call. The first time, it was from inside a restaurant. The second time she was outdoors. I heard traffic. Next time, no background sounds at all. Different places, same phone each time." Julie shrugged.

I smiled. "You're brilliant."

"That's true," she said.

I went back into my office and called the number.

After two rings, a female voice said, "Hello," making it three syllables. Her tone suggested she was trying to sound outgoing and friendly and having a hard time carrying it off. In the background, I heard muffled voices and the clink and clatter of glassware and crockery.

"It's Brady Coyne," I said. "You've been trying to reach me?"

"Oh, jeez," she said. "I'm glad it's you."

"Who is this?" I said.

"Huh? Oh, sorry. It's Misty. Remember me?"

I remembered. Black hair. Red beret. Slash of lipstick to match. Short skirt, fake fur jacket. A few nights earlier I'd given her sixty dollars and my business card.

"Sure," I said. "What's up? Everything okay?"

"You're a lawyer, right?"

"Yes."

"So I can talk to you without . . ."

"If you were my client, it would be confidential."

"Can I be your client?"

"Misty," I said, "is everything all right?"

"Not really, no. I — hang on a minute."

I had the sense that she'd covered her phone. When she came back on, her voice was soft and guarded. "I have some information."

"About what?"

"Remember that van?"

"The one with the bear logo."

"Yes. Well, not the van. The guy in the van. He . . . it's about Kayla. I'm — look. I can't . . . not on the phone."

"Tell me where you are," I said, "and I'll be there."

"I can be your client?"

"It'll cost you a dollar to retain me."

"Then you can't tell anybody what I say?"

"It's a little more complicated than that, but basically, yes. Anything you tell me will be privileged. I can't tell anybody unless you give me permission."

"Where are you?" she said.

"Me? In my office."

"Where's that?"

"Copley Square. Where are you?"

"You don't want to come all the way down here. I'll meet you halfway."

"Chinatown, right?" I said. "Didn't you tell me you liked to hang in Chinatown?"

"Right," she said. "Beach Street. Look, there's a Dunkin' on the corner. Boylston and Tremont? You know where I mean?"

"Sure."

"Let's meet there," she said. "At the Dunkin'. You say when."

I looked at my watch. It was few minutes after five. I'd have to ransom my car from the parking garage across the plaza from my office, negotiate the traffic to my regular garage at the far end of Charles Street, then from there walk the length of Charles and diagonally across the Common to the Dunkin' Donuts.

"Six," I said. "I'll be there around six. Whoever gets there first, grab a table."

"Six," Misty said. "Good." She paused. "Hey?"

"What?"

"Nothing," she said. "I'll tell you then." She hesitated a moment. "I'm kinda worried about Kayla, that's all."

By the time I bumper-to-bumpered my way to my slot in the parking garage near the end of Charles Street, it was ten minutes of six. It's a brisk fifteen-minute hike from the garage to the Dunkin' Donuts on the corner of Boylston and Tremont, so it was about five past six when I walked through the door.

Seven or eight people were lined up at the counter ordering their coffees. This time on a Tuesday night, most of them would be to-go orders, a coffee or a cappucino or a hot chocolate for the walk to the T station or the parking garage.

Misty wasn't in the line. I looked around at the tables, and she wasn't sitting at any of them.

This time I was a little late, but I had tried to be on time. I always try to be on time. Some people are constitutionally unable to be where they say they'll be at the time they agree to be there. I supposed Misty was one of them. It was no more than a ten-or fifteen-minute walk even from the Atlantic Avenue end of Beach Street in Chinatown to this Dunkin'. Or maybe, streetwise girl that she seemed to be, she was lurking outside somewhere, waiting to see me come in before making her own appearance.

I got a medium black coffee, house blend, and took it to a table-for-two near the window. I draped my topcoat over the back of my chair, popped the top off the cardboard coffee cup, took a sip, and watched the people and the traffic go by on the other side of the window.

I'd had the foresight to copy Misty's cell-phone number into the little notebook I always carry in the inside pocket of my jacket. After sitting there for about ten minutes, I tried to call it from my own cell phone. It rang five or six times. Then her breathy recorded voice said, "It's Misty. Please leave a message."

I said, "It's Brady Coyne, and it's, um, twenty after six, and I'm here, at the Dunkin'. Where are you?"

I tried to rationalize the bad vibes I was beginning to feel, but it wasn't going well. Misty had said she was worried. She'd sounded nervous. Maybe frightened. She had information about the man who drove the van with the bear logo — the man who might have been looking for Dana the night I saw the van.

Now she'd connected the man in the van and her friend Kayla. She said she was worried about Kayla.

I told myself I shouldn't worry about Misty, but it didn't work.

Six-thirty came and went. No Misty. No phone call.

Okay. I'd give her until seven. If she hadn't made an appearance by then, or at least called, I was going home.

As the minutes ticked away, the vibes got worse.

At ten of seven I called her cell number again, and again her voice mail answered, inviting me to leave a message.

I said, "It's Brady again. Now it's ten of seven. I'm still here at Dunkin'. I'll wait another fifteen minutes. If you can't make it, give me a call, okay? Or you can call me at home." I gave her the number. Then I said, "You got me worried. I hope everything's okay. Let me know, please."

I snapped my phone shut and shoved it into my pocket. I noticed that for the moment there was no line at the counter, so I went up and got myself another cup of coffee.

If she hadn't shown up by the time I

finished the coffee, I decided, I'd leave.

*Come on, Misty. Where the hell are you?*

I nursed that cup of coffee until seven-twenty. We'd agreed to meet at six.

She wasn't coming.

I tried her cell number again. When her message came on, I told her I was going home and she could call me any time to reschedule our meeting. I said I'd meet her any time, any place.

Then I stood up, put on my topcoat, and walked outside onto the Boylston Street sidewalk.

I waited for a gap in the one-way traffic, then trotted across Boylston. I stopped there at the head of the diagonal pathway that would take me across the Common to my home on Beacon Hill. There were a lot of Tuesday-evening folks milling around, crowding the sidewalks, heading for the restaurants and the theaters and the MBTA stations.

I looked all around, studied each of the faces.

Misty's was not among them.

I tried calling Misty's cell phone when I got home. I tried again after dinner, and a couple of times after that. I kept getting her voice mail.

It was around midnight when I went up to the bedroom. Evie had gone up an hour earlier, and now she was mounded under the blankets. The lights were off, and she was breathing rhythmically.

I slid in beside her and lay there on my back looking up at the streetlight shadows flickering on the ceiling.

After a few minutes, she sighed and rolled onto her side. Her hand slithered under my T-shirt and rested lightly my chest. "What's up?" she whispered.

I turned to her and kissed her forehead. "Nothing, babe. Go back to sleep."

"You're worried about that girl, huh?"

"I am, yes."

"She was probably just trying to get some money out of you."

"That's not what it sounded like. She sounded worried. Scared, maybe."

"She's a streetwalker, Brady."

"She's not what you'd expect."

"The hooker with a heart of gold?"

"I don't know about that," I said. "But she's smart and interesting. I think she's the kind of kid, she'll save her money and stay off drugs, and in a few years she'll quit the business and go to college."

"How well do you know her, anyway?"

"Not well at all. You're right."

Evie snuggled against me and buried her face against my shoulder. "You are such a lovely idealist."

"I am not."

"You are too," she said. "It's really quite endearing." She pushed me onto my back, slid her long bare leg over mine, and then she was straddling me.

I watched her lift her arms and peel off her nightgown. Her skin was silvery in the ambient light from the streetlights outside. I touched her naked breasts, and she shivered. She bent to me so that her hair curtained our faces, and she kissed me deeply.

I moved my hands down her back, over her hips, then back up along her spine.

She reached down and put me into her.

I held her hips as we moved together. Then she took in a sharp breath, and I felt all of her muscles harden, and then mine did, too.

She sprawled on top of me while we got our breathing under control. We dozed that way for a while.

Sometime later, she kissed my cheek, whispered, "I love you," slid off me, and laid her cheek on my shoulder.

I had my arm around her, and she kept her bare leg hooked possessively over mine as she went to sleep.

# FOURTEEN

The next morning, Wednesday, instead of climbing into my lawyer suit and heading for the office, I stayed home. At five after nine, when I knew she'd be at her desk checking the morning's e-mails, I called Julie.

"Where are you?" she said.

"Still home. I don't have any appointments this morning, right?"

"So?"

"There's something I've got to do," I said. "I'll be in after lunch. Do you have a copy of yesterday's phone log in front of you?"

"Right here in my computer. Hang on . . . okay. I'm looking at it now."

"The young woman who called three times, wouldn't leave her name?"

"Yes," said Julie. "What about her?"

"What time was the first call she made?"

"Ten-thirty-five in the morning."

"And it was from indoors, you told me, right?"

"That's right," she said. "She was inside a restaurant. Restaurant sounds are quite distinctive."

"Tell me what you remember about those sounds."

"Muffled voices. I couldn't distinguish any words. Plates and cups and saucers clinking together. Um, music, too. In the background. Soft music. It was barely audible."

"What kind of music?"

Julie was silent for a minute. Then she said, "Plucked strings. And a flute. Minimalist music in a minor key. Sort of spooky. Haunting, you know?" She paused. "Asian. It was that Asian, New-Agey type of music that goes on and on, no beginning, middle, or end. They play that kind of music at the spa where I get my nails done. It's supposed to be soothing."

After I hung up with Julie, I tried Misty's cell phone. Got her voice mail. Declined to leave another message.

I left the house a little after nine-thirty. It was one of those mythic January-thaw days that come along once every three or four years in Boston, and when it does, it's usually in February. For a day or two, the sun blazes out of a cloudless blue sky and the temperature soars into the fifties. Snowpiles shrink, sending miniature trout streams flooding down the sides of hilly streets, and the world, as e.e. cummings observed, is mud-luscious and puddle-wonderful.

It's a cruel illusion, of course. Cold fronts and northeasters and ice storms inevitably come surging in behind January thaws.

There were no goat-footed balloonmen whistling far and wee on the Common, nor did I notice any on Boylston Street after I crossed Tremont at the Dunkin' Donuts where I'd waited for Misty the previous evening. I turned right onto Washington, then took a left onto Beach Street — and suddenly, as they say, I was in a whole nother world.

Boston's Chinatown is compressed into ten or a dozen irregular city blocks between the Common and the waterfront. It's a rough rectangle bounded by Washington, Boylston, Purchase, and Kneeland streets. Part of one block is taken up by the Registry of Motor Vehicles building, and it's partly bordered on the Kneeland Street side by the New England Medical Center.

Chinatown is all about food. There are close to fifty restaurants, mostly Chinese but a scattering of Vietnamese, Cambodian,

Japanese, and Korean. There are markets with plucked chickens hanging in the windows and fresh fish laid out on ice, bakeries, greengrocers, fast-food noodle and rice shops, dim sum and sushi, Chinese delis.

There are herbal-medicine shops and book shops and souvenir shops, too, and massage parlors and acupuncture parlors and palm-reading parlors.

But mostly, Chinatown is about food.

I strolled slowly down Beach Street with my jacket open and my face turned up to the warm sun, savoring the January thaw. Beach Street was where Misty said she and her two friends — Kayla and Zooey — hung out.

I was looking for a restaurant that would be open at 10:35 in the morning. That's when Misty had called yesterday. That eliminated the majority of them. Most of the restaurants, according to the little signs hanging in the windows or on the doors, served lunch and dinner and opened at eleven o'clock or eleven-thirty.

I crossed back and forth, methodically checking out all the Beach Street restaurants. I went into every one that I found open at that hour. The first thing I did was listen for New-Agey, Asian music. Plucked strings and a flute. Minimalist, in a minor key.

Whenever I went into a restaurant and heard that kind of music, I found a hostess and did my best to ask her about three young women, one of whom was probably Asian, who liked to hang out there.

At the first four or five places, the hostesses had barely-serviceable English. But they indicated that they understood my question, and they denied knowing the girls.

I realized that they could have been lying, thinking they were protecting the three girls. I tried to explain that I was their friend, that I was worried that they might be in trouble. I showed them my business card, told them I was a lawyer, said that they'd asked me to help them.

The hostesses looked at me with solemn black eyes and shook their heads. Very sorry.

The sixth or seventh open restaurant I tried was in sight of the Chinatown Gate near the end of Beach Street. Underneath the Chinese characters on the restaurant's sign were the English words: Happy Family. Translated literally from the Chinese, I assumed.

When I stepped inside, I noticed the soft music coming from speakers. Plucked strings and woodwinds. It sounded like a forest stream bubbling over smooth stones with a soft breeze sifting through hemlocks. It was unmistakably Asian, haunting and comforting at the same time.

The hostess of Happy Family was an Asian woman whose age was impossible to guess. Her black hair was long, straight, and shiny, her skin unwrinkled, her body slender, her teeth white. But there was something old and worn-out in her eyes, and her voice, when she spoke, rasped with a lifetime of cigarettes and disappointments.

She told me her name was Bonnie. She spoke flawless English, if you consider an East Boston accent flawless . . . which I do.

She asked if I wanted a table.

I told her I just wanted to ask her some questions.

Her eyes slid away from mine. "What kind of questions?" she said.

"I wonder if you know three young women," I said. "Misty, Zooey, and Kayla are their names. Or at least those are their, um, professional names. Pretty girls, maybe twenty? One's a brunette, one's blond, and one's Asian."

"Who are you?" she said.

I said I was a lawyer and gave her one of my cards.

She looked at it, then she looked up at me

and nodded. "What can I do for you?"

"I'm worried that one of these girls — or maybe all three of them — might be in trouble."

Bonnie looked at me for a long moment, measuring me, it seemed, with her dark eyes. Then she nodded. "What about some tea?"

I smiled. "Sure. Tea would be nice."

She gestured toward a table by the front window. The place was entirely empty of patrons.

I sat down. She disappeared.

She was back a minute later with a teapot and a platter of little pastries. She poured some tea for each of us in little cups without handles, then sat across from me.

I took a sip. It tasted smoky. I told Bonnie I liked it. Then I asked her what she could tell me about Misty, Zooey, and Kayla.

"Hookers, I assume," she said. "Nice kids. They're here a lot. They like to sit over there." She gestured toward an L-shaped corner booth. "Talking on their cell phones, sometimes all three of them talking at once. Doing business. They have tea, rice cakes, now and then a bowl of sweet-and-sour soup. Sometimes they're here — or one or two of them are, anyway — all day, all evening until we close. We don't mind. They behave, keep it quiet, dress nice. Classy kids. Always leave a tip."

"They're here a lot, you said."

She shrugged. "Two or three times a week. I think they have a few other places they hang out."

"What about yesterday?" I said.

"Yes," she said. "All three of them were here in the morning. Came in around nine-thirty. They were having some kind of argument. They left after an hour or so. A few hours later — I didn't notice the time, but it was after the lunch hour — the brunette and the Japanese girl came back."

"Misty and Zooey," I said.

She smiled. "Yes."

"What about the blond? Kayla?"

Bonnie shook her head. "She didn't come back with them."

"How about later? Did Kayla ever show up?"

"No. I haven't seen her since yesterday morning when all three of them were here."

"When Misty and Zooey came back after lunchtime, how long did they stay?"

"Most of the afternoon. They were still arguing."

"Could you tell what they were arguing about?"

"Not really. It was one of those quiet argu-

208

ments. Didn't raise their voices, didn't bang around. The two of them, sitting there across from each other, leaning over the table with their faces close together, very serious. Didn't seem exactly angry, but you could see by their expressions and their body language they were tense, upset. At first I didn't even realize they were upset with each other. Then suddenly Zooey slides out of the booth. She starts to leave, then she turns around as if she forgot something. She marches back to the table, bends over so she's right in Misty's face, and she says something and shakes her finger at her."

"She shook her finger?" I said.

Bonnie lifted her hand, made a little fist, stuck out her index finger, and shook it at me.

"Did you overhear anything at all?" I said. "A word, a phrase, a name?"

Bonnie stared down into her teacup for a moment. Then she looked up at me. "It was about Kayla," she said. "She'd done something and Misty was worried about her, thought they should do something. Zooey disagreed. Said it was none of their business. That's what I thought at the time, anyway."

"Any idea why they were worried about Kayla?"

"No."

"Or what it was Misty wanted to do that Zooey disagreed with?"

She shook her head. "I really didn't hear more than a word or two of what they said. I wasn't trying to listen. It was none of my business."

"So Zooey left?"

"Yes. After she — she shook her finger — she marched out."

"And didn't come back?"

Bonnie shook her head. "Haven't seen her since then."

"What time was it that she left?"

She looked up at the ceiling for a moment. "Middle of the afternoon sometime, I think. I didn't really notice."

"What about Misty?" I said. "When was the last time you saw her?"

"Misty?" Bonnie narrowed her eyes and looked up at the ceiling for a minute. "We were starting to get the early dinner crowd. It got busy, and I wasn't paying too much attention to Misty. She was over there in their usual booth, pot of tea, working the phone. Then, next time I looked over, she was gone."

"Do you think you could pin down a time?"

"Five-thirty? Could've been closer to six."

She shrugged.

"Have you seen any of them since then?" I said. "Later last night or this morning?"

"No."

"I'm interested in a certain panel truck," I said. "It's got a logo painted on its side. Bears. A big one and a little one."

"Bears?" she said. "What kind of bears?"

I took a pen from my pocket, and sketched on a napkin — crudely — the bear logo as I remembered it. I showed it to Bonnie. "They're sort of generic bears. Mother and cub, probably. The truck has New Hampshire license plates."

She looked at my sketch. She seemed to be fighting back a smile. "Those are bears?"

I shrugged.

"I don't remember seeing any truck with bears on it," she said.

"Did you know Sunshine?"

She frowned.

"Her real name was Maureen Quinlan. She was homeless. They called her Sunshine."

Bonnie blinked. Then she nodded. "Okay, I know who you mean. The poor woman who was murdered. She — they found her body not far from here a few days ago. Behind the Moon Garden over on Tyler Street. Is that who you mean?"

"Yes. You didn't know her, then?"

"No. I don't think she hung around here. What I heard, she probably wandered into somebody's territory, they took exception to it."

"They killed her for being in the wrong place?"

"They've got all the Dumpsters staked out," she said. "You better not go dipping into somebody else's Dumpster."

"Did you hear anything else?"

"About . . . Sunshine?"

"Yes."

Bonnie gazed up at the ceiling. Either she was trying to remember, or else she was trying to appear to be trying to remember.

"No," she said. "There hasn't been much talk about it, at least among the people who talk to me. Homeless people die in alleys." She shrugged.

I had thought to bring Dana Wetherbee's morgue photo with me. I took it from my shirt pocket and put it on the table in front of Bonnie. "Do you recognize her?"

She frowned at the picture, then looked up at me. "She's dead, isn't she?"

"Yes."

"I don't recognize her."

"You've never seen her?"

"I didn't say that. I might have seen her.

212

But if I did, I don't remember. I don't recall her face. Who is she?"

"She died in an alley, too."

She sighed. "Oh, dear."

"Yes," I said.

"And this girl," she said, tapping Dana's photo with her forefinger, "is connected to Misty and the other two girls . . . how?"

"I don't know," I said.

"You think Misty and Zooey and Kayla? . . ."

"I hope not," I said.

Bonnie looked at me for a long moment. "Can I ask you a question?"

"Sure."

"What's your interest in these girls?" she said. "I mean, you're a lawyer . . ."

"Misty called me yesterday," I said. "I think she was calling from here. She wanted to talk to me. Left several messages. We didn't connect till later in the afternoon. I agreed to meet her at six at the Dunkin' Donuts on the corner of Tremont and Boylston. She never showed up. I tried calling her cell a few times, but she didn't answer." I shrugged. "I'm worried about her."

"You think something happened to her."

"That's what worries me, yes."

Bonnie shook her head. "Girls who live

that way, it always seems, sooner or later . . ."

"I know," I said. "That's what I keep thinking."

When I stepped outside the Happy Family Chinese restaurant, the sun was high in the sky and you could almost smell springtime in the air. A cruel illusion, I knew, but it still turned my thoughts to green fields and apple blossoms, mayflies and trout streams.

As I walked back to my home on Beacon Hill, I tried to figure out what I should do. Something had happened to Misty, I was convinced of it. Maybe it was connected to the guy who drove the panel truck with the bear logo and New Hampshire plates. Maybe it was also connected to what happened to Sunshine and to Dana Wetherbee.

I thought about telling Saundra Mendoza about it. I tried to play out our conversation.

Coyne: "There's this girl, Misty. I'm worried about her."

Mendoza: "Misty who?"

Coyne: "I don't know her last name. I don't even know if Misty is really her first name. She's got two friends. Kayla and Zooey. I'm worried about them, too."

Mendoza: "Last names also unknown, I suppose?"

Coyne: "Well, yes."

Mendoza: "And you're worried why?"

Coyne: "Misty wanted to meet with me. We made a date. Except she didn't show up."

Mendoza: "You never been stood up by a woman before?"

Coyne: "Hardly the same thing."

Mendoza: "These girls. Where do they live?"

Coyne: "I don't know. They sometimes hang out in the Happy Family restaurant on Beach Street."

Mendoza: "And what do they do?"

Coyne: "They're hookers, I think."

Mendoza: "So you got stood up by a hooker . . ."

I decided that if I was going to talk to Saundra Mendoza, I better have more to tell her.

I tried to convince myself that Misty was a resourceful kid. She could take care of herself. She'd probably worked out whatever was bothering her, or just decided she didn't need me to help her. It would have been considerate of her to return my calls. But I had no reason to believe that she was considerate.

I almost believed myself.

# FIFTEEN

That evening Evie and I were sitting at our kitchen table eating home-delivery thin-crust pizza — Vidalia onion, sun-dried tomatoes, and goat cheese for Evie, sausage, pepperoni, and eggplant for me, between us covering all of the important food groups except chocolate. I was telling her about my adventures in Chinatown and how I found the restaurant that Misty had called me from on Tuesday.

"Sam Spade," she said.

"Yes," I said. "Exactly."

"So what did you learn?"

I shook my head. "Hardly anything."

Right then the phone rang. Evie started to get out of her chair.

"Leave it," I said. "We're eating. Probably somebody trying to foist another credit card on us. They always call at dinnertime."

It rang again.

Evie put down her pizza slice and looked

at me. "What if it's important?"

"They'll leave a message. We can call them back."

"I'm going to get it."

"I know," I said.

She got up, went over to the counter, picked up the cordless phone, and said, "Hello?"

She looked up at the ceiling as she listened. Then she glanced at me, gave her head a quick shake, said, "Yes, of course," and wandered into the living room with the phone pressed against her ear.

I could hear the occasional murmur of Evie's voice from the other room, but I couldn't tell what she was saying. She seemed to be doing more listening than speaking. I inferred that she was not talking to a credit-card salesman.

She was gone for the length of time it took me to drink half a glass of beer, eat two slices of pizza, and feed a crust to Henry. When she came back and took her seat at the table, she looked at me and said, "That was Shirley Arsenault."

"Who?"

"Dana Wetherbee's grandmother. Verna's mother. I called them last night, remember?"

"Sure I remember," I said. "I just didn't

remember her name. I thought you said she didn't want to talk to you."

"She didn't. That was yesterday. This afternoon a Rhode Island State Police officer dropped by their house."

"Oh, jeez."

Evie nodded. "Your Lieutenant Mendoza faxed him a copy of that morgue photo. He showed it to Shirley. She confirmed that it was Dana. Now she wants to talk to me."

"Why?"

Evie shrugged. "She's pretty upset."

"Of course she's upset," I said. "That's her dead granddaughter. She's already buried her daughter. That's way too much. What I meant was, why you?"

"I suppose it's because I knew Dana, and because I called her. She needs to talk to somebody."

"Grief counseling," I said.

Evie shrugged. "Call it whatever you want. I told her I'd be there tomorrow afternoon around four." She arched her eyebrows at me.

"Where is there?"

"Edson, Rhode Island."

I nodded. "Okay. I'll go with you."

Evie was poking me. "Brady, the phone," she said. "Get the damn phone."

219

Then I was aware of it ringing on the table beside our bed. I fumbled for it, pressed it against my ear, and mumbled, "Yeah?"

"Mr. Coyne," came a woman's voice. "This is Marcia Benetti. Roger Horowitz's partner?"

I pushed myself into a half-sitting position. It was still dark in the bedroom. "What the hell time is it?"

"Around five-thirty. Roger wants to talk to you. I'm on my way over to pick you up. Please be ready."

"Who died?" Horowitz and Benetti were state-police homicide detectives. If they were up and about at five-thirty on a January morning, it meant somebody had died under circumstances that usually amounted to murder.

"I'm on Storrow Drive, Mr. Coyne. I'll be in front of your house in ten minutes."

"Young woman," I said, "maybe twenty, maybe younger, dark hair, goes by the name of Misty?"

"You can talk to Roger when you see him," she said. Then she disconnected.

I hung up the phone. Beside me, Evie rolled onto her side and flopped an arm across my chest. "Wha's up?" she grumbled.

"That was Roger Horowitz's partner," I said. "She's coming over to pick me up."

"Why?"

"Go back to sleep, babe."

"You have to go?"

"Yes." I leaned over, kissed her cheek, and slid out of bed.

By the time I'd pulled on my T-shirt and boxers, Evie had rolled back onto her belly and resumed snoring.

Henry was curled up in his usual spot on the rug at the foot of the bed. He opened an eye, considered following me downstairs, thought better of it, and went back to sleep.

The automatic coffeemaker had not started brewing when I got to the kitchen. I turned it on, hoping Marcia Benetti would have the courtesy not to arrive until I could pour myself a mugful.

But when I peeked out the front door, her gray sedan was sitting there under the streetlight.

I pulled on my parka, went outside, and climbed into the passenger seat. "Hope I didn't keep you waiting," I said.

She handed me a giant-sized Dunkin' Donuts cup. "The Starbucks wasn't open," she said. "Hope this is okay. Roger said you needed black."

" 'Need' is the operative word." I popped the lid and sniffed. "Plain house blend, right?"

"He said you didn't go for the fancy stuff," she said. "He said get you two-day-old cop coffee if they had it. But they didn't."

I took a sip. I could feel the caffeine surge through my blood vessels and zap happy little sparks into my brain. "Thank you," I said. "You're an angel." I took another sip. "So tell me what's going on. Where are we headed, anyway?"

"The coffee was Roger's idea," she said. "You can tell him he's angelic, if you want. As far as what's going on, all I can really tell you is what he told me. Cleaning service found a body in back of an office building on Route One in Danvers. He wants you there."

"Why me?"

"He didn't tell me, Mr. Coyne. You know Roger. He called me, told me to get my ass up there, pick you up on the way. That's all I know, okay?"

"I guess you've had enough conversation for now, huh?"

"More than enough," she said. "Drink your coffee and stop asking me questions I can't answer."

Marcia Benetti drove up Route One through Charlestown and Chelsea, Revere and Everett, Saugus and Peabody and Lynnfield, and a little after six-fifteen, she took a left, cut across the southbound lane, and followed a driveway around to the back of a low-slung brick-and-glass office building.

Eight or ten official-looking vehicles were parked randomly down at the far end of the lot with their doors hanging open and their headlights sending cones of light into the predawn darkness. Running engines puffed clouds of exhaust into the cold winter morning, and blue and red lights flashed on the dirty snow.

Benetti stopped beside a Danvers cruiser. I opened the car door and started to get out.

"Hang on," she said. She picked up her car phone, pecked a number into it, paused, then said, "We're here." She listened for a moment, glanced at me, said, "I don't know. I didn't ask," then put the phone back.

"Didn't ask what?" I said.

"He'll ask you himself."

A minute later Horowitz appeared from behind the vehicles. He was wearing a camel hair topcoat, a multi-colored knitted scarf, and a floppy felt hat with the brim turned down all the way around. He stopped in front of the car, lifted his hand, and crooked his finger at us.

"He wants you," said Benetti.

I got out and went over to where Horowitz was waiting. "Who's dead?" I said. I didn't offer to shake hands, and neither did he. Roger Horowitz had little patience with empty gestures of civility.

"If I knew," he said, "I wouldn't need you. She had your business card in her pocket."

"I was afraid of that," I said. "Young girl?"

"Late teens, I'd say. Brunette." He cocked his head and peered at me. "You think you know who it is?"

"Yes," I said. "Let's have a look."

"This way." Horowitz flicked on the footlong flashlight he was carrying, turned, and headed toward the back corner of the parking lot. I trailed along behind him.

At least a dozen men and women were standing around hunching their shoulders, stamping their feet, and sipping from Styrofoam coffee cups. Nobody seemed to be saying much.

Out of the corner of his mouth, Horowitz said, "Still waiting for the M.E." Then he mumbled, "Excuse us," and shouldered his way through the circle of onlookers. I followed behind him.

A big circle of yellow crime-scene tape had been strung around the corner of the parking lot. It encompassed the snowbanks where the plow had cleared the lot and a large area of drifted snow beyond the snow-banks.

Horowitz ducked under the tape, held it for me so I could bend under it, and then led me to the edge of the lot. He played his flashlight on the ground.

She was sprawled on her side on the packed snow on the parking lot near the snowbank. Her head was twisted awkwardly to the side, and her legs were bent in a running position. She was wearing a hip-length fake-fur jacket, a short black skirt, fishnet stockings, and leather boots. A red beret lay beside her body. She had long dark hair. Her skin was unnaturally white.

"Shit," I said.

"Recognize her?" said Horowitz.

"You better let me see her face."

"Don't touch anything."

I kept my hands in my pockets and scootched down beside the body. Horowitz shone his flashlight on her face.

It was Misty.

"I know her," I said.

"You got a name?"

I stood up. "She called herself Misty. That's all I know. She was a pro, hung out in Chinatown. How'd she die?"

"Beaten and strangled. Looks like they dumped her here. Killed her somewhere else, loaded her into a vehicle, and tossed her out. Cleaning service spotted her in their headlights when they were leaving around four this morning." Horowitz looked at me. "Misty? That what you said?"

"Yes. I assume it's her, um, professional name."

He narrowed his eyes at me. "A hooker named Misty with your business card in her pocket?"

"It's nothing like that, for Christ sake."

"Better not be. Jesus, Coyne."

"If it was, would you tell Evie?"

"Bet your ass."

"Evie knows all about Misty."

"Well," he said, "I don't. Let's go over to my vehicle, turn on the heater, and you can talk to me."

On the way to Horowitz's car, he stopped, poked a uniformed policeman in the chest, and said, "Run down to the Dunkin' and get me and Mr. Coyne here some coffee and a couple sugar-covered crullers. You might as well pick up something for yourself, too." He fumbled in his wallet and handed the cop a twenty-dollar bill.

The motor was running and the driver's door of Horowitz's sedan hung open. We got in, closed the doors, and cracked the windows so they wouldn't steam up.

"Okay," he said. "Talk to me."

I told him how Henry found Dana Wetherbee's body in my backyard, how she died from blood loss and exposure to the cold. When I told him how she'd been on fertility medication and the M.E. surmised that she'd miscarried because her fetus had outgrown her uterus, Horowitz said, "Humph."

When I mentioned Saundra Mendoza, he muttered, "Yeah. Good cop."

I told him about Sunshine, and the Shamrock Inn, and running into Misty, Zooey, and Kayla, and seeing a van with New Hampshire plates and a logo with bears on the side. I told him that Evie was the one who identified the girl as Dana Wetherbee and that she and I were planning to drive down to Rhode Island that afternoon to talk with Dana's grandmother.

About then the cop came back with our coffee and crullers. Horowitz and I stopped talking long enough to take a couple bites of cruller.

When I started up again, I told him about finding the photo in the baggie stapled onto Henry's collar.

Horowitz's head snapped up at that. "In your backyard?"

I nodded. "I haven't told Evie about it."

"Yeah," he said. "Don't blame you. You told Mendoza, though, I hope."

"I did," I said. Then I told him how Misty had called my office on Tuesday, how she said she needed to talk with me confidentially, something about the guy who'd been driving the van with the bear logo. She was concerned about her friend Kayla, but she didn't tell me why. I told him that she agreed to meet me at Dunkin' Donuts on Tremont and Boylston but never showed up. I told him how the next day I'd tracked down the Happy Family Restaurant on Beach Street where, according to Bonnie, the hostess, the three girls hung out. I summarized what Bonnie had told me. "You should talk to her," I said. "And Kayla and Zooey. They were Misty's best friends. The three of them were there together the day she called me."

"Never would've occurred to me," he grumbled. "Thanks."

"You don't need to be sarcastic," I said. "I'm just trying to help."

Horowitz was taking notes in his pocket-sized black notebook. Without looking up, he said, "Yeah, sorry. That was excellent detecting."

"I thought so, too," I said. "Evie called me Sam Spade."

He snorted.

"Dana Wetherbee weighs heavy on my heart," I said. "So does Sunshine. And now Misty."

"I don't blame you," he said. He snapped his notebook shut and shoved it into his jacket pocket. "These women, they run into you, next thing you know, they're dead."

"I appreciate your sympathy," I said. "But I don't think I'm the important connection among the three of them."

"That wasn't sympathy."

"Gee," I said. "You could've fooled me."

"So did she have a pimp?"

"Misty? I have no idea. You think? . . ."

"Beaten and strangled. A pimp or a customer, huh?"

"Funny," I said. "She's a prostitute. But I never really thought about it. About what she did, I mean."

"You didn't, huh?"

"No. She was just this pretty young woman. She was smart and savvy, she had friends, she liked Chinese tea . . ."

Horowitz was shaking his head.

"Yeah," I said. "Evie called me naïve." I took a bite of cruller. "You think whoever did this picked her up in the city and drove up here to dump her?"

Horowitz shrugged. "She worked in the

city, right?"

"Right," I said. "But why pick a place on the opposite side of the road where you've got to cut across traffic? I mean, there are plenty of office buildings on the northbound side."

"We're checking out this building," said Horowitz. "Assume it's not random. Assume our killer specifically chose this building. Maybe he works here, or used to work here. Maybe his ex-wife or the guy who fired him works here."

"That's not exactly what I'm saying."

"What *are* you saying?"

"That panel truck I mentioned, the one with the bears? It had New Hampshire plates."

"Heading south on Route One, coming down from the Granite State," said Horowitz. "Stops along the way to dispose of a body. That what you're thinking?"

I shrugged. "What do I know?"

He sighed. "What do any of us know."

"So what're you going to do?"

"Do?" He shook his head. "We've got to solve this damn murder, that's what."

"I mean —"

"Look, Coyne. I'm sorry to drag you out of bed, and I appreciate all your help. I really do. But I don't need your advice on investigating homicides, and I sure as hell don't want you hanging around getting in my way. Understand?"

I nodded. "Sure."

He looked at me and rolled his eyes. "I know you, Coyne."

"Don't worry about me," I said. "I just want to know what happened to Dana Wetherbee."

"Sam Spade, my ass," he grumbled. He flipped through his notebook, then looked up at me. "Okay, so let's go over your story again."

# Sixteen

Edson, Rhode Island, turned out to be a little postcard-pretty New England village similar to dozens of quaint New England villages on the Massachusetts South Shore and in Vermont's Champlain Valley and New Hampshire's Monadnock region. To get to the Arsenaults' house, Evie and I had to drive through what passed for the center of town. The rectangular village green featured a statue of a man on a horse and a World War I cannon with a pyramid of cannonballs. A white-spired Congregational church, a rambling nineteenth-century inn, a general store, a post office, a town office building, and several well-tended colonial houses encircled the green. A graveyard rolled across the hillside behind the church, and villagers were ice skating on the little frozen pond in back of the post office. The roads were lined with giant maple trees and old stone walls, and everything was draped with pristine white snow that glistened in the late-afternoon January sunshine.

Edson, Rhode Island, looked like the kind of place where nothing bad could ever happen to anybody.

Evie was driving her Volkswagen Jetta. I was navigating with the directions I'd printed out from MapQuest.

Most of the way down we'd talked about Misty.

First Dana. Then Sunshine. And now Misty. They were all connected, and the connection seemed to be me.

Brady Coyne, KOD. The kiss of death.

"You're not that powerful," said Evie. "Everything doesn't revolve around you. You're just some guy. A nice guy, true. A fairly lovable guy, most of the time. And cute. But still, just a guy. You can't save the world."

"I don't know why the hell not," I muttered.

Shirley and Richard Arsenault lived in a white dormered Cape at 27 Marlboro Road, one-point-three miles past the center of town according to MapQuest and confirmed by the Jetta's odometer. An old blue Ford Escort wagon was parked in the driveway beside the house.

Evie pulled in behind it. She turned off

the ignition, blew out a breath, and said, "Okay. Here we go."

We walked up the steps to the front porch and she rang the bell.

After a minute, the door opened, and a boy — he looked twelve or thirteen — stood there. He was small and pale with just the beginnings of fuzz on his upper lip. "You're Mrs. Banyon," he said to Evie. "You're here about Dana."

"Yes," she said. "I'm very sorry." I noticed that she did not bother correcting him about the "Mrs."

He nodded. "I remember you from the hospital."

"I remember you, too," she said. "This is Brady."

He looked at me, then held out his hand. "I'm Bobby Wetherbee."

I shook his hand. "Brady Coyne. Good to meet you."

Bobby Wetherbee's hand was small but his grip was manly. "Come on in," he said.

We followed him into the house. The front door opened directly into a small, dim living room.

Bobby took our coats and gestured at the sofa. It had a faded slipcover featuring large brownish flowers. "Have a seat," he said. "My nana will be right there."

We sat, and Bobby left the room. A little gentleman.

An upright piano dominated one corner of the room. On one wall a brick fireplace was flanked by built-in bookcases with glass doors. A braided rug covered the pine-plank flooring. A single copy of *Reader's Digest* and an empty green-glass candy dish sat on the coffee table.

The only wall decoration was a picture of Jesus on the cross. He had a crown of thorns and a halo around his head, and his blood was bright red. A sprig of dried palm fronds had been tucked behind the frame.

From somewhere inside the house came the hum of a refrigerator and the loud tick of a clock. Otherwise, it was ghostly silent.

Evie squeezed my leg. I covered her hand with mine.

After a minute, a woman came into the room. She was short and stout, with tightly permed white hair and sharp pale eyes. She wore gray sweatpants and a blue Providence College sweatshirt and white sneakers. Her eyes were red, as if she'd been crying. She nodded at us without smiling.

Evie stood up. "Mrs. Arsenault, hello. I'm Evie Banyon. We met a couple years ago."

The woman nodded. "Yes. In the hospital. I remember. When Verna was dying. You were kind to all of us." She glanced at me and arched her eyebrows.

"This is Brady Coyne," said Evie. "My husband. Brady's a lawyer."

I stood up, smiled at Shirley, and held out my hand.

She shook it quickly, then took a step backwards, as if she was afraid to get too close to me. "Did Bobby offer you coffee?"

I shook my head.

"It's all made," she said.

"Thank you," said Evie. "Coffee would be great."

Shirley Arsenault shuffled out of the room.

"Husband," I whispered to Evie.

She smiled.

Shirley Arsenault was back a couple minutes later with a tray bearing an aluminum carafe, three mugs, a pitcher of milk, a matching bowl of sugar, a plate of Fig Newtons, and a stack of napkins. She set it on the table and poured the mugs full of coffee. Then she sat on the rocking chair across from us. She perched on the edge of the seat with her knees pressed together, holding her coffee mug in both hands. "This is all my fault," she said softly.

Evie said nothing. Neither did I.

"I should have stopped her. I know Verna would never have allowed it. She was just a child." She looked at Evie.

"You mean Dana?" said Evie.

She nodded.

"Dana ran away?"

She nodded. "I didn't stop her. I let her go."

"Where did she go?"

Shirley Arsenault shook her head, then plucked a handkerchief from the cuff of her sweatshirt and dabbed at her eyes with it. "I didn't ask for my daughter to die, Lord knows, and I didn't ask to have two young children to take care of. I've already got Richard. That's my husband. Since he had his stroke, he's worse than a child. I have to feed him and bathe him and change him, and . . ." She was looking down into her coffee mug. "I'm just tired all the time," she said. "I can't do it all by myself."

"You've been taking care of Dana and Bobby since Verna died?" said Evie.

"Obviously doing a poor job of it," she said.

"What about their father?" I said.

"Benjamin?" Shirley looked up. Sparks flashed in her eyes. "Benjamin drives trucks back and forth to Oklahoma and Utah and places like that. He doesn't have time to raise children. Never did. Sends me a little money once in a while. Very little. That's about it for Benjamin. It's not as if I had a choice, mind you. Somebody had to take the children. Now Bobby, he's a good boy. Helps his old nana out around the house, sits and reads to his grandfather, gets good grades in school. But Dana . . ." Shirley blinked, then picked up her mug and took a sip.

"Dana wasn't a good girl?" said Evie.

"She used to be," said Shirley. "When her mother was alive, Dana was a sweet, serious girl, helpful and obedient and, you know, just nice. But always a sad, private child. You never knew what she was thinking. It was hard to blame her. Her mother was sick all the time, in and out of the hospital. Then when Verna died, Dana became even more . . . quiet. Moody. I know I should have tried harder to help her, but I was awfully sad myself. Verna was my only child." She stared hard at Evie. "There's nothing worse than outliving your children." She glanced up at the picture of Jesus. "I tried to get Dana to go to Mass with me, but she wouldn't. That was another thing. When Verna died, Dana stopped going to church. Then she turned sixteen, and next thing I know, she tells me she's not going back to school, she's found a job, and she's leaving, and then . . . she just left. And I never saw her again."

"What was this job?" said Evie.

Shirley shook her head. "I don't know. I remember she said it was important work, whatever that meant. She said she'd keep in touch with me. I asked her about this job, where she'd be, what she'd be doing. She said she'd tell me more when she got settled down."

"She ran away," said Evie.

"It took me a while to realize that's what it was. I guess I wasn't thinking very straight."

"Did you report it?" I said.

Shirley narrowed her eyes at me. "Yes, of course I did. After a few days, I realized what Dana was doing. I called the Edson police. I gave them a photo, answered a lot of questions, and they said they'd keep an eye out for her. But they said if she was sixteen, she could quit school and leave home, and unless she'd been abducted or something, there wasn't much they could do." She shook her head. "I called them a few times after that to see if they knew anything. But they didn't. And then . . . then yesterday this policeman comes to my door with that awful photograph. . . ."

"When did this happen?" said Evie. "When did Dana leave?"

"At the beginning of the summer. Her

birthday was in June. The nineteenth. I gave her a jacket. I think she liked it. We don't have much money. She left a week or so after that. It was a Saturday. When I came downstairs that morning, Bobby told me she was gone."

"Did you hear from her after she left?" I said.

Shirley swiveled her head to look at me. "Just once," she said. "A few days later. She called me on the phone, told me she was fine, and asked to speak to Bobby. Bobby wasn't here at the time." She shrugged. "I told her it was wrong for her to be gone, that she should finish school first. I asked her to come back home. She said she would, but not yet." She shrugged. "After that one phone call, I never heard from her again."

"You must have been worried," said Evie.

Shirley looked at her. "Of course I was worried. But she said she was fine, and I just prayed that she was. I spoke to the police. I didn't know what else to do."

"She said it was important work?" I said.

"Yes. Important. That was the word she used."

"Any idea what she meant?"

Shirley shrugged. "All I can tell you," she said, "is that ever since I can remember, Dana wanted to be a doctor. I suppose it was because her mother was always sick."

"She used to tell me that, too," said Evie. "She was very interested in Verna's disease and how she was being treated. She asked very good questions."

"I doubt that Dana left home at sixteen to enroll in medical school," said Shirley. She leaned forward and put her coffee mug on the tray on the coffee table. Then she sat back in her rocking chair and looked at us. "That policeman yesterday, he said I'd have to go to Boston to identify her body."

"If you want," said Evie, "I'll go with you."

Shirley looked at Evie. "You were always kind to Verna. Dana loved you. I — I don't have anybody. Nobody at all. You're very kind. Thank you."

"Happy to do it."

"That policeman," said Shirley. "The man who came to my door yesterday with that terrible photograph?"

Evie nodded.

"He said Dana was pregnant. He said she had a miscarriage or something. He said she died in the snow in some alley in the city. He said . . ." Shirley stopped, bowed her head, and covered her eyes with both hands.

Evie got up and went over to her. She knelt beside the rocking chair and took both of Shirley's hands in hers.

Shirley looked at her. Her eyes were wet. "Is all that true?"

"It is true," said Evie. "Dana came to our house in Boston. I assume she was looking for me, but I was away on a business trip. It was the middle of the night. She'd had a miscarriage, and she died in our backyard."

Shirley was shaking her head. "This is too awful," she said. "I don't know what to do."

"I blame myself," said Evie. "I wasn't there for her."

I cleared my throat. "I wonder if Dana left anything behind that might help us figure out where she went," I said. "Something that might tell us what her important work was, who she went with, anything like that."

Shirley looked at me. "Like what?"

"I don't know," I said. "Letters? A diary?"

She shook her head. "Yesterday, after that policeman left, I went up to her room. I looked everywhere. In her desk, in the closet, under the bed, in her school notebooks. There was nothing."

"Did Dana have a computer?"

"Lord, no. We can't afford computers."

"How about her telephone?"

"She didn't have her own telephone. We have just the one phone. It's in the kitchen.

Nobody ever called for her except Benjamin."

"Her father," I said.

She nodded. "He'd call every few weeks from wherever he happened to be to say hello to his children."

"Did he call after Dana left?"

Shirley nodded. "He asked to speak to her. I told him she wasn't living here anymore. He said, Oh, really? And I said, Yes, really. Sarcastic-like. Those children need a father. And Benjamin, all he said was, Well, okay, and then he asked to talk to Bobby."

"That was it? He didn't even ask where she went?"

"No. It was as if he didn't care."

"What about Dana's friends?" I said.

"I don't know about her friends," she said. "Dana never invited friends to the house. I don't even know if she had any friends. She was always alone."

"How about Bobby?" said Evie. "Maybe he knows something."

"I asked him," said Shirley. "Bobby says he doesn't know anything. When Verna was sick, Dana was practically Bobby's mother. She was wonderful with him. But after Verna died . . ." She took a deep breath. "I just don't think I can. . . ." She was rocking, hugging herself. Her eyes glittered with tears.

Evie looked at me and shook her head, her way of saying, *Enough. No more questions.* To Shirley she said, "That's all right. We'll see what we can find out. When the police in Massachusetts want you to go to Boston, give me a call. Okay?"

Shirley nodded. "Thank you. Yes. I will."

"We can talk some more, too, sometime, if you want," said Evie.

"That would be nice. Thank you."

We all stood up. Shirley left the room and came back a minute later with our coats.

At the front door, I turned to Shirley. "I'm wondering if you might have a recent photograph of Dana that I could borrow."

She looked up at me. "What in the world for?"

"If we're going to try to figure out where she went and what happened to her," I said, "I'll need to have something other than the picture that the policeman had to show to people."

"Oh, yes," she said. "Of course. I do have one. I'll be right back."

She left the room, and then I heard her stomping up the stairs.

She was back a few minutes later. She handed me a three-by-five snapshot. It showed Dana leaning against the side of a blue car, possibly the Escort that was parked in the driveway. She was wearing white shorts and a pale blue T-shirt, and she was squinting into the sun and smiling shyly. She looked young and pretty and vulnerable.

I tucked the photo into my shirt pocket. "Thanks," I said to Shirley. "I'll return it to you if you want."

She waved that idea away. "I have others. You can keep that one."

We said good-bye, promised to keep in touch, and then Evie and I climbed into her car.

Just as she started up the engine there was a tap on the window beside my head. I turned. Bobby Wetherbee was standing there.

I rolled down the window.

"You were talking to my nana about Dana, right?"

I nodded. "We're trying to figure out where she went, who she was with when she left. Did she say anything to you?"

He shook his head. "Not really. Just one day she told me she had to leave for a while. She said it was something important, something she wanted to do."

"Important how?" I said.

"I don't know," said Bobby. "I asked her. I asked her where she was going, what she was doing, but she just said that I shouldn't worry, she'd be okay and she wouldn't be gone long. It was me she was worried about. Ever since our mother died, she was always worrying about me, asking if I was okay, trying to get me to talk about how I was feeling and everything. I know she was sad, too, but she never talked about herself. Anyway, I don't know if this would help, but . . ." He stuck an envelope into the half-open window. "I got this around Christmas. It's from Dana. You can keep it if you want."

I took the envelope from him. "Thank you," I said.

Evie leaned over to my window and said, "Did you talk to Dana after she left?"

He shook his head. "My nana said she called once when I was out. She didn't leave a number, and she never called again."

"So you have no idea where she went, or why, or with whom?"

"No," he said. "She didn't tell me anything. I'm sorry. Look, I gotta go." Bobby Wetherbee waved his hand, then scurried down the driveway and disappeared behind the house.

"What is in the envelope?" said Evie.

It was addressed in green ink to Bobby

Wetherbee, 27 Marlboro Road, Edson, Rhode Island. Inside was one of those religious Christmas cards with a nativity scene on the outside and the words "Wishing You a Blessed Christmas" printed on the inside.

Under that sentiment, in the same green ink, she had written: "Be good. Love, Dana."

I turned the card over, but there was no other message, no information, no clue.

I handed it to Evie.

She read it, shrugged, and said, "Let's see the envelope."

I handed it to her.

She glanced at it, then looked at me. "Where's Churchill, New Hampshire?"

"I don't know," I said. "But that van, the one with the bears on it? It had New Hampshire plates."

# SEVENTEEN

When we got home, Evie and I opened our Rand McNally *Road Atlas* on the kitchen table and looked for Churchill, New Hampshire. We needed our magnifying glass to locate it. The name was marked in the small, faint print reserved for a town barely worthy of Mr. McNally's notice. It was tucked into the northwestern corner of the state near the place where the border between Vermont and Quebec touch it. Churchill straddled an unnamed thin blue line that appeared to be a tributary of the Connecticut River.

I estimated that Churchill, New Hampshire, was a little more than 200 miles from Boston. The index in the back of our two-year-old atlas said the town's population was 941.

"What in the world was Dana Wetherbee doing there?" said Evie.

"That's the question," I said.

"Pregnant and alone and far from home," she said.

"Maybe she was just passing through when it was time to mail her Christmas cards."

"Mm," she murmured. "Let's see what we can find out."

I followed her upstairs to our guestroom, which doubled as Evie's home office. Besides the twin beds, nightstand, and bureau, there was a small desk for her beloved iMac in the corner by the window that looked down onto Mt. Vernon Street.

She sat at the desk. I sat on the end of one of the beds. From there I could see the pictures on her monitor but couldn't read the words.

"Tell me what you're doing," I said.

"Googling Churchill, New Hampshire," she mumbled. A minute later she said, "Hm. The town doesn't even have a Web site."

"Should it?"

"Most towns do."

"Too small, huh?"

"Not necessarily," she said. "A lot of towns with populations under a thousand have very nice Web sites."

"Too backward, then."

"Or poor," she said. "Or stubborn, or

249

indifferent."

I watched the images and colors change on her monitor as she popped up Web sites.

"Would you mind getting me a beer?" said Evie.

"It would be my honor."

I went downstairs, snagged two bottles of Long Trail from the refrigerator, popped their tops, and took them upstairs.

I put one of them on Evie's desk and resumed my seat on the bed.

"Interesting," she said.

"What?"

She swiveled around in her chair, picked up her beer bottle, and took a long swig. "Churchill, New Hampshire," she said, "is a very old town with a long history. A crucial battle in the French and Indian War was fought there. In the nineteenth century, it had a big lumber mill that employed a couple hundred people, mostly Canadians. They were running pulp down the Skiprood River through Churchill as recently as the nineteen-fifties. The paper company had a factory on the river there."

"Sounds like your typical old northern New England village," I said. "Run down and worn out."

She nodded. "When the paper company shut down, it's as if the town died. As near as I can determine, aside from a gun shop, a boat builder, a café, an auto-body shop, a gas station, and a few dairy farms, there's not much enterprise in Churchill."

"So what do nine hundred citizens do?"

"Work somewhere else, I guess." She took another gulp of beer. "Raise cows. Grow corn. Collect welfare checks and food stamps. The question remains. What was Dana Wetherbee doing there?"

Before I left for the office the next morning — Friday — I called Gordon Cahill.

Cahill was the best private investigator I knew. Over the years I'd hired him to do some jobs for me, typically researching financial records for clients who were in the middle of contentious divorces. You might hide an asset or two from the IRS, but you couldn't hide it from Gordie Cahill.

He used to do surveillance and missing-persons and bodyguard work, but a couple of years earlier — while tracking down a client's husband for me, in fact — some bad guys smashed his leg with the blunt end of an axe and locked him up in their cellar. By the time I found him and got him to a hospital, the infection had nearly killed him, and as a condition of remaining married to

251

him, his wife demanded that he quit the business.

Gordie hated that idea, but he loved his wife, and they ended up compromising, as functional couples do. Gordie, they agreed, could keep his business, but he'd stick to the office and restrict his sleuthing to computer and telephone work.

As it turned out, the whole issue was moot. Gordie ended up with a chronically aching leg and a severe limp. He leaned heavily on his cane and hired freelancers to do his legwork. Gordie always made a joke out of the word "legwork."

He liked to compare himself to Nero Wolfe, Rex Stout's famously sedentary detective. He called his freelancers "Archies."

When he answered the phone, I said, "It's Brady. I got a little job for you. Interested?"

"How little?"

"I don't know," I said. "For you, it's probably easy. For me it'd be impossible. I want to put names and faces and places and dates on a logo."

"Sounds like fun," he said. "What kind of logo?"

"A company logo, I assume. It looks like a pair of bears. A big one and a little one. I saw it on the side of a panel truck."

"I'll need more than that, my man."

"I can give you a sketch."

"No words?" he said.

"There were words," I said, "but I didn't catch them."

"That's good," he said. "Words would make it too easy. You want to fax me that sketch?"

"I can drop it off on my way to the office."

"Even better," he said. "I've got the coffee, you bring the donuts. Glazed or jelly. One of each, preferably."

"That's a deal. I'll be there in an hour."

"Hey," he said, "you're a big fisherman, right?"

I found myself smiling. Gordie loved to inflict bad puns on his friends, and I suspected one of them was coming at me. "Sure," I said. "I'm a very big fisherman. Why do you ask?"

"Well," he said, "this buddy of mine, guy name of Crockett, he's like you, a fanatical fisherman. So he's telling me how he's out bass fishing in his rowboat one afternoon last August and he accidentally drops his wallet overboard. He's anchored in shallow water, so he leans over the side, hoping he can spot the wallet so he can reach down and grab it, or maybe snag it with the treble hooks on one of his lures. So Crock's shading his eyes and peering down into the water and he sees this big orange carp swim along and pick up the wallet in its mouth. Next thing Crock knows, another carp swims over and grabs the wallet away from the first one. So carp number one starts chasing after carp number two, and then a third carp comes along, and Crock's poor old wallet is going back and forth between those fish like a volleyball." He paused. "So he's telling me about this, and —"

"Gordie," I said, "I'm warning you."

"Crock," he said as if I hadn't spoken, "says to me, Gordie, he says, you should've seen it." He paused. Then, "It was carp-to-carp walleting down there."

"You are a seriously disturbed person," I said.

"See you in an hour," he said. "Don't forget the donuts."

Gordon Cahill's office used to be on St. Botolph Street around the corner from Symphony Hall, where he rented a dingy second-floor suite over a Thai restaurant. He welcomed the shabbiness and the pungent odors of Thai cooking that wafted up from below, he claimed, because they nauseated him and encouraged him to get out of the office and onto the streets, where the action was.

After his accident, out of deference to his gimpy leg and his wife's ultimatums, he moved to a first-floor storefront on Exeter Street between Boylston and Commonwealth. Donna, Gordie's wife, helped decorate the new office. She installed comfortable furniture, divided the open space with movable partitions, hung watercolor seascapes on the walls, painted it in orange and tan earth tones, and created a workplace for a man who could no longer roam the streets.

It was bright and airy and altogether cheerful, and so was Gordie when I walked in. "Hooray," he said. "The donut man."

I plopped the bag of donuts onto his desk. He ripped into it, fished out a glazed, and took a giant bite. "Pour us some coffee, why don't you." He pointed what was left of his donut at the aluminum urn on the table in the corner.

I poured two mugfuls and brought them back to Gordie's desk.

"So lemme see this bear thing," he mumbled around a mouthful of glazed donut.

I unfolded the sketch I'd made and put it in front of him.

He looked at it and laughed. "This is supposed to be bears?"

"It's pretty much what I remember the logo looked like," I said. "When I saw it, I thought they were bears. What else could they be?"

"You don't have to be defensive," he said. "Maybe they're wolverines or groundhogs or something."

"What do wolverines look like?"

"How the hell should I know," he said. "I'm a city boy."

"They were bears," I said.

He squinted at my sketch, then touched it with his finger. "And this here, these squiggles, that's where the writing was?"

"Across the bottom. Yes. It was fancy writing. Cursive, like handwriting. Not printing."

"But you don't remember what it said, huh?"

"Look," I said, "I only saw it once. Just a glimpse, really. It was night, the street was poorly lit. What the hell do you want?"

"Nothing. I wasn't being critical. It's actually an excellent sketch. You're a talented artist, no doubt about it. If you gave me any more detail, there'd be no challenge."

I rolled my eyes.

"I'll give you a call when I've got something for you," he said.

"When might that be?"

Gordie shrugged. "Sometime today. Later this morning if we're lucky. I got a couple other things to clean up first." He pulled another donut out of the bag and took a big bite. Then he wiped his mouth with a napkin, put his forearms on his desk, and leaned forward. "So these two frogs are sitting beside a pond —"

"Must you?" I said.

"This'll just take a minute," he said. "It's a pretty summer's day and these frogs are crouching there on their lily pads, their long tongues flicking in and out, finding plenty of bugs to eat, basking in the warm sunshine, living the good amphibian life, and one frog turns to the other frog and says, You know, Charlie, time's sure fun when you're having flies."

I got the hell out of there.

Gordie called a little after noontime. "I got some information for you if you want it," he said.

"Of course I do."

"It'll cost you a ham and Swiss on pumpernickel, hot mustard, dill pickle."

"You want something to drink?"

"Nah. I got a fridge full of drinks."

"I'll stop at the deli," I said. "Be there in

half an hour or so."

Gordie's office was just a short walk across Copley Square from mine. I took a detour to Manny's deli on Boylston and got us both a ham and Swiss. When I got to Gordie's, I clomped the slush off my boots, hung my coat on the hook beside the door, and put the bag of sandwiches on his desk. Gordie was peering at his computer monitor. He didn't bother looking up. "Grab me a Dr Pepper," he said, gesturing at the mini-fridge against the wall near the coffee urn. "Help yourself."

I got a Pepsi for myself, a Dr Pepper for Gordie, took them over to his desk, and sat down.

He swiveled around in his chair and grinned at me. "Don't suppose you want to hear about the baby who was born without a torso or limbs, do you?"

"No. Sounds sick."

He nodded. "Sure. It is. Later, maybe." He took his sandwich out of the bag, unfolded the waxed paper, and bit into it. With his other hand, he shuffled through some papers and pushed one of them across his desk to me. "That logo. Something like this?"

The logo I'd seen on the side of the panel truck was printed on the sheet of paper. It was in the shape of an oval. The bears, I was pleased to see, more-or-less resembled those in the sketch I'd made from my memory. They were crouching there with a couple of pine trees in the background.

Curving under the bears were the words "Ursula Laboratories Cambridge, Massachusetts."

"That's the one," I said. "Ursula, huh? That's how you tracked it down?"

"Google needs words," he said. "I tried plain old bear, bruin, Kodiak bear, brown bear, black bear, polar bear, grizzly bear, panda bear, koala bear, Winnie-the-Pooh bear, teddy bear. Got millions of hits, of course, which I had to plow through. To no avail. So then I tried *ursa, ursus, ursine,* like that." He arched his eyebrows at me.

"Latin for bear," I said.

"Yes. And lo, Ursula popped up, and there you are."

"But this place is in Cambridge," I said. "I'm positive those were New Hampshire plates on that truck."

"They did business in Cambridge," said Gordie, "but actually, Ursula Laboratories was a New Hampshire corporation."

"Aha," I said. "The New Hampshire connection."

"You can incorporate anywhere, you

know," Gordie said, "and do business any-where. It's not necessarily a connection at all. Most likely, all it means is that their lawyers thought being a New Hampshire corporation was favorable tax-wise."

"And they registered their truck in New Hampshire for the same reason?"

He shrugged. "I don't think it works the same way."

"Wait a minute," I said. "Did you say it *was* a New Hampshire corporation? Past tense?"

"Yes I did," he said. "Urusula Laboratories was incorporated in June of 1996 and closed down in October of 2002."

"Closed down? Or moved?"

"Closed down, near as I can tell," Gordie said. "The corporation was dissolved and the laboratories stopped doing business. I couldn't find any Ursula Laboratories do-ing business currently anywhere in the United States. No hits on the Internet except that defunct one."

"Well, shit."

"Sorry."

"That's okay," I said. "I appreciate what you did. It's just a dead end, you know?"

"No, I don't know," he said, "since I don't have any idea what this is all about."

"Do you want me to tell you all about it?"

"Actually, no," he said. "I don't want to know any more than I need to know. That's always been my policy."

"And a sound policy it is," I said.

"Helps me avoid confidentiality issues," he said.

"I'm the same way myself."

Gordie shuffled through some papers on his desk. "Some notes I made," he mumbled. He picked up a yellow legal pad. "President of the corporation was a guy named Judson McKibben, M.D. The vice president was, da-da, Ursula McKibben. From what I can decipher of the technical gobbledegook, they did DNA testing and stem-cell research. Biogenetics. Pretty cutting-edge stuff, I infer. Ursula McKibben, the V.P., died in May, 2002, and the corporation dissolved the next October, and since then the doctor appears to have fallen off the face of the earth."

"Who was Ursula? His wife?"

"Daughter, I think."

"Why do you think that?"

"Because she was twelve years old when she died."

"Jesus," I said.

"Yeah," said Gordie. "It's a bitch, all right. Might explain why he decided to shut down the business. Must've loved his daughter a

261

lot to name it after her. Hard to keep yourself going after something like that."

"They live in Cambridge, though, huh?"

"I don't know. Did I say that?"

"It's on the logo," I said.

"The laboratory was in Cambridge," said Gordie. "Who the hell knows where Dr. McKibben lives." He looked at me. "I bet you could figure that out for youself."

"You think so?" I said. "Me?"

He smiled. "I take it back. Probably not a completely geekless person such as you. But I bet Julie could do it for you."

# EIGHTEEN

When I got back to the office, I told Julie what Gordie had told me. "He thinks you could track down this Dr. Judson McKibben."

"Me?"

"He called me geekless. But you're a whiz at that stuff."

"Geekless." She smiled.

"So will you —"

"Wait a minute," she said. "The girl, his daughter, Ursula, she died four years ago, you said?"

"That's right."

"She was twelve?"

I nodded.

"So," said Julie, "if Ursula had lived, she would've been the same age as Dana Wetherbee was when she died."

I looked at her. "Sometimes you amaze me."

"I hardly ever amaze myself," said Julie.

"That does seem significant, though, doesn't it?"

"It surely does," I said. "See what you can find out about Dr. McKibben, okay? Maybe that will help us understand its significance."

I went into my office and fooled around with some paperwork, and about an hour later Julie thumped on my door, then pushed it open with her hip. She was holding a mug of coffee in each hand. A manila folder was wedged into her armpit.

She sat in my client chair across from me, slid one mug across the desk to me, and kept the other one for herself. She opened the folder, removed a sheet of paper, and laid it flat on my desk in front of her. I could see that it was covered with handwritten notes.

She studied her notes for a minute, then looked up at me and cleared her throat. "Dr. Judson McKibben," she said. "He's forty-one years old. B.S. University of New Hampshire, Phi Beta Kappa, Summa Cum Laude, major in biology. Ph.D. from Harvard in genetics. M.D., also Harvard."

"Smart man."

"Good student, anyway," said Julie. "Not always the same thing. Anyway, he got married when he was in medical school, woman named Greta Gottfried, a med student herself. Judson and Greta had a daughter, and then Greta died. McKibben didn't remarry. Raised the child, Ursula, himself. The doctor never did practice medicine. After medical school he worked for a biomed outfit for a few years before he started up Ursula Laboratories in Cambridge. Dissolved the corporation when Ursula died. Drowning accident." Julie blinked at her page of notes, then looked up at me. "Since then, the past four years, Google came up with no hits on Dr. McKibben."

"No hits," I said. "Isn't that unusual?"

"It's extremely unusual for Google to come up with zero hits on a businessman like this McKibben. It's not particularly unusual for ordinary people who don't have things published about them." Julie looked up at me. "You could Google me, for example, and you wouldn't get a single hit."

"But in McKibben's case," I said, "the fact that you got no hits on him is significant."

"Yes," she said. "It definitely is."

"It means he's trying to be invisible."

"A man like him," she said, "he'd have to make an effort. That's right."

"Mourning his dead daughter," I said. "His only child. The light of his life. Already lost his wife. That's pretty rough. So he sells his business, gives up his life as a public person, avoids publicity, goes into seclusion."

Julie nodded. "It would be understandable." She hesitated. "There was something else."

"What?"

"Guess where Judson McKibben grew up, went to public schools, and where he still owns property."

"I bet you're going to say Churchill, New Hampshire."

"Bingo," said Julie. "There's a house and a hundred-forty-nine acres that's been in the family since 1877."

"This is excellent," I said. "Anything else?"

"The rest is details," she said. "I'll type up my notes for you if you want."

"Good," I said. "Thank you. I do want. Hold my calls for a while, okay?"

She stood up and collected our empty coffee mugs. "Gonna talk to Detective Mendoza?"

"If she'll let me."

After Julie left my office, I called Saundra Mendoza's cell phone.

"What do you want, Mr. Coyne?" was how she answered.

"How'd you know it was me?"

"It's a feature on my phone," she said.

"Alerts me to nuisance calls. So naturally your name pops right up. I thought I warned you about calling my cell phone."

"I've held off calling you," I said, "until I thought I had good information. I'd hate to be a nuisance."

"Ah, come on, Mr. Coyne. I'm yanking your chain. What's up?"

"I've learned a couple things."

"Give me a hint."

"Where Dana Wetherbee went when she ran away, maybe. That van with the bear logo."

"Okay," she said. "I'm on the road. Can't talk now. I'll be there in an hour."

Saundra Mendoza actually arrived less than three-quarters of an hour later. Julie ushered her into my office.

"Where's your partner?" I said.

"In the car. We're double-parked in front of the library."

"Did Julie offer you coffee?"

"Yes," she said. "I declined. What've you got for me?"

"Did Roger Horowitz talk to you about a girl named Misty?"

"The hooker up in Danvers?" She nodded. "He did. What's that got to do with anything?"

I told her that Misty called, said she

wanted to hire me, claimed she had information that somehow related to the van with the bear logo and her friend Kayla. She was worried about Kayla, and even though she denied it, I'd sensed that she was worried about herself. I told her that Misty didn't show up after we agreed to meet, so the next day I tracked her back to the Happy Family restaurant on Beach Street. Thirty-six hours later she was dead. I told her how Bonnie at the restaurant said Misty, Kayla, and Zooey had been arguing. I told her about talking with Dana Wetherbee's grandmother, how Dana had been more-or-less abandoned by her father after her mother died, how she'd been living with her grandparents in Edson, Rhode Island, how she left home when she turned sixteen and sent a Christmas card to her brother that had been postmarked from Churchill, New Hampshire. I reminded Mendoza that the panel truck with the bear logo had New Hampshire plates, and I told her how I'd learned that the logo was for an outfit called Ursula Laboratories out of Cambridge, Massachusetts, which did DNA testing and stem-cell research and went out of business four years ago. The president of the company, I told her, was an M.D. named Judson McKibben, and the vice president was his daughter, Ursula McKibben, who drowned at the age of twelve. I pointed out the interesting age coincidence between Dana Wetherbee and Ursula McKibben. I told her that Judson McKibben had deep roots in Churchill, New Hampshire.

"Where's Churchill, New Hampshire?" she said.

"Way up north near the Canadian border."

"A long ways from Chinatown."

I nodded. "Over two hundred miles."

She looked at me for a minute out of those big somber brown eyes. Then she shook her head and smiled. "It's really interesting information. Intriguing. I'm glad you shared it with me. I think you're onto something. But you know, Mr. Coyne, I'm just a Boston cop, stuck here in the city limits, and my case, the Maureen Quinlan case, my only actual case here, is only indirectly connected to all of this."

"It's directly connected," I said. "Don't forget Dana's photo, the one I gave to Sunshine, was stapled on Henry's collar."

"I didn't forget that," she said. "Have you talked to Lieutenant Horowitz?"

"Not yet," I said. "I intend to. I just thought —"

"Please talk to Roger," she said. "Tell him all this. Ask him to call me. We can work together on this. He can liase with the New Hampshire police, if it comes to that." She stood up and reached her hand across my desk. "It's good information, Mr. Coyne. Thank you."

After Saundra Mendoza left, I tried Roger Horowitz's cell phone.

He answered the way he always did. "Coyne? Whaddya want?"

"I don't want anything," I said. "I have some information you might be able to use."

"Use how?"

"On the Misty case."

"Go ahead."

I repeated to Horowitz what I'd told Saundra Mendoza.

When I finished, he said, "New Hampshire, huh? Very interesting. I'll check it out."

"When?"

"Whaddya mean, when? I'll do it when I do it. Since when am I required to report to you?"

"I just —"

"Look, Coyne. You know how it works. I'll make some phone calls. I can't just go slamming around in some other jurisdiction without being invited, but I know some New Hampshire state cops."

"Meanwhile," I said, "while you guys are

arguing about jurisdictions, I'm worrying about Kayla. That's the one thing Misty said to me. She was worried about her friend Kayla. She linked Kayla to the guy in the van with the New Hampshire plates. My guess is, he's got Kayla."

Horowitz didn't say anything.

"Misty got killed, for Christ sake," I said. "So did Maureen Quinlan. Dana Wetherbee, she died, too."

"You're worried about Kayla," he said.

"Yes. And Zooey, for that matter."

Horowitz was silent for a minute. Then he said, "Thanks for the information. Mendoza and I will take it from here."

"Okay," I said. "Good."

"You hear me, Coyne? We've got it now. Thanks for all the help."

"I hear you," I said.

I bought a loaf of fresh-baked anadama bread from the bakery on Newbury Street and picked up a dozen eggs, a hunk of extra-sharp cheddar, a yellow onion, a green pepper, a dozen oranges for fresh-squeezed juice, and a pound of unsliced bacon at Savenor's on Charles Street. It was my turn to cook, and I had Friday-night omelettes on my mind.

Henry wagged his tail and gazed hungrily

at my bag of groceries when I walked in the front door. I took the bag into the kitchen, where a pitcher of Bloody Marys sat on the table.

I heard the shower running upstairs.

I put the omelette makings in the refrigerator, poured two glasses of Bloody, added some ice cubes, took them upstairs, and set them on the bedside table. I hung my necktie and jacket in the closet, took off my shoes, and lay down on the bed.

Pretty soon the bathroom door opened, a cloud of steam billowed out, and Evie emerged like a redheaded ghost in the fog. She was wrapped in a giant pink bath towel.

When she saw me, she smiled and unwrapped herself.

Afterwards, we dozed. When we woke up, we lay there propped up on our pillows sipping our Bloody Marys. The ice had melted, but they still tasted good.

I told Evie about my conversations with Gordon Cahill and Saundra Mendoza and Roger Horowitz.

"So you don't think the detectives will do anything?"

"Jurisdictions," I said. "There's not a lot they can do without something solid. Roger will probably talk to his counterparts in

New Hampshire. That's about it."

She was quiet for a minute. Then she said, "So now what?"

"I think tomorrow I'll head up to Churchill, New Hampshire," I said, "poke around a little."

"Why did I know you were going to say that?"

"You love me," I said. "You know me inside and out."

"What do you mean, poke around?"

"Just try to get some information. Don't worry. I won't do anything stupid."

"Ha," she said. "Can I come?"

"Nope."

"I knew you were going to say that, too." She studied my face for a minute, then shrugged. "The Lone Ranger rides again."

After breakfast the next morning, I opened my overnight duffel on our bed. I packed it with underwear, socks, sneakers, sweatshirts, flannel shirts, blue jeans, and woolen long johns, along with my tattered copy of *Moby-Dick* and my toiletry kit.

Then I wandered around the house gathering the other stuff I wanted to bring and piling it on the bed — binoculars, tape recorder, Swiss Army knife, cell phone, digital camera, flashlight, spare batteries,

Space blanket, Leatherman.

Evie was sitting there watching. "I see you put a padlock on the back gate."

"I've been meaning to get the lock fixed."

"To keep out pregnant teenagers?"

I shrugged.

"Kind of a horse and barn door thing, isn't it?"

"I suppose so," I said.

"So how long do you expect to be gone?"

"I'll be back tomorrow night."

"Does Roger know what you're doing?"

I smiled. "I didn't tell him. He would've just ordered me not to."

"But he knows."

I nodded. "Probably."

"Because he knows you."

I shrugged.

"You're just going to ask questions, right?"

"That's all."

"You've got enough stuff for a month of espionage."

"Probably won't need any of it," I said. "I just want to see what I can find out. Talk to Dr. McKibben if I'm lucky." I looked at my stuff. "What'm I forgetting?"

She rolled her eyes.

I stuck my cell phone in my pocket and tucked the other tools and gadgets in among the clothes in the duffel so they wouldn't rattle around and scrape against each other. "All set," I said. "I'm outta here."

Evie followed me downstairs and watched while I pulled on my parka and laced up my old Herman Survivors boots.

"You gonna be warm enough?" said Evie.

"Plenty of layers," I said. "My boots are insulated and waterproof. I'm good."

"Got your gloves?" she said.

I fished in the pockets of the parka and showed my fur-lined leather gloves to her.

"A warm hat?"

"It's in the car, Mom."

We headed for the front door. When I turned to kiss her good-bye, Evie was grinning at me.

"What?" I said.

"You love this stuff, don't you?"

"What stuff?"

"Sleuthing. Answering the call. Setting forth on quests. Being out there on your own. Having adventures. Testing yourself."

I smiled. "Probably a guy thing."

"Well," she said, "have fun, then." She put her arms around my neck, went up on tiptoes, pressed the entire front of her body against the entire front of mine, and gave me a long wet kiss on the mouth. "You better remember to come home," she said.

I gave her a squeeze. "How could I forget?"

"Please be careful."

"I will. I promise."

Henry was sitting there beside the door with his head cocked to the side and his ears perked up. I scootched down beside him and gave his forehead a scratch. "Sorry, pal," I said. "You can't come."

He looked at me for a minute, then lay down, put his chin on his paws, and refused to make eye contact.

I picked up my duffel and got the hell out of there right then, before my resolve evaporated. It's hard enough to resist a woman when she presses her body against you and puts her tongue in your mouth, but sulking dogs are almost impossible.

It was a gray Saturday morning in Boston, damp and raw and chilly, and the sharp wind that was funneling down Charles Street blew against me all the way to the parking garage and made the skin on my face cold and stiff. The air smelled like more snow was coming.

I pulled out of the garage, drove down Charles, turned right onto Beacon, and cut over to Boylston via Mass. Ave. I found an empty meter around the corner from the

Public Library, grabbed my duffel off the front seat, and went into my office building.

On weekends you needed to punch the security code into the keypad in the lobby lest you set off alarms. They changed the code every Friday, and Julie always insisted that I write the new one down and carry it in my wallet. It was her perpetual hope that I'd be inspired to sneak into the office over the weekend and catch up on my paperwork.

Weekends came and weekends went, and I kept not doing it. But Julie didn't discourage easily.

I went into my office, ignored the stack of paperwork on my desk, and opened the wall safe that I kept cleverly hidden behind a big framed photograph of my two boys. I took out my Smith & Wesson Chiefs Special .38 revolver. I kept the gun wrapped in a terry-cloth dish towel that was lightly impregnated with Hoppe's gun oil. The evocative aroma of Hoppe's filled my office whenever I opened my safe. Sometimes I went into my safe just for a whiff of Hoppe's. Once in a while I stowed some particularly important documents in the safe, and when I removed them, they smelled good.

I broke open the gun. The Chiefs Special cylinder held five cartridges. Four of the chambers had bullets in them. I always kept the hammer down on an empty chamber, a precaution that I'd been told was entirely unnecessary, but I did it anyway.

I kept a few boxes of .38-caliber bullets in my safe, too. I took out one box and put the bullets and the revolver into my parka pocket. Then I shut the safe, twirled the dial, evened up the picture, locked the office, and headed back to my car.

I was feeling furtive and clever. Armed and dangerous. Ready for action. I had to resist the impulse to slink down the sidewalk with my back against the wall.

My gun was licensed, and I had a permit to carry it — in Massachusetts. When I crossed the state line into New Hampshire, I'd become an instant criminal. New Hampshire had no reciprocity agreement with the Commonwealth on the matter of concealed-weapons permits.

If I got caught in New Hampshire with that gun, I'd be guilty of a felony. And I couldn't very well plead ignorance of the law. I was, after all, a lawyer.

Actually, I'd be committing a felony whether I got caught or not, which should have bothered the conscience of a lawyer, not even to mention the risk of disbarment.

My plan was to not get caught, which is

probably a sign of a criminal mind.

I'd owned the revolver for about twenty years and had used it just twice. Killed two men. A single shot in the chest each time. The Chiefs Special packed a wallop.

Both of my victims were evil men who murdered people for a living and were prepared to murder me, and I had no regrets about killing either of them. But shooting people was an unpleasant business, and I profoundly hoped I'd never have to do it again.

When I got back to the car, I stuffed the gun inside a sock, leaving the handle sticking out. I shoved it and the box of bullets into my duffel, which I left half unzipped on the front seat beside me. If I needed the revolver, I could reach in, grab its handle, and be shooting in about two seconds.

Evie had me pegged. I did thirst for adventures. Negotiating divorces, settling estates, and suing companies that had screwed my clients was useful and sometimes rewarding work. I liked helping people. Justice always made me feel good.

But practicing law, even when the stakes were high and the adversaries were formidable, hadn't really pumped my adrenaline for many years.

Smuggling a handgun across a state line

was not exactly my idea of adrenaline-pumping adventure, but it was a start.

# NINETEEN

I headed north on Route 93. I'd loaded the CD changer with an assortment of stuff I liked — The Beach Boys, Beethoven, Oscar Peterson, ZZ Top, The Band, Sibelius, Miles Davis, Bob Dylan. I was facing four or five hours in the car, and I intended to do some serious daydreaming. I wanted to put Dana Wetherbee and Shirley Arsenault and Dr. Judson McKibben, Misty and Zooey and Kayla, Sunshine and Patricia McAfee and Dr. Rossi — all of them out there on the periphery of my consciousness where they could mix and mingle and match, and maybe a serendipitous association might occur. My mind sometimes performed interesting creative tricks when I wasn't paying attention to it.

The sky hung heavy with ominous gray clouds, and about the time the highway passed through the outskirts of Concord, New Hampshire, I noticed that dry snow as fine as baby powder was swirling on the pavement. I didn't remember seeing it before then, but it must've started sometime earlier.

I didn't have much of a plan. Hang out in Churchill, New Hampshire, and talk to people. Ask about trucks with bear logos on the sides, see if anyone knew anything about Dr. Judson McKibben and his dead daughter, Ursula, or remembered seeing a pregnant young blond girl mailing a card back around Christmas time. I'd show Dana's photo around, the one her grandmother gave me in which Dana was looking young and cute and alive. Maybe I'd pull out her morgue shot, too. That might get a rise out of somebody. I had them both with me.

Thrashing around, Gordie called it. The modus operandi of the diligent private investigator. Keep asking questions. Annoy people. Turn over rocks, kick the underbrush, shake the branches, rattle the cages. Disturb things and see if anybody reacted.

By the time the highway began rising and twisting into the foothills of the White Mountains around Plymouth, the snow was blowing across the highway and accumulating on the pavement. I slowed down to forty-five, turned on my headlights and windshield wipers, and stuck to the right lane. Now and then an oil tanker or a ten-wheeler pounded past me at its usual cruising speed of seventy-five, and I gripped the wheel hard against the sucking backdraft and the clouds of swirling snow and resisted the impulse to touch the brakes.

Somewhere around Franconia, while The Band and I were singing "It Makes No Difference," history's saddest and most beautiful song of lost love, my mind unexpectedly linked the puzzling fact that Dana Wetherbee had been taking a fertility drug called clomiphene with the fact that Ursula Laboratories of Cambridge, Massachusetts, had been in the business of stem-cell research. There seemed to be a link there somewhere.

I pondered those two facts but drew no conclusions. So I pushed them to the outskirts of my consciousness and went back to singing.

The snow petered out and then stopped as I was coming down out of the mountains, but the sky still hung low and heavy and dark and foreboding. I turned off the highway onto the winding two-lane northbound road that my atlas promised would take me to Churchill. It cut through a board-flat valley that I guessed would be planted with hay and corn in the spring. Widely-scattered mailboxes poked out of the high snowbanks at the ends of long straight driveways that led to trailers and boxy ranch-style houses and farmhouses with barns and silos. Here and there a rocky ice-rimmed brook passed under the road.

It was a little after three-thirty in the afternoon when I stopped at a gas station to fill my tank. When I went inside to pay, I found a coffee urn and some donuts in a transparent plastic case. A hand-lettered sign claimed the donuts were "fresh today." I poured a large container of coffee, balanced two plain donuts on a napkin, and took them to the front of the store

A boy wearing a Phish T-shirt sat behind the counter reading a *Sports Illustrated* magazine. I paid him for the gas and the coffee and donuts.

When I asked him how far it was to Churchill, he said, "Huh? Where?"

Back in the car before starting up, I consulted Mr. McNally again. By my crude calculation, Churchill lay seventy-five or eighty miles to the north.

Head-high snowbanks on both sides of the road crowded against the shoulders and made the lanes barely wide enough for two cars to pass.

I drove slowly, sipped my coffee, and munched my donuts. Some lunch. The least healthful kinds of fat and empty calories washed down with muddy concentrations of caffeine. Evie would not approve.

That got me thinking about Evie, which reminded me how her body felt when she pressed it against mine, and that reminded me of how she believed that what I was doing was immature and macho.

I had to admit that she was pretty much right. It was all about adventure. Brady Quixote Coyne on his noble quest, rattling around in his squeaky suit of armor, driving through the snow-covered countryside on a gray Saturday afternoon in the middle of January . . . two hundred miles from his loving woman and his faithful dog and his warm hearth.

I fished out my cell phone and hit speed-dial for our home number. I wanted to hear Evie tell me she missed me in that unbearably sexy telephone voice of hers, see if she'd try to tempt me to turn around and come home and then force me to articulate the reasons why I wouldn't do it.

The phone didn't ring. On the display it said, "No Service." Oh, well.

No road sign told me that I had entered Churchill, but according to my odometer, I had traveled seventy-six miles since leaving the gas station where I bought my donuts.

I did appear to be entering a town of sorts, the first one in the past eight or ten miles. A medium-sized river appeared along the east side of the road and then passed under it at an old iron bridge. On the downstream side of the bridge the river widened into a frozen millpond. The pond was bounded on one side by a brick building that had once been some kind of factory. Now the windows on the flat wall that faced the millpond were covered with plywood.

On the other side of the bridge there was an intersection too insignificant to warrant a traffic light. This seemed to be the commercial heart of Churchill. Here were a mom 'n' pop grocery store, an animal hospital, a hardware store, a Catholic church, a lumberyard, and a couple of boarded-up storefronts.

I drove through the intersection, passed a post office and an Exxon station, and found myself in the country again. I'd been driving with my headlights on since the snow squalls in the mountains. Now it was a little after five o'clock in the afternoon, and darkness had already settled over the land. Nighttime came early in the middle of January up near the Canadian border. Here and there specks of pale light shone from houses set back from the road. My headlights burrowed down the dark, narrow highway.

Two or three miles north of town I came upon a low rambling log building. A brightly-lit sign out front said "Nick's Cafe." Floodlights lit the entire area, and warm orange lights glowed from the windows. Half a dozen vehicles were nosed up to the big snowbank in front.

I pulled in and parked between two pickup trucks. One truck had a snowmobile tethered in its bed. A plow was bolted to the front of the other one.

My forest-green BMW with its Massachusetts plates bracketed by those banged-up old Live-Free-Or-Die trucks was a neon sign screaming "Yuppie City Slicker."

That was all right. I didn't care about blending in. I'd never been any good at role playing, and I didn't intend to try it now.

I went inside and stomped my boots on the mat. It was a large dimly-lit rectangular room with a low ceiling and a wooden floor. The walls were raw pine planks stained brown from years of smoke and sweat. They were hung with stuffed brook trout and deer heads and neon beer signs. To the left was the dining area — a bar against the back wall, a few square tables by the front window, and some plain wooden booths along the side wall.

Three or four men wearing baseball caps and flannel shirts perched on stools at the bar. They had beer bottles in front of them, and they were leaning on their elbows and gazing up at the television where a college basketball game was in progress. The booths and tables were all empty.

There was a pool table at the other end of the room, plus a row of old-fashioned pinball machines. A couple of men were playing pool. I watched them for a minute. A young guy with a ponytail and an earring seemed to be running the table. A cigarette dangled from the corner of his mouth, and when he leaned over his cue stick to line up a shot, he squinted against the smoke. A bulky guy with a big droopy mustache and a bald head was sitting on a high stool against the wall chalking his cue and looking up at the ceiling.

There were some wooden pegs on the wall inside the doorway. I hung up my parka, went into the dining area, and slid onto an empty stool down at the end of the bar.

The guy beside me turned his head and said, "Howya doin'?" He had a scraggly red beard and a rumbling voice. A green John Deere cap was pulled low on his forehead.

I nodded. "Good. You?"

He mumbled, "No complaints," and returned his attention to the basketball game.

A minute later a woman appeared from the kitchen behind the bar area. She had short blond hair and a wide, generous mouth. She was wearing skin-tight blue jeans and a little leather vest over a snug-fitting black T-shirt, and it was hard not to notice her body.

She wiped the bar in front of me with her rag, and without looking up said, "What can I get for you?"

"Coffee," I said. "And some advice."

She lifted her head and looked at me. Late thirties, early forties, judging by the squint lines at the corners of her eyes. "Coffee's cheap," she said. "Advice is free, which is just about what mine's worth most of the time." She turned, poured a mugful of coffee from a pot on a burner, and slid it in front of me. "Cream and sugar?"

I waved my hand. "Black is good."

"Haven't seen you around," she said.

"First time I've ever been to Churchill," I said. "My name's Brady. Brady Coyne."

She nodded slowly, as if she intended to memorize my name. "I'm Nick."

"Nick."

She smiled. "Short for Niccola. I own this dump. This plus my daughter are all I got left from a crappy marriage. Both of 'em cost me more money than they're worth, but I love 'em anyway. So what kind of advice you looking for?"

"I'm a long way from home," I said. "Is there a motel or inn or something near here?"

"Where's home?"

"Boston."

She nodded as if she already knew that. She pointed off to the right. "There's a motel up the road. Keep on going north five or six miles, you'll come to it. Big red neon sign out front. You can see it a mile before you get there. Bruce and Joanne Sweeney been running it for twenty years. You want me to see if they got a vacancy?"

"That would be nice," I said. "I appreciate it."

She took a cordless phone from under the bar, pecked out a number, listened, then said, "Hey, hi, it's Nick . . . Yeah, not too bad. You know how it goes. Look, I got a fella here from Boston needs a bed. . . ." She listened for a minute, then looked at me. "They got a couple units vacant. She wants to know, twin beds or a double, and for how long."

"Double, I guess," I said. "Just one night."

"He'll take the double," Nick said into the

phone. "Yeah, just tonight. His name is Brady. No, that's his first name. Brady —" She looked at me with her eyebrows arched.

"Coyne," I said. "With a Y."

"Coyne," said Nick into the telephone. "Brady Coyne. Right." She spelled it, listened for a moment, then looked up at the ceiling and smiled. "Oh, yeah. More comin', too, they're saying. Hey, what the hell, it's winter in Siberia, you know?"

She hung up, put the phone back under the bar, and said, "You're all set. It sure isn't fancy, but it's pretty comfortable. They got satellite TV and a little coffeemaker in every room. Joanne says if you don't get there by seven the key'll be under the mat in front of unit four."

"Thanks a lot," I said. "They didn't want my credit card or anything?"

Nick shrugged. "Around here we assume people are honest until they prove otherwise. You can pay up in the morning. So where're you headed?"

"Here, actually. Churchill."

She smiled. "That's pretty funny." She turned to the guy who was sitting beside me. "You hear that, Jerry?"

He looked at her. "Hear what?"

She rolled her eyes. "Never mind." She picked up Jerry's empty beer bottle. "Ready

291

for another?"

Jerry nodded, and the guy beside him said he needed another beer, too.

Nick fetched two bottles of Budweiser from the ice chest, snapped off the caps, and put them in front of the two men. Then she came back to where I was sitting. She braced her elbows on the bar, put her chin in her hands, and looked at me. "So seriously," she said. "You on some kind of secret mission or something, you can't tell me where you're really going?"

"I told you," I said. "I have arrived at my destination."

"Churchill, huh?"

I nodded.

"Churchill is nobody's destination," she said. "Even those of us who ended up here didn't do it on purpose."

"I'm here on purpose."

She smiled. "Really?"

"Yes."

"I don't even want to ask."

"You can ask." I said. "I'm looking for somebody. Man named McKibben. Dr. Judson McKibben."

Nick narrowed her eyes at me for a quick moment, then shrugged. "How's your coffee?"

"You can top it off," I said.

She picked up the coffeepot, filled my mug, then wandered down to the other end of the bar.

I leaned toward the red-bearded man named Jerry on the stool next to me. "What about you?" I said to him.

He turned. "What about me?"

"Do you know Dr. Judson McKibben?"

He shook his head and looked back up at the television.

"Does that mean you don't know him," I said, "or that you don't want to talk to me?"

With his eyes still on the TV, he said, "I got money on this basketball game."

"So what about McKibben?"

"Jesus Christ," he muttered. "I'm just trying to enjoy my beer and watch my game, okay? I don't want to talk to nobody. I just wanna relax, because pretty soon I'm gonna have to go home and have supper with my wife, and it's for damn sure that I'll have to talk to her, and then I won't be all that relaxed."

"I'm sorry I bothered you," I said.

Jerry shrugged. "Don't worry about it."

Nick wandered back to my end of the bar. "Hey, Boston. You ready for something to eat?"

I glanced at my watch. It was a few minutes before six. "Good idea," I said. "Let's see your menu."

She shook her head. "No menu. Most folks who come here to eat know what we got and what they like. What do you like?"

"What do you recommend?"

She smiled. "This isn't exactly your Boston gourmet dining experience, you know. This is just your basic roadside café out here in the sticks. We got chicken and pork chops and steaks. Ribeyes and New York sirloin. You pick your meat, we can fry it or bake it or broil it, rare, medium, or well. Nice big salad, choice of dressings. Peas or carrots or green beans depending on what night it is. Beans tonight, I think. Fries or mashed. Or pasta or rice, if you prefer. Or we can make you a sandwich."

"A ribeye sounds good," I said. "Medium rare. Fries, Russian dressing on the salad."

She shrugged. "You got it. I'd grab a booth if I were you. Sometimes it gets pretty cramped and rowdy at the bar on a Saturday night."

"Nick," I said, "you didn't answer my question about Dr. Judson McKibben."

"You didn't ask any question that I remember," she said. "You said you were looking for him, and that doesn't matter to me one way or another."

"So would you know how I might find

him, then?"

She looked at me, and at that moment somebody from the other end of the bar yelled, "Hey, Nick. We're gettin' dry down here."

She touched my arm and said, "Catch you later," and she went to take care of them.

I picked up my coffee and took it to one of the booths against the wall. A couple of minutes later a slender dark-haired girl came over and put a paper placemat and some silverware wrapped in a napkin in front of me and filled a glass with water. She was wearing a long-sleeved yellow jersey and tight black jeans tucked into cowboy boots. She looked about fifteen.

"You ordered the ribeye, right?" she said.

"That's right."

"Ready for some more coffee?"

"I'm all set for now," I said. "Are you Nick's daughter?"

She smiled. "You think I look like her?"

I held up both hands. "That's a trick question, and I refuse to answer it. She mentioned that she had a daughter, that's all."

"I wouldn't be insulted if you said I looked like her," she said. "I think she's gorgeous, don't you?"

"She's very attractive," I said. "You both are."

"Hey, thanks. You were right. Nick's my mom. Most people don't see it because she's blond and I'm a brunette, you know? I'm Gaby. Gabrielle. I help out on weekends. She won't let me work during the week. She says my full-time job is school. Let me go see about your salad. I'll bring you some bread, too." And before I could open my mouth, she was gone.

I went into the men's room to wash my hands. When I came back, a man was sitting in my booth. It was the big guy with the bald head and the bushy mustache who'd been playing pool.

He was holding a can of Coke. His big hand went all the way around the can.

I slid in across from him. "How you doing?" I said.

He nodded. "I'm good. Name's Harrigan. Nate Harrigan." He held out his hand.

I reached across the booth and shook it. "Brady Coyne," I said.

"Haven't seen you in here before."

"Nope," I said. "First time. Nice place."

"On your way through," he said, "or staying for a while?"

"Staying overnight."

"You got business here in Churchill?"

"Actually," I said, "I'm looking for somebody, and —"

"Dr. McKibben, huh?"

"Yes. That's right."

"So you got business with the doctor?"

I shrugged. "You could say that."

"What kind of business?"

"It's personal."

"Between you and him, huh?"

"That's right. That's pretty much what personal means."

He stared at me for a moment. "So, you and him old friends or something?"

"Not exactly. We have mutual acquaintances."

"Mutual acquaintances," he said. "You said you were looking for him?"

I nodded.

"Meaning you don't know where he is."

"That's right. I don't. I hoped I'd find him here in Churchill. I know he's from here, and I know he owns property here. Assuming he's here now, I figured I'd give him a call, set up an appointment, transact our business."

"I doubt if he'd appreciate that," said Nate Harrigan.

"Oh? Why's that?"

"Dr. McKibben likes his privacy, that's all." Harrigan's mustache was so bushy that you couldn't see his mouth move when he spoke. "He likes to be left alone, and we here in Churchill, we all respect that."

"You're telling me I should leave him alone."

Harrigan smiled and nodded. "That's it."

"Why does he want to be left alone?" I said. "Is it because of his daughter?"

"You're pretty nosy, aren't you?"

"I just want to talk with McKibben. What's the big deal?"

"The big deal is simple. He doesn't want to talk to you. He likes his privacy."

"And you're — what? His guardian?"

Harrigan nodded. "You might say that." He reached into his hip pocket, took out a leather wallet, flipped it open, and showed it to me. It held a badge.

"You're a cop?"

"Chief of police," he said.

"Okay," I said. "Let me tell you why I want to talk to Dr. McKibben." I took out the photo of Dana Wetherbee that Shirley Arsenault had given me and slid it across the table to him.

He looked at it, shrugged, then arched his eyebrows at me. "Who's this?"

"Her name is Dana Wetherbee. She was here in Churchill last month."

"Yeah?"

"Yes," I said. "She mailed her brother a Christmas card. It was postmarked from

Churchill."

"I don't recognize her," said Harrigan. "Anyway, what's this got to do with Dr. McKibben?"

"I don't know," I said. "Maybe nothing. His name came up, that's all. I'd just like to ask him about her. Take another look at that photo. She was just a young girl. Sixteen. Now she's dead. She had a miscarriage and died in the snow in my backyard in Boston a week ago Tuesday."

"She's dead?"

"Yes."

Harrigan touched the photo with his fingertip. "Jesus," he muttered. "In your backyard?"

I nodded. "My dog found her. She was covered with snow. I carried her inside, laid her on my sofa, put a blanket over her, called 911. But it was too late. It's not clear whether she bled to death or froze to death. I feel kind of responsible."

Harrigan looked up at me. "That's a rough one, all right."

"Yes, it certainly is," I said. "Very rough. And since then, two other women have died. Murdered, actually. They seem to be connected to Dana." I tapped the photo. "So now maybe you can understand why I'm so anxious to get ahold of Dr. McKibben. All I need is his phone number or an address."

Nate Harrigan pushed the photo across the table to me. "Sorry," he said. "I don't see what good it would do. All it would accomplish would be upsetting Dr. Mc-Kibben. I'm pretty sure talking to some stranger from Boston about the death of another pretty young girl wouldn't make him very happy, and next thing you know, the chief of police who let it happen finds himself back where he started, driving a fork lift at Sullivan's lumberyard."

I took the printout of the Ursula Laboratories logo that Gordie had given me. "Do you recognize this?"

He looked at it and shrugged. "Sure."

"You do?"

"Dr. McKibben's old business. That was his logo. He sold the company three or four years ago."

"I saw a truck with this logo on it in Boston a week ago," I said.

"So?"

"I don't know. There's a connection, but I don't know what it is. That's why I want to talk to Dr. McKibben."

"I'm telling you," he said, "just leave it lay."

"I was hoping, in the interest of truth and justice, you'd want to help me here."

"All I want," he said, "is for you to leave Dr. McKibben in peace."

I shrugged. "I guess I'll have to find another way, then. When I talk to him, I'll be sure he knows that you did your best to keep me away."

"I guess you don't get it." Harrigan leaned across the table. "Let me put it this way. Stay away from Dr. McKibben. How's that? Clear enough? Get it?"

"I get it," I said.

"Good." He put his hands on the table and pushed himself into a standing position. "So we understand each other?"

"I understand you," I said. "But I don't think you understand me."

"No? How's that?"

"I don't do well with threats."

"I don't remember threatening you," he said.

"Excuse me, then," I said. "I guess I didn't understand you after all."

"I gave you an order," he said. "It wasn't a threat."

"Ah," I said. "Well, in the spirit of clarifying our understanding, let me explain it to you this way. I don't do well with orders, either."

"Let me clarify, too, then." He put both hands flat on the table, bent down, and pushed his face close to mine. "When you wake up tomorrow morning in unit four in Bruce and Joanne Sweeney's motel, mister lawyer, you will pack up your stuff, climb into that green BMW of yours, and you'll start driving south, and you won't stop until you get to Mt. Vernon Street, and —" He stopped and glanced over his shoulder.

Gaby, the waitress, was standing there with a bread basket in one hand and a bowl of salad in the other.

"Sorry, honey," said Harrigan. He stepped back.

Gaby put the bread and the salad in front of me. "You want more coffee? A drink, maybe?"

"More coffee would be good," I said. "Thanks."

"I'll be right back." She turned and walked away.

Harrigan watched her go, then turned to me. "Just go home, Mr. Coyne. Best for everybody."

"I appreciate the advice," I said.

He held out his hand. "Sorry how I spoke to you. People tell me I'm not very tactful."

"You're not." I shook his hand. "How do you know those things about me?"

He smiled through his mustache. "I'm a cop. It's my job to know things."

"And you're good at your job."

"I am." He touched his forehead with the side of his forefinger, a little mock salute. "Enjoy your ribeye," he said. Then he turned and walked away.

# TWENTY

I watched Chief Nate Harrigan lumber over to the door. He waved at Nick behind the bar, patted a couple of men on the back, shrugged his beefy shoulders into his coat, and stomped out of the restaurant.

The place was filling up. The booths along the wall and the tables by the front windows were occupied — couples of all ages, the young ones with two or three kids — and more people were milling around the bar and the pool table and in the entryway.

Saturday night at Nick's Café. I suspected this was it for excitement in Churchill, New Hampshire.

I finished my salad and was munching on a hunk of bread when Gaby delivered my ribeye. She slid it in front of me, picked up my empty salad bowl, turned to leave, then hesitated.

She was looking down at the table where I'd left Dana's photo.

"Do you know her?" I said to Gaby.

"Huh?" She looked at me. "Oh, this girl? No, I don't think so. Should I? Who is she?"

"Her name is Dana."

"She your daughter or something?"

"No," I said. "She's a friend of a friend. She ran away from home a while ago."

"And you're looking for her? Is that it?"

I shrugged. "Kind of, yes."

"You think she's here? In Churchill?"

"She might have been."

She smiled. "Here? Really?"

"I don't know." I picked up the photo and handed it to her. "Take a good look."

She frowned at it. "She's cute." She shook her head and handed the photo back to me. "I guess not. Sorry." She glanced over her shoulder. "I gotta go. We're getting busy. Can I get you something else? Steak sauce?"

I shook my head. "All set."

"Okay. Enjoy your meal."

I did. It was a good ribeye, thick and juicy, marbled with fat, and cooked perfectly. The fries were crispy, and so what if the beans came from a can.

I was sopping up steak juice with the last fry on my plate when Nick slid into the booth across from me. She took an idle swipe at the tabletop with her bar rag and cocked an eyebrow at me. "So how was your ribeye?"

I nodded. "Good. Excellent."

She looked down at the table, then up at me. "You were asking about Dr. Mc-Kibben."

I nodded.

"Get any answers?"

"Not many."

"Nate Harrigan give you a hard time?"

"Threatened to run me out of town."

She smiled. "You scared?"

"No. Curious."

"Nate's a pussycat. He thinks, because he's a cop, he's supposed to be tough, but it doesn't come naturally to him. He's actually a pretty good officer. He's fair, he's good with kids, he cares about people. He just wants things to be peaceful."

"Protect and serve," I said.

"Really," she said. "Don't worry about Nate."

"I wasn't. It's just, you mention Dr. Judson McKibben around here and the air suddenly gets chilly. Makes you wonder."

"It's not a secret," she said. "Just small-town stuff, you know?"

"No," I said. "I really don't know."

Nick slid out of the booth. "You want some more coffee?"

"Sure."

"Sit tight. I'll be right back." She gathered up my empty dishes and walked away.

She was back a minute later with two mugs. She put them on the table and resumed her seat across from me. She picked up one of the mugs, took a sip, and looked at me over the rim. "The McKibbens are an old Churchill family," she said. "Settled here right after the Civil War, bought up a big hunk of land, grew apples, raised sheep, built the cider mill down on the river, did better than most. Over the years they gave a lot of money back to the town. People around here have always felt obligated to the McKibben family."

I sipped my coffee and nodded.

"Up until recently," she said, "a kid from Churchill who actually graduated from high school was considered some kind of prodigy. A few of them might go off to the state college in Plymouth. Once in a while somebody got accepted at the University in Durham or maybe lucked into some school in Florida or California that's looking for geographical diversity. Mostly they quit school and joined the army or went to work for their uncle or got married and had babies or had babies without getting married, or they took off for Boston or New York and never came back again. So when Judson McKibben got into Harvard — medical school, no less — well, he was pretty much a hero."

"Local boy makes good," I said. "Nice story."

She nodded. "He said he intended to come back, be a family doctor here in town, and I supposed that's what he did plan to do originally." Nick paused, sipped her coffee, looked up at me.

"Didn't happen," I said.

"He got married, had a child," she said. "And then his wife died, and he had the little girl to raise, and I guess he felt he had to make some money. So he set up his business down there in Massachusetts. But he kept the family homestead after his parents died, and he came back to town every now and then, him and his little girl. He'd come in here, have lunch, shoot the breeze with the locals, and little Ursula, she was cute as a button. Skinny, pale little thing, with these great big blue eyes, blond hair practically white. Sometimes, if it was a nice day, she and Gaby would go outside and play. They were about the same age." Nick shrugged. "Anyway, Ursula died, terrible thing, drowned in somebody's pool at a birthday party, and pretty soon after, the doctor, he moved back into his old place and made it clear that he just wanted to be left alone. We respect that. It's been three, four years now. I suppose he's still grieving. No one ever sees him. We just steer clear of his place, and try to protect his privacy if some stranger should come snooping around." She looked up at me and smiled.

"Lots of strangers come snooping around?" I said.

"Far as I know," she said, "you're the first."

I picked up the photo of Dana Wetherbee and showed it to Nick. "Did Ursula look anything like this girl?"

She took it from me, held it up, and frowned at it. "This the picture that Gaby was talking about?"

I nodded.

"Mm." Nick was shaking her head. "I mean, there are similarities. Both fair, blond, cute. Ursula might've looked something like this girl if she . . . had she not died." She looked up at me. "Who is she?"

"It's a long story," I said.

"Are you looking for her? Is she missing?"

"I'm trying to figure out where she's been. I was hoping somebody might've seen her."

Nick shook her head. "I'm not sure I'd remember her if I did see her."

"Is there a bus line or a train near here?"

She nodded. "There's a bus."

"Where does it go?"

"It comes down from Quebec, goes to New York and D.C. Stops at about a hundred places along the way, if anybody's waiting."

"It doesn't go to Boston?"

"Nope. You want to go to Boston, you get off in Springfield and change buses. The bus stop's right there across from the post office." She reached across the table and touched my arm. "Do you feel like telling me what this is all about?"

"Sure." I told Nick about finding Dana in my backyard. I told her about the Christmas card that had been postmarked from Churchill. I told her about the truck with the bear logo that I traced to Ursula Laboratories in Cambridge, owned and operated by Dr. Judson McKibben, who was now living in seclusion in Churchill.

I did not tell her about Sunshine and Misty being murdered.

"Dana was pregnant," I said. "She died of a miscarriage. I feel like I should have saved her life. But I didn't. I feel responsible."

Nick was shaking her head. "That's a terrible story. I'm sorry."

I nodded.

"Maybe she was on a bus passing through,

and when it stopped across from the post office . . ."

I nodded. "That's when she mailed the Christmas card. Maybe that is what happened."

"I don't know what to say." Nick shook her head. "It just makes me want to go hug my daughter, you know?" She blew out a breath, smiled quickly, and stood up. "Anyway, I really gotta get back to work. How about a piece of pie? We got apple and banana cream. Fresh today. The apple's still warm."

"Warm apple pie," I said. "Perfect."

It was around eight o'clock when I stepped outside the restaurant. It had been snowing for a while, and it was still coming down, big soft flakes drifting down in the floodlights that lit the area out front and mounding over the parked vehicles.

I zipped my parka up to my chin and went over to where I'd left my car. Two or three inches of fluffy new snow covered it. When I went to the door to get in, I noticed that a patch of snow had been cleared off the driver's-side window. I pictured Chief Nate Harrigan's gloved hand brushing away the snow, then Harrigan bending over and shining his big cop flashlight around inside my car.

My duffel still sat on the passenger seat. I'd left it half unzipped so I could easily reach my .38 revolver — a silly and unnecessary precaution, of course. Careless of me not to zip it up tight when I went into the restaurant.

I wondered if Harrigan's flashlight had shone on the checkered end of the revolver's butt protruding from the socks and T-shirts I'd buried it in. And if he did see it, I wondered if he recognized it for what it was, and if he did, what his reaction was.

If he wanted to, Chief Harrigan could stop me, search my car, find that gun that he already knew was there, and run me in for a firearms violation.

I unlocked the door, slid in, and pulled the duffel onto my lap. I shoved the gun down toward the bottom and zippered the bag all the way shut, which I realized amounted to latching the kennel door after the dog had run away.

I got the car started, turned on the defroster and the wipers, popped the trunk, picked up the duffel, and got out. I went around to the back of the car and shoved the duffel in behind the spare tire. Then I brushed the snow off the windows, headlights, license plates, and brake lights.

I would drive slowly and carefully, violate no motor vehicle laws, and give Chief Nate Harrigan no cause to stop and hassle me. But if he did, my duffel would not be sitting there in plain sight where he could legally search it, and he couldn't force me to open my trunk without some kind of probable cause.

I pulled out of the lot and onto the road. A fresh layer of snow covered the pavement. I crept along in third gear, following the snowbank on the righthand side, and after about fifteen minutes the Motel sign loomed up on the right, its red lights fuzzy in the swirling snow. I put on my directional, slowed way down, recognized the driveway by the rounded snowbanks, and crept up the incline to the parking area in front.

The Sweeney's motel appeared to have twelve units — six in front and six around back. There were three other vehicles parked out front. The office was down on the end. The neon pink Office light in the window was lit, but the room behind the window was dark.

I parked in front of unit four, got out, retrieved my duffel from the trunk, and went to the door. The key, as promised, was under the mat. I unlocked the door, flicked the light switch inside the doorway, went in, shut the door behind me, and hooked the security chain.

Typical motel room. I'd stayed in a hundred just like it. Standard double bed against the inside wall under a large framed print of round-topped New England mountains and autumn foliage, a table in the corner with a good-sized television set on it, a small chest of drawers, an upholstered chair in the other corner, a bedside table with an alarm clock and a lamp on top and a Bible in the drawer, a big front window with heavy orange curtains pulled shut over it, a small bathroom with a plastic shower stall, no tub.

There was a little four-cup coffeemaker on the counter in the bathroom, with half a dozen coffee bags, a handful of packets of artificial sweetener and powdered creamer, two ceramic mugs. No minifridge, but I'd noticed a Coke machine in front of the office.

I set my duffel on top of the chest of drawers, tossed my parka on the chair, kicked off my boots, and flopped down on the bed. I found the remote on the bedside table, flicked on the television, surfed through the channels, and stopped at a basketball game. The announcer's voice was familiar and comforting, although I knew nothing and cared even less about the Providence and Seton Hall teams that were playing.

I watched for a few minutes, then muted it. I wanted to talk to Evie. I reached over to the bedside table and groped for the telephone.

Right. The room had no telephone.

I fished my cell phone from my pants pocket and checked the screen.

"No service," it said.

I closed my eyes and saw, beside the Coke machine, a pay phone on the outside wall under the overhang beside the motel office.

I pulled on my boots, hunched into my parka, made sure my room key was in my pocket, and went outside.

The wind seemed to have picked up, and the snow was still coming down, hard little kernels now, blowing sideways and biting the backs of my hands. At the pay phone, I faced the wall, putting my back to the storm. I pecked in the numbers from my calling card, then the numbers for my house in Boston, and a minute later Evie said, "Hello?"

"Hi, baby."

"Hey, it's you," she said. "Are you all right?"

"Sure. I'm fine. Why wouldn't I be?"

"I just sort of expected to hear from you before now. That you'd arrived safely. That you hadn't gone skidding off the road somewhere in the White Mountains. It's been a stormy day."

"I'm sorry," I said. "There's no cell-phone signal up here. This is the first crack I've had at a pay phone."

"It's stupid to worry," she said.

"It's sweet and loving to worry. But I'm fine. No problems. I'm at a motel in Churchill."

"Sounds exotic."

"Satellite TV, no phone."

"Perfect." She hesitated. "Learn anything?"

"I learned that Dr. Judson McKibben lives here in Churchill," I said. "He's some sort of recluse, mourning his daughter's death. I had a nice dinner at the local café, talked with the owner, who's very nice, and the chief of police, who's not so nice."

"Wow," said Evie. "You've been busy."

"I haven't actually learned much," I said.

"But you will."

"I'm going to try."

"And to hell with the bad guys."

"I don't know if there are any bad guys."

"There are always bad guys."

I paused. "Honey?"

"Yes?"

"Do I detect a note of . . . cynicism in your voice?"

"No," she said. "It's a note of loneliness, spiced with a soupçon of resentment and a pinch of apprehension. Don't worry about it. I'm fine. I love you. Oh. Roger Horowitz called."

"What'd he want?"

"He wanted you."

"Did you tell him — ?"

"Of course I did. I told him you were off on a quest."

"Jesus," I said. "I wish you hadn't. What'd he say?"

"What do you think? He's pissed at you, which I take to mean he's worried, which I understand. He said he tried your cell. I told him I was positive I'd be talking to you, did he want me to give you a message or have you call him. He said I should tell you to turn around and come home."

"If he calls again," I said, "tell him that Dr. McKibben does, in fact, live here in Churchill. The local police chief is named Nate Harrigan. He knows about McKibben. Roger might want to talk to Harrigan."

Evie paused, then said, "Okay. I wrote it down. Harrigan. Anything else for him?"

"Can't think of anything."

She hesitated. "So you gonna do what Roger says? You gonna turn around and come home?"

"Sure."

"When?"

"Tomorrow."

"I will not consider that a promise."

"I'll see you tomorrow," I said. "I miss you."

"That's nice."

"However," I said, "I'm freezing my ass out here. Gotta go. I love you."

"Me, too."

"Pat Henry for me."

"You bet. Sleep tight."

Back in my room, I lay down on my motel bed with the TV muted and the basketball game still going on. I clasped my hands behind my neck and stared up at the ceiling. I didn't know exactly what I'd been expecting from Evie, but whatever it was, I didn't get it.

Maybe something more effusive than "Me, too," when I told her I loved her.

I closed my eyes. It had been a long day, and my shoulders and neck were stiff from white-knuckle driving over narrow mountain roads in the snow.

A pounding noise came at me through the fog of sleep. I blinked and pushed myself into a sitting position. The basketball game was still going on.

More pounding. "Mr. Coyne." A man's voice at the door.

"Hang on," I called.

I swiveled around, sat on the edge of the bed, stretched, took a couple of deep breaths, then pushed myself to my feet.

"Mr. Coyne," came the voice from outside again. "I need to speak to you, sir."

I went to my duffel, unzipped it, fished around inside, found the handle of my Chiefs Special, pulled it out, and peeled the sock off it.

I went to the door and opened it a crack, leaving the chain hooked. I kept the gun behind my leg.

"Who are you?" I said.

"My name is Albert Cranston." He moved so I could see his face through the crack in the door. He looked to be in his forties, clean shaven, glasses, brown hair cut short. A pleasant, nondescript face, neither smiling nor frowning. He was wearing a dark ski parka, no hat. The snow was white on his shoulders. "Dr. McKibben would like to talk with you, sir."

"When?" I said.

"Now, if you wouldn't mind," he said. "I've come to drive you there."

# Twenty-One

"I'll be with you in a minute," I said to Albert Cranston. I shut the door and went over to where my duffel was sitting on the chest of drawers. I stuck my gun in its sock and started to shove it down among my underwear.

Then I had a second thought. I went over to the bed, lifted up the mattress, and slid the gun in between the mattress and the box spring. An unnecessary precaution, no doubt, and futile, probably. If somebody really wanted to toss my room, under the mattress was the second or third place even an amateur would look.

On the other hand, if I left the camera and the tape recorder and the binoculars there in the duffel, maybe they'd think they'd found everything there was to find.

On the third hand, if they did find my gun under the mattress, they'd not only know that I'd brought a gun, but they'd also know that I was a cautious and suspicious person with something I thought I needed to hide.

On the fourth hand, they'd also conclude that, cautious and suspicious as I might be, I was also too inept to be taken seriously, hiding my weapon in such an obvious place.

I have a tendency to overanalyze things sometimes. Most likely, nobody would search my room in the first place. If they did, they could think whatever they wanted to think, as long as they didn't steal anything.

I pulled on my boots and parka, patted my pants pocket to be sure the room key was there, and went outside.

Albert Cranston was standing under the overhang with his arms folded across his chest.

I held out my hand to him. "Brady Coyne," I said.

He looked at my hand, then gave it a quick shake. "This way, please," he said, and he walked over to a big Lincoln SUV that was parked beside my little BMW. The SUV's motor was running. The wipers were keeping the windshield clear. Snow swirled in the headlights.

I went over to the passenger side and climbed in beside Cranston. "What's this all about?" I said.

"Dr. McKibben wants to talk to you."

"Why?"

"He's under the impression that you want to talk to him," he said. "Please fasten your seat belt."

I did, and he did, too, and then the door lock beside me clicked. I wondered if I tried the handle I'd be able to open the door. I didn't bother trying.

Cranston backed out of his parking slot, eased down the motel driveway, and turned right onto the highway, heading north. The illuminated clock on the dashboard read 9:58.

The road was surrounded by blackness. No streetlights, no lighted buildings, no road signs along the way. No moon. No starry night sky. No other traffic moving in either direction. Just our headlights boring a tunnel of light straight ahead through the dark and the swirling snow between the high white snowbanks.

Once he was on the road and up to speed, Cranston kept the odometer on forty MPH.

He drove with both hands on the wheel at ten and two. He leaned slightly forward and kept his eyes on the road. He didn't seem inclined to talk, which was all right by me.

At 10:09, he took a right turn onto a narrower secondary road and eased back to thirty MPH. At 10:12 he took another right. Both were ninety-degree rights, which, if I visualized it accurately, meant that we'd doubled back and were now moving due south, parallel to the highway we'd started on.

It occurred to me that Cranston was driving in circles to confuse me.

If so, it wasn't working.

From where I sat, I couldn't read the small numbers on the odometer, but I was doing the math in my head. Forty miles per hour was two-thirds of a mile per minute. He'd taken that first right eleven minutes north of the motel. A little under eight miles.

Thirty MPH translated to a mile every two minutes. The second right came three minutes later. A mile and a half.

At 10:16 — four minutes and two miles later — he slowed down and took an oblique left onto a narrow sloping driveway. It curved up a hill through a thick stand of dark evergreens and stopped about half a mile later in a turnaround in front of a big rambling farmhouse.

A wide stairway led up to an open wrap-around porch. The house had three stories and two dormers and a big fieldstone chimney at each end. A pale light was flickering behind one of the dormer windows. A candle, maybe.

Floodlights up in the eaves bathed the turnaround out front in yellow light and left the surrounding area in absolute darkness.

"Here we are," said Cranston. He shut off the ignition, and then the door locks clicked. "Follow me, please."

I climbed out of the car and looked around. One branch of the driveway curled around the side of the house to the back, where I could make out a couple of roof-lines silhouetted against the dark sky. An attached barn, I guessed, and beyond it a lower building with a less steeply pitched roof. A stable, perhaps.

A dog yipped a couple of times. The sound seemed to come from the direction of the barn. It could have been a coyote.

Cranston moved behind me and kind of herded me up the steps onto the porch. He rang the doorbell, and a minute later it opened and a woman wearing a baggy UNH sweatshirt and blue jeans was standing there. She smiled and said, "Come on in, Mr. Coyne. The doctor is expecting you." She held out her hand. "I'm Jeanette Perkins."

I shook her hand. She had large brown eyes and olive skin and shiny black hair, cut short. Up close I saw the crinkles at the corners of her eyes and mouth and the flecks of gray in her hair, and I guessed she, like Cranston, was somewhere in her early forties.

She turned and led me through the front living room to a smaller room toward the back corner of the house. This room was lined with bookshelves and furnished with a big leather sofa, several upholstered soft chairs, and a couple of sturdy wooden rocking chairs. A few braided rugs were scattered on the pine-plank floor. A fire crackled in the fieldstone fireplace, and a black-and-white cat was curled up in one of the soft chairs.

"Please make yourself comfortable," said Jeanette Perkins. She held out her hand. "Let me take your coat."

I took off my parka and handed it to her.

"What can I get you?" she said. "Wine? Beer? Soft drink?"

I waved my hand. "I'm fine, thanks."

"You sure? How about a nice cup of tea?"

"Actually," I said, "I guess I could use a mug of coffee, if you have it. Albert, there, he woke me up." I looked around, suddenly aware that Albert Cranston had not followed us into this little parlor. "Where is Albert?"

"Mr. Cranston's waiting to take you

back," she said. "I'll get your coffee. The doctor will be right with you."

She left through a doorway in the back of the room. I went to the fireplace to look at some framed photos on the mantel. One showed a young couple sitting on a bench on a porch that might have been this very house I was in. The woman was blond and pale and thin. The man had a long angular face, with a crooked nose and a small mouth. Neither of them was smiling in the photo. The doctor and his wife, I guessed. Greta, I remembered her name was. She died soon after their daughter was born.

There were three other photos in cheap metal frames. All pictured the same blond girl. The girl as a toddler, her hair a helmet of blond curls, sitting on some steps licking an orange Popsicle, with orange stains covering the front of her white T-shirt and a big yellow teddy bear sitting beside her. The girl was older in the next photo, six or seven, I guessed, wearing a little plaid skirt and white blouse, her blond hair longer and less curly and pulled back in a ponytail. She was standing beside a mailbox with a pink backpack over one shoulder. First day of school, maybe. And the same blond girl — Ursula, I assumed, Judson McKibben's daughter — on the cusp of womanhood,

326

wearing jeans and a sleeveless jersey and a backward baseball cap, sitting bareback on a horse and looking fearlessly into the camera. This photo must have been taken close to the time she died. She was twelve when she drowned. She looked comfortable on the horse.

Something about this photo bothered me. I took it down from the mantel and —

"Ah, Mr. Coyne," came a deep voice from behind me. "There you are."

I turned. It was the man in the photo with the angular face and crooked nose and small mouth, except now his face was deeply creased, with half-moon glasses perched down toward the tip of that long meandering nose.

He held out his hand. "I'm Jud Mc-Kibben."

I shook it. "Brady Coyne."

"Yes," he said. "I know." He took the photograph I was holding from my hand. "Ursula, my daughter." He touched the glass with his forefinger. "She died two days after that photo was taken. It's the last image of her I have." He arched his eyebrows at me, as if he expected me to say something.

I didn't.

He gave me a quick smile, then waved at

one of the rocking chairs that was facing the fireplace. "Have a seat, please," he said.

I sat.

"It was a birthday party," he said. "I didn't want her to go. There were going to be boys there, and they had a swimming pool. Ursula had bought herself a new bathing suit for this party. My daughter was not naïve. On the contrary. She was wise way beyond her years." He looked at the photo he was holding. "She knew exactly how she looked in that bathing suit, how the boys would react to it. It was a two-piece. You wouldn't call it a bikini, but . . ." He shook his head. "She was turning into a woman, and she was quite aware of it, and she knew that it . . . it bothered me, and so when she came prancing into the living room that afternoon in this skimpy little bathing suit and did a couple of pirouettes with one hand on a hip and this smile on her face, I said to her, just as she expected me to, I said, 'I absolutely forbid you to wear that.' " McKibben looked at me. "She just laughed. She knew she'd end up doing what she wanted to do. And she did. I spoiled her. I couldn't say no to her. So I drove her to the party, and all the way there, and afterwards, after I drove away and went home, I was feeling this horrible dark foreboding. I thought it was about boys seeing her in that skimpy bathing suit, and I felt foolish and overprotective. And then the telephone rang."

He looked at the photo he was holding for a moment, then put it back on the mantel. He touched the corner, adjusting it, then gave his head a small shake, turned around, and sat on the sofa across from me. "Jeanette will bring your coffee in a minute," he said. "Me, I can't drink coffee in the evening."

I smiled and nodded.

"Do you have children, Mr. Coyne?"

"Two boys," I said. "Both grown."

"Do you see them often?"

"No. Nowhere near often enough."

He nodded. "You should correct that."

"Nothing to correct," I said. "They are independent, autonomous adults. They're living their lives. It's what I've always wanted for them. I miss them, but that's my problem."

"And your wife? Their mother?"

"She doesn't see them much, either." I looked at him. "She's no longer my wife."

"I'm sorry."

"We're not."

At that moment Jeanette came into the room. She was carrying a tray with two mugs on it. She gave one to me and the other to McKibben. "Can I get you something else?" she said to him.

"Thank you, no, my dear."

She bowed quickly, flashed a quick smile at me, turned, and left the room.

"Jeanette's my cousin," McKibben said.

I shrugged.

"She's been a comfort," he said.

I sipped my coffee. I was curious to see how he would proceed.

He dipped his teabag in his mug a few times, then put it on the tray that Jeanette had left on the table beside him. He took a sip, gazed up at the ceiling, put down his mug. He sat back, crossed his ankle over his knee. "I understand you wanted to talk with me," he said.

"Word travels fast in Churchill."

He smiled. "So how can I help you?"

"Do you know a girl named Dana Wetherbee?"

He sat still and expressionless for a minute. Then he said, "You were asking about this girl at Nick's."

"That's right."

"I don't know her," he said. "I never heard her name before today. I am very curious to know why you think I might have."

"Let me explain," I said, and I proceeded to tell him about finding Dana in the snow

330

in my backyard, and seeing the truck with the Ursula Laboratories logo on the side in the same part of the city where Dana had been seen on the night that she died, and learning that Dana had mailed a Christmas card from Churchill. I told him that Dana died, but I did not tell him that she'd had a miscarriage. I did not mention Sunshine or Misty.

As I talked, McKibben watched me without expression. He had pale, intense eyes. They were the color of ice.

"Dana," I said, "was sixteen. She looked remarkably like your Ursula." I pointed at the photo on the mantel. "Ursula would be about sixteen now, is that right?"

He nodded. "She died four years ago last July. You find this to be an important coincidence?"

"I don't know that it *is* a coincidence."

"You think Ursula and Dana — what? — knew each other?"

"I don't know. I'm just trying to figure out what Dana's story is. She died in my backyard. I need to understand. I thought you might be able to help me."

He shook his head. "I don't see how, Mr. Coyne. I'm sorry. Truly I am. I think I understand how you feel. You feel responsible. You should have rescued her. What happened to her is your fault. When you analyze it, of course, you know that's not true. But in your heart, you can't help feeling that way. I carry that same guilt, that same burden of responsibility. It's with me every minute of every hour of every day, and I don't think it will ever change."

"Tell me about your company truck."

"My truck?"

"Yes."

He smiled. "What do you want to know?"

"Where is the truck now?"

He stared at me for a minute, then shrugged. "Trucks," he said. "Plural. My company had three panel trucks with our logo painted on their sides. When I dissolved the corporation, I turned the trucks, along with all the furnishings and the laboratory equipment, over to a firm that specializes in liquidations. I have no idea where those trucks are or who owns them now. I must say, though, I would find it odd if the new owners didn't paint out our old logo."

"Where'd that logo come from?"

He looked away for a moment. "Ursula designed it. I told her I was naming my new company after her. She knew that her name derived from the Latin word for bear. She sketched the design herself, the two bears, a mother and a cub. She didn't really remember her mother. Greta was her name. Greta died when Ursula was a baby. Ursula was very curious about Greta, and I know not having a mother was important to her." He shrugged. "My designer took Ursula's sketch and created our logo. She was very proud of it."

"Why did you dissolve your corporation?"

He gazed into the fire. "When Ursula died, I guess I just lost my . . . my zest for doing business. My motivation. We were making a lot of money. In my mind, that money was for her. For her future. Her . . . her life. Do you see?"

"Sure."

"Without Ursula, making money seemed . . . frivolous."

I nodded. "And now?"

He turned his head and looked at me. "What do you mean?"

"You're not working? Doing business?"

"I work," he said. "I cut firewood, and I split it and I stack it. I patch holes in the roof of my barn. I repair my stone walls. I grow vegetables and flowers. Albert helps with the heavy lifting. Jeanette takes care of the house." He shrugged. "I have more money than I can use. I don't want any more. I like to give it away. I'm trying to live a quiet, anonymous life here in

Churchill, New Hampshire. Simplify, simplify, Thoreau said. I try to be a good neighbor. Really, all I want is to be left alone."

"To avoid being bothered by people like me," I said.

He shrugged.

"I'm sorry."

He waved his hand. "It's all right. I understand. I suppose I'd do what you're doing if I were you."

I took a sip of coffee, then put down the mug. "Thank you for seeing me and helping me to clear this up."

"You haven't cleared up anything," he said. "I haven't told you anything that helps you."

"No, I guess you haven't. But you've helped me to eliminate some possibilities. That's a start."

"It's a shame you had to come all this distance."

"It was doing something," I said. "Doing something is always better than doing nothing, even if it doesn't pan out."

He looked at me for a moment, then said, "Now you won't have to bother me anymore."

"Sure."

"Good." He nodded. "Albert will take you back."

"Thank you."

He stood up, went over to the door, and pushed it open. "Jeanette, dear," he said, speaking into the other room. "Mr. Coyne is ready to leave."

A moment later, Jeanette came into the room. She was carrying my coat in both arms like she might lug a load of firewood.

I stood up, took my coat from her, and put it on. Then I held out my hand to Judson McKibben.

He took it. "Good luck on your quest."

"Thank you."

"Please," said Jeanette. "Follow me."

I followed her through the house. She opened the front door. Albert Cranston was waiting there on the porch for me.

"This way," he said, and he turned and went down the front steps. The big Lincoln SUV was parked where he'd left it.

"Have a nice evening," I said to Jeanette.

She dipped her head slightly. "You, too, Mr. Coyne," she said. Then she smiled, went back inside, and closed the door.

I went down to the car. Cranston got in behind the wheel, and I opened the door on the passenger's side. As I bent to get in, I glanced up at the attic dormer. The light was still on up there, and as I looked, I thought I glimpsed a shadow sliding away from the window.

# Twenty-Two

Albert Cranston turned on the ignition. The lock on my door clicked. "Seat belt, please," he said.

I buckled up.

He rolled down the long curving driveway. It had stopped snowing, but the night was dark, and all I could see was what the headlights showed straight in front of us. Snow and woods.

At the foot of the driveway, he turned left, which meant he was taking me back a different way. I wasn't sure why he felt he needed to confuse me. I'd already indicated that my interest in Dr. Judson McKibben had been satisfied.

The clock on the Lincoln's dashboard read 11:22. I'd been there a little more than an hour.

I watched the clock and the odometer and kept track of the lefts and rights that Cranston took. We didn't talk at all. By the time he pulled up in front of unit four at Sweeney's motel, I had a clear mental map of the round trip from the motel to McKibben's house and back, even though I hadn't identified a single landmark along the way.

"Here we are," said Cranston.

I unsnapped my seat belt. "Thanks for the ride."

"Now you'll leave him alone," he said. "You have no more business in Churchill." It was neither a question nor a request. It was a statement.

"I'm pretty tired," I said, "and I've got a long drive facing me tomorrow."

"I hope you sleep well," he said. "Have a pleasant trip home."

The locks clicked. I opened the door and got out.

Cranston sat there in his big square Lincoln SUV with the headlights blazing on the front of the motel while I went to my door, unlocked it, flicked on the light, and went inside.

I stood there for a minute, as if some sixth sense might kick in and tell me if somebody had snuck in while I was gone. Not surprisingly, I received no subliminal messages.

I went to the bed and dug around under the mattress. My Chiefs Special was still there, as nearly as I could tell in exactly the same place it had been when I hid it there. I slid it out and put it on the table beside the bed.

Nor did it seem that anybody had been digging around in my duffel. Nothing was missing or out of place.

I tossed my parka onto the chair, sat on the edge of the bed, and pried off my boots.

It was almost midnight on a snowy Saturday night in January, and here I was, alone in a motel room in godforsaken Churchill, New Hampshire. If there had been a phone in the room, or if my cellular was functioning, I would've called Evie again. I could've pulled my boots back on, hunched into my parka, gone out to the pay phone and called her. Maybe she'd be happy to hear from me. Maybe not. Most likely she was already asleep, flopped on her belly, hugging her pillow, with Henry curled up against her hip, and if I woke her, she'd be grouchy, and I'd end up feeling lonelier than I already did.

So I turned on the television, found an old Clint Eastwood movie, took off my clothes, and crawled into bed . . . and the next thing I knew, gray daylight was filtering in around the blinds and the digital alarm clock on the table beside me read 8:23.

I plugged in the coffee, and while it was brewing, I showered and got dressed. Woolen long johns, woolen socks, heavy woolen shirt, woolen turtleneck sweater, wool pants. I was a big fan of wool. No space-age synthetic I'd ever tried could match wool for warmth. Even when it was wet, wool continued to do its job.

I watched the news while I drank my coffee. Then I packed up my duffel, pulled on my boots and parka, and went down to the motel office.

A pretty gray-haired woman was behind the counter. She looked up and smiled when the bell over the door dinged. "Mr. Coyne?" she said.

"Yes." I held out my hand. "You're Mrs. Sweeney?"

"Joanne, please," she said. "Everything was okay, I hope."

"Great," I said. "Slept like a log. Thanks for leaving the key for me." I took out my room key and my credit card and gave them to her. "Do you know anyplace around here where a man could rustle up some bacon and eggs and hot coffee on a Sunday morning?"

"Nick's," she said as she slid my card

through her machine. "She's open all the time." She gave me my card and a receipt to sign. "Heading back today?"

"Right after breakfast," I said. "It's a long drive."

She smiled. "Come back soon."

I ate at a small table by the front window at Nick's. Three eggs over easy, home fries, double order of bacon, wheat toast, a giant glass of orange juice, two mugs of coffee. A fisherman's breakfast, loaded with proteins and fats and evil carbohydrates. It would keep me going all day.

Four or five men — they might have been the same guys in flannel shirts and baggy blue jeans and faded baseball caps who'd been there drinking beer the previous night — were having breakfast at the bar. A young couple with a baby in a high chair occupied one booth, and a middle-aged couple sharing a Sunday newspaper sat at one of the tables. Nick waited on all of us.

I was on my second mug of coffee when she came over and sat across from me. "How was the motel?" she said.

"Good. Comfortable."

"So you heading back home?"

I nodded. "By popular demand."

She arched her eyebrows. "Huh?"

I waved the back of my hand. "Everybody seems pretty anxious for me to leave."

"That's not what *I* meant," she said.

"It's okay. I'm just hoping I can get back to Boston before it starts snowing again."

She pushed back her chair and stood up. "It's in the forecast for later. Drive carefully."

"I will."

I paid my bill, and when I stepped outside, I saw that tiny little flakes of soft snow had begun sifting down while I was inside. Already a thin coating had covered the vehicles in Nick's lot.

I climbed into my car, turned on the windshield wipers, pulled out of the lot, and turned south. The sky was low and gray, heavy with moisture, as it had been quite consistently since New Year's Day. It looked like it was planning to snow for a while.

I stopped at the Exxon station next to the post office and filled up my tank. Inside, I found two bottles of orange juice and three Hershey's bars and took them to the counter. When I paid the old guy who was sitting there working on the Sunday crossword puzzle, I asked him how long he thought it would take me to get to Boston.

He scratched the side of his neck and pondered the question, then said, "If it don't snow, four and a half, five hours. If this snow decides to get serious, who knows? What in hell you want to go to Boston for, anyway?"

"I live there."

He nodded, as if I'd said something profound. "Good reason, I suppose."

I pulled away from the gas station and continued south. I passed the intersection and crossed the bridge by the frozen mill-pond, and a little over two miles later I came to a side road that veered off to the left.

I slowed down, checked my rearview mirror to be sure nobody was behind me, and took that left. According to the map in my head that I'd sketched from the clock and the odometer in Albert Cranston's Lincoln SUV the previous evening, in about two minutes I should come to another left that would take me north, parallel to the road that cut through the middle of Churchill, and if I kept my odometer on thirty, it would take me thirteen minutes to get to the right turn, and another minute-and-a-half to find the left that would take me past the long driveway that curved up the hill and through the evergreens to Judson Mc-Kibben's big farmhouse.

I drove past a couple of roadside farm stands bearing "Closed for the Season" signs, and a little over thirteen minutes later I came to the right turn I was looking for.

An old metal building shaped like a small airplane hangar sat on the corner. I hadn't seen it the previous night in the dark. Twenty-five or thirty snow-covered vehicles — sedans, sports cars, SUVs, pickup trucks, and one yellow school bus — were parked haphazardly in a big side lot. The sign over the door read "Don's Auto Body." The area was surrounded by a tall chain-link fence, but the front gates, I noticed, hung unlocked and half open. No lights glowed from inside the garage. It was Sunday. Even tin-knockers took Sundays off.

Perfect.

I continued following the map in my head. The narrow road twisted through woodland and swamp, and according to my odometer it was one-point-two miles from Don's Auto Body to the rocky ice-rimmed stream that tumbled out of the woods and passed through a culvert under the road about a hundred yards before I came to the end of Judson McKibben's driveway.

I continued past the driveway for another half mile, then made a three-point turn and headed back to the auto-body shop.

McKibben was smart and suspicious, and I was pretty sure Nate Harrigan, the chief of police, was no dummy. My impression was that Albert Cranston was the smartest of them all.

If I'd done everything right, McKibben and Cranston now believed that they'd satisfied my curiosity, and Harrigan believed he'd intimidated me. Joanne Sweeney at the motel and Nick at the cafe and the guy at the gas station would all be able to report that the nosy lawyer from Boston had said he was going home, and in fact, they'd seen him driving south. He was worried about getting back to Boston before the snow got too heavy.

I stopped in front of the auto-body place, got out, and pushed the chain-link gates all the way open. Then I got back into my car and drove into the lot. I found a space between a Dodge pickup and a Ford Explorer and nosed my BMW into it. The front of the Dodge was pushed in as if it had plowed straight-on into a brick wall. The sides and roof of the Ford were dented and crumpled, and all the windows were smashed, as if it had rolled down a rocky slope.

By comparison, my BMW looked — well, it looked like a spiffy new BMW amid a bunch of banged-up old American vehicles, not even taking the Massachusetts plates into account. But like the other vehicles that were parked there, the roof and hood of my car were covered with snow, and I was fairly confident that nobody driving by would take a second look at it.

I dug around in my duffel, found my digital camera, binoculars, tape recorder, Leatherman, Swiss Army knife, Smith & Wesson .38, extra bullets, flashlight, and Space blanket. The aluminum-lined Space blanket was an amazing invention that folded into a neat little square about the size of a pack of cards and weighed less. I looped the binoculars around my neck and tucked them inside the front of my parka. Everything else went into the deep pockets, including the juice and candy bars. I tried to distribute the weight evenly.

I pulled on my black knit hat and fur-lined leather gloves, then slid out of the car and locked it. I walked to the front of the building, then turned and looked back. Aside from the tire tracks I'd left in last night's snow leading into the auto-body lot, nothing looked amiss. At the rate today's snow was falling, those tire tracks, plus my boot prints, would disappear in an hour.

I adjusted the gates so that they hung half open the way they had when I'd driven in. Then I began trudging along the side of the road toward McKibben's house.

It was a snowy Sunday morning in January, and this appeared to be a little-traveled roadway. If everything went perfectly, I'd be able to walk the mile and a half to McKibben's without anybody driving by. Moving briskly under normal conditions, I knew I could walk a mile in twelve to fifteen minutes. On this snow-packed road wearing my heavy insulated boots and many layers of woolen clothing, I figured it would take me closer to twenty minutes.

It was probably asking too much for nobody to come along in twenty minutes. Nothing ever went perfectly.

The snowbanks along the sides of the road were about waist-high. The forest — a mixture of hardwoods and hemlocks, with alders and swamp maples in the low places — crowded close to both sides.

A soft breeze murmured high in the hemlocks. In the distance a couple of crows cawed at each other. My boots crunched on the snow-packed roadway. Otherwise, the snowy world seemed uninhabited and still.

I had been walking for about five minutes when I heard the growl of an engine in low gear coming from around the bend behind me. I didn't wait to see what it was. I launched myself over the snowbank, rolled under a hemlock bough, and lay flat on my belly.

I peeked up as the vehicle came close. It was a dump truck with a yellow light revolving on its roof. A logo on the door indicated that it belonged to the Churchill department of public works. A plow was mounted up front and the truckbed was piled with sand, but the plow was up and it wasn't spreading sand. If the snow persisted, it would soon have to go to work.

I waited for the truck to pass and for the sound of its engine to fade around the corner before I slipped back out onto the road.

A few minutes later I heard another engine. The sound was muffled by the snow and the hemlocks, and I couldn't tell whether it was coming from behind me or ahead of me. I didn't wait to see. I again slithered over the snowbank and crawled behind a brushy clump of alders.

It was a big square SUV coming from the direction of McKibben's house, and as it got closer, I saw that it was the same Lincoln SUV that Albert Cranston had driven when he shuttled me from the motel and back the previous night.

Cranston was behind the wheel. He was driving very slowly, and I could see his face behind the windshield. He was hunched forward, tense and alert, and it looked like his eyes were darting from side to side, although I could have been imagining that.

I lay flat on my belly behind the alders and tried to burrow into the snow. My parka was olive, my jeans were faded blue, my cap was black — all neutral natural colors that should not draw attention.

If Cranston spotted me, I'd have to do some quick thinking to explain why I was hiding in the woods beside the road that led to Judson McKibben's house with binoculars around my neck and a .38 revolver in my pocket.

I tried to think quickly, just for practice, but nothing occurred to me.

He was poking along in second gear, driving cautiously on this narrow snow-covered road. But he didn't slow down or give any indication that he'd spotted something worth noticing as he approached and then passed my hiding place. He just kept going, and after a few minutes the sound of his engine faded and disappeared.

I crawled back out to the road and started walking again. I walked fast. I didn't want to encounter another vehicle.

Soon I came to the place where the rocky brook curled out of the woods along the bottom of a hillside and passed through the culvert under the road. The end of McKibben's driveway, I remembered, was just around the bend.

If I figured it correctly, I could follow the brook into the woods for a couple hundred yards, then cut off to the left and climb up the hill. McKibben's place was on the other side of the hill.

The winter brook was running low and clear over a meandering sand-and-gravel streambed. It ranged in width from about five to ten feet. In most parts it ran just a few inches deep, although here and there the water quickened and funneled between some boulders and spilled into a pool deep enough for a trout to hide.

I climbed over the snowbank and held on to some branches as I skidded down the slope to the brook.

My leather Herman Survivors boots came up over my ankles. They were absolutely waterproof. When I stepped into the brook, I didn't feel any cold, even though the water temperature was probably one degree above freezing.

I picked my way carefully up the stream, feeling the stone-cobbled bottom with my toes before shifting my weight forward, as I had learned to do from a lifetime of wading

— and slipping and falling more than once — in slick-bottomed trout streams. In places where it ran too deep I got out of the water and stepped from boulder to boulder. My aim was to leave no boot prints in the snow.

Assuming the snow kept falling, it would eventually cover the tracks I would have left if I'd decided just to walk off the road and trek through the woods. But this was better. Even bloodhounds couldn't follow me as long as I walked in the water and on the bare rocks.

By looking back to the roadway, I judged that I'd gone far enough. I left the stream and began slogging up the wooded hillside. It was slow going. The snow was thigh deep, and within minutes I was sweating heavily under all my woolen layers.

After fifty yards or so my route intersected a well-used game trail running diagonally up the hill ahead of me. It looked like the local deer herd had been following it since the year's first snowfall, and hares and squirrels and turkeys had also been using it. It wasn't exactly a boulevard, but the snow was packed enough to make the going easier for a human animal such as I.

The crest of the hill grew thick with a mixture of scrubby oaks and big hemlocks. On the far side, it sloped down to Mc-

Kibben's clearing. The game trail had taken me to a vantage overlooking the rear of his rambling buildings.

A low structure with double-wide doors that seemed to be a horse stable was attached to a big barn. The barn had glass windows and wide weathered boards and a couple of aluminum stovepipes poking through the roof. It was attached to Mc-Kibben's farmhouse by a long one-story ell.

I didn't know what I expected to see, but I was prepared to spend the day looking.

I glanced at my watch. It was about half past ten on this Sunday morning. I would watch until dark. It would be better to walk out in the dark. I wouldn't even need my flashlight. I could follow the game trail, then cut down the slope to the brook, and then follow the brook back to the road.

In mid January, darkness fell around five in the afternoon. Earlier on an overcast afternoon. Six, six and a half hours. I could do that. I had juice and chocolate and warm clothes and patience, and I didn't mind peeing in the woods.

McKibben told me he lived there with his cousin, Jeanette Perkins, his housekeeper, and Albert Cranston, his caretaker. He was still mourning the death of his Ursula, he said, and he just wanted to be left alone.

Everything he told me was plausible. He really did seem to be a sad, grief-stricken man.

But he had lied to me. I was sure of it. I just didn't know which things he said were the lies or how significant they were.

I chose a large hemlock on the crest of the ridge and crept under its bottom boughs. There was very little snow on the ground near the trunk of the tree. I brushed it away, and underneath was a soft bed of dead needles. I used the blade on my Leatherman to cut out a few branches to give me a clear look at McKibben's buildings and yard and the big sloping field behind the barn. Then I opened my Space blanket and spread it on the hemlock needles. It would insulate my butt from the cold ground.

I wiggled around so that I could lean my back against the trunk of the tree and scan the area below me with my binoculars.

I took a few photos with my digital camera — some wide-angle shots, and then, through the zoom lens, shots of windows, doors, and any other details that might be worth blowing up on my computer later.

I put my camera back in my pocket.

Ate a Hershey's bar and took a sip of juice.

Sat there and watched.

Nothing happened.

About five hours later, or so it seemed, I checked my watch. It was eleven-thirty. The same day. The same morning, in fact.

A chickadee landed on a hemlock branch so close I could have reached out and touched it. I made little kissing sounds and he turned to look at me.

Then he flew away in a soft whirr of wings.

Sometime later a door on the side of the barn opened and a person wearing a knit cap, a hip-length parka, blue jeans, and boots came out. Through my binoculars I could see it was a young, plain-looking woman. She had a blond braid hanging halfway down her back.

She wasn't Jeanette and she certainly wasn't Albert Cranston. Which meant that McKibben had definitely lied to me.

I barely had time to ponder why he hadn't mentioned this blond girl when the door opened again and another young woman came out. This one wore no hat. She had short brown hair and a round face. I didn't recognize her, either. She was carrying a broom.

Both girls were teenagers, I guessed. Seventeen or eighteen, at the most.

The blonde picked up the snow shovel that was leaning against the side of the barn and began scraping off the walkway. The other girl swept the snow off the steps.

I got out my camera, zoomed in on them, and took a few photos.

From my hiding place I could hear them talking, although I couldn't make out their words. They didn't laugh or fool around the way a couple of carefree teenage girls might, and their body language in general suggested to me that they weren't, in fact, carefree.

After a while they went back inside.

A few minutes later a different young woman came outside. She was also a blonde. I put the binoculars on her, and when she turned her face in my direction, I was pretty sure I recognized her. I'd only seen her that one time outside the Shamrock Inn. It had been dark, and most of my attention was on Misty. But I was pretty sure this was Kayla, Misty's friend.

She disappeared behind the stable, then reappeared lugging an armload of cordwood. She took it to the door. She pushed it open with her shoulder and took the wood inside.

A few minutes later smoke began to curl out of one of the barn's stovepipes.

I continued watching and waiting. But now I had a puzzle to occupy me.

Why was Kayla here? Who were the other

girls? What were they doing here? Did they live with Dr. Judson McKibben? And why did McKibben want to keep them secret? What was going on here, anyway?

I watched and pondered and sipped my juice. I got a cramp in my leg, which I pounded with my fist until it went away. I ate another Hershey's bar. I wiggled my butt around, trying to find a more comfortable sitting position.

Nothing happened for at least a week and a half.

When I looked at my watch, it was a little before one in the afternoon.

A few minutes later I heard a creaking noise. As I watched, a double-wide door on the side of the stable building swung open and a vehicle backed out. It was a panel truck.

The driver got out and went back to the garage door. I looked through my binoculars. It was Albert Cranston. He was wearing the same parka he'd had on when he came to my motel to pick me up.

I remembered how Misty had described the man driving the van, and her description fit Cranston, right down to the round wire-rimmed glasses.

I dropped my binoculars and fished my little digital camera from my pocket. I snapped a couple of quick shots of Cranston as he was shutting the heavy door and then getting back into the truck.

He put it in gear and started down the driveway, and when the truck turned sideways to me, I saw the Ursula Laboratories logo painted on its side.

# TWENTY-THREE

My first instinct was to slip out of the woods, sneak back to Don's Auto Body, rescue my car, get the hell out of Churchill, New Hampshire, and find a pay phone. Call Horowitz and tell him that I'd found Kayla and had tracked down the van with the bear logo. Try to convince him that McKibben was linked to the murders of Sunshine and Misty, and that Kayla was in danger.

My second, smarter thought was that trying to sneak out of the woods and get back to my car in the daylight was too risky. I'd been lucky to get this far without being seen. Whatever danger Kayla and those other young women might be in, it didn't seem immediate. After it got dark I could get away from there without being spotted. Meanwhile, I could continue hunkering there under the big hemlock, safe and unobserved, and see what else might happen.

So I waited. I ate my last Hershey's bar, sipped some water, adjusted my position on my Space blanket. Light snow was still sifting down, but I was snug and comfortable and warm, leaning my back against the trunk of the hemlock tree.

I couple of times my eyelids grew heavy, and I allowed them to fall down for a minute. Nothing was happening. Nobody came out of the house. Nobody went in.

I daydreamed about a donut and a big mug of hot black coffee.

I was resting my eyes, drifting on the muffled silence of the snowy woods, mind-surfing about a steamy shower, silky sheets, Evie's warm skin, her lips and tongue light on my chest, murmurs in her throat, her musky earth-scent filling my head, a mingling of images all mixed up with each other —

"Put your hands on top of your head, Mr. Coyne."

*Oh, shit.*

I opened my eyes, looked behind me.

Albert Cranston was standing about ten yards away. He'd snuck up the hill through the woods behind me. Now he was holding a pump-action shotgun at his hip. I was looking right down the barrel. Twelve-gauge, I guessed. The bore looked as big as a howitzer.

I put my hands on my head.

"Okay," he said. "Come out from under there. Slowly. I wouldn't mind an excuse to shoot you right where you are. It would save me a lot of aggravation."

A man who'd use the word "aggravation" when pondering whether to shoot a trespasser would also use the word "seek" when talking to some young streetwalkers in Boston.

I crawled out of my hiding place and stood up. I noticed that Cranston was standing on snowshoes.

"Take off your parka," he said.

"You want me to freeze?"

He smiled. "Actually, I think that would be an excellent solution. Take it off and put it down."

I did.

"Now," he said, "move over there." He gestured with his shotgun.

I took a few steps away from where my coat lay.

He jerked his gun barrel, and I stepped back another few feet.

Cranston knew that standing knee-deep in the snow, I couldn't make any sneaky moves at him from where I was standing, nor could I run away. A load of buckshot from an open-choked 12-gauge would blow a hole the size of a basketball through a man at ten yards, and you didn't have to be any kind of sharpshooter to hit your target with that armament."

He went to where I'd laid my parka on the snow and squatted beside it on his snowshoes. He held the shotgun in one hand like a pistol, with his finger on the trigger and the barrel resting on his shoulder. With his other hand he rummaged through the pockets.

He dropped my flashlight and Swiss Army knife and Leatherman and water bottle into the snow. He slid my digital camera and my tape recorder into his pocket.

When he found my Chiefs Special, he glanced up at me, and I thought I detected surprise — maybe it was admiration — in his expression.

He shoved the revolver into his pocket, then straightened up. "Take off those binoculars," he said.

I lifted the strap from around my neck and held them out to him.

"Drop 'em."

"These are top-of-the-line," I said. "I paid a lot of money for these glasses. I don't want them to get wet."

"You're not going to need them anymore," he said. "Drop 'em."

I let them fall to the snow.

"Empty your pants pockets. Slowly. Show me what you've got."

I took my car keys from my right front pocket and held them out to him.

"Toss them there, onto your coat."

I did.

"The other pocket."

I showed him the change from my left front pocket.

"Throw it over your shoulder."

I obeyed.

"Now your back pockets."

I had a handkerchief in my right hip pocket. My wallet was in my left. He told me to drop the handkerchief and toss the wallet onto my parka, which I did.

Without taking his eyes off me, Cranston bent down, scooped up my keys and my wallet, and put them into one of his pockets.

Then he picked up my parka and tossed it to me. "Put it on."

I did.

"Okay. Let's go." He jerked his head in the direction of McKibben's buildings. He kept the shotgun pointing at me.

I considered running. The woods were dense, and the terrain was rough and rocky, and even though Cranston had a shotgun, if I ran fast and dodged and darted evasively, I had a reasonably good chance of not getting hit.

But, of course, I couldn't run fast or dart and dodge evasively in snow up to my crotch. The best I could manage would be a slow-motion lumber, and he'd have no problem blowing a hole in me.

This, I decided, wasn't the time to try something. It wouldn't be daring or heroic. It would be stupid.

So I started plowing down the hill through the snow.

Cranston, clomping along easily on his snowshoes, stayed about ten yards behind me. It took about five minutes to slog down the slope through the snow to the cleared area in front of the stables where the girls had shoveled and later the panel truck had backed out. By then my woolen underwear was soaked with sweat and I was sucking deep breaths.

A door opened, and Judson McKibben stepped outside. "Ah, Mr. Coyne," he said. "How disappointing to see you again."

"Likewise," I said.

Cranston poked my back with the muzzle of his shotgun. "Inside," he said.

McKibben held the door open. I went in.

It was a long, low, dimly-lit building, obviously a stable, although it didn't appear that any horses were living there. It had thick, time-stained wood-plank walls, a few bare light bulbs hanging from the rafters, a dirt floor. The big Lincoln SUV was parked there facing a garage-sized door. A wide corridor ran down one side of the long narrow building. The other side was lined with heavy swinging double doors, so that you could open the top half and leave the bottom half closed. Or the other way around, for that matter.

"This way, Mr. Coyne," said McKibben. He went down the corridor, stopped outside one of the stalls, and opened both the top and bottom doors.

Cranston came along behind me. When I glanced back, I saw that he'd put down his shotgun. Now he was pointing my own Chiefs Special at me.

"Go ahead in, please, Mr. Coyne," said McKibben.

I entered the stall. It was a square room, with wood-plank walls, dirt floor, wooden trough along one wall. It smelled of moldy hay and old manure and sour urine. There was one small window high up on the outside wall. It was covered with wire mesh. On the sides, the spaces above the head-high walls were covered with chicken wire.

I stood there looking around. Cranston had come up behind me. I started to turn to speak to him when something hard and heavy slammed down on the top of my head. An arrow of red pain shot down through my head to my stomach and radiated into my arms and legs, and I felt myself tumbling, numb and weightless, through black, empty space.

My legs were icy cold. My stomach churned acid. I tentatively slit open my eyes. Shafts of thin yellow light sent darts of pain zipping through my eyeballs into the center of my brain.

I closed my eyes and the pain became fuzzy.

Sometime later I tried again. The light still hurt, but I forced myself to keep my eyes open. I was sprawled on the hard-packed dirt floor of the stall with my shoulders leaning against the rough wood-plank wall. They'd removed my parka and taken away my boots. A cold draft was blowing over me, and the dirt floor felt damp, and I was shivering.

I tried to move and failed. My ankles were wrapped with duct tape up to my knees. My arms were pulled behind my back and my wrists were bound together at the small of my back. Several turns of tape had been taken around my torso, pinning my upper arms at my sides.

All four of my limbs were numb. My throat felt like I'd swallowed a Brillo pad. A lump the size of a volleyball was throbbing and zapping darts of pain from the top of my head into my face and eyes.

I turned my head gingerly and looked up at the window. It was dark outside. I had no idea how long I'd been lying there.

After a while I heard the rumble of male voices from somewhere outside my stall. Then the door opened, and Judson McKibben came in. Albert Cranston was right behind him.

McKibben was holding a bottle of spring water. "Thirsty, Mr. Coyne?"

"Yes," I croaked.

He came over, knelt beside me, and held the bottle to my mouth.

I took a swig, sloshed it around in my mouth, turned my head, and spit it out onto the floor. Then I took another drink and let it slide down my throat. When it hit my stomach, I had to swallow back a wave of nausea.

"Enough?" said McKibben.

I nodded.

He stood up, looked down at me, and shook his head. "You are a problem," he said. "We don't quite know what to do about you." He turned to Cranston.

"Sure we do," Cranston said.

"Albert's a little angry with you," said McKibben. "I myself am simply disappointed. I opened my home to you, extended my hospitality to you. We had a pleasant and productive conversation, and I thought we'd come to an understanding." He shook his head. "And then we find you lurking on our property, spying on us, with binoculars and cameras and guns, for heaven's sake. Very disappointing."

"I'd appreciate it if you'd take this damn tape off me," I said. "I've got no circulation in my arms or legs."

McKibben nodded. "I understand. Albert will take care of you. I do want you to be comfortable. But first, if you wouldn't mind answering a few questions?"

"I don't see how," I said. "My head hurts too much. My brain's all fuzzy. I can't think very well."

McKibben shrugged. "Albert?"

Cranston came over and squatted down beside me. He was slapping his palm with a blackjack. That, I guessed, was what he'd used to whack the top of my head.

Suddenly he flicked his wrist and the sap crashed against the side of my knee.

It felt like he'd hammered a spike into the bone. I was sure he'd cracked it. I howled against the pain.

McKibben reached out and touched my arm. "Let's try again, Mr. Coyne," he said. "First, please tell me who knows you're here in Churchill."

I was drenched with sweat, shivering from the pain, chilled to the marrow. I gasped for breath.

Cranston showed me his blackjack.

"Horowitz," I said between clenched teeth. "Massachusetts State Police Lieutenant Roger Horowitz. Him and Saundra Mendoza. She's a Boston homicide detective. They know I'm here. They'll come looking for me."

"So who's your client?"

"Huh?"

"Your client, Mr. Coyne. You're a lawyer. Who's paying you to come snooping around my house, my town."

"Nobody pays me to snoop," I said. "They pay me to probate their estates and negotiate their divorce agreements. You said it. I'm just a lawyer."

"You go snooping on your own time, then," said McKibben. He grinned as if he'd cracked a great joke.

"Sure," I said. "That's it."

"Who did you call from the pay phone at the motel last night?"

"Horowitz," I said. "I told him all about you. He's talking to the New Hampshire cops."

"And what exactly did you tell this Horowitz about me?"

"That you're keeping girls here."

McKibben peered into my eyes and shook his head. "You called your girlfriend in Boston," he said. "It's not a good idea to lie to me." He turned to Cranston and nodded.

Cranston whacked the point of my left shoulder with his sap. There was a moment of numbness, a moment when I felt nothing. Then lightning bolts of pain zinged through my body. My stomach flipped. I gagged and swallowed back the acid that rose in my throat.

"Want another drink?" said McKibben.

I nodded.

He held the water bottle to my lips.

I took a mouthful, sloshed it around, swallowed a little, spit the rest out.

"Let's try again, Mr. Coyne," said McKibben. "I understand you're upset about poor little Dana Wetherbee, but really, what

369

in the world compelled you to come slinking around on my property?"

"She was here, wasn't she?" I said. "Like those other girls you've got here. They're prisoners, right? Are you fucking all of them? Is that how Dana got pregnant?"

McKibben smiled. "What a vivid imagination you have. But you have not answered my question. I bet Albert would like to see how you'd react to getting tapped on your elbow." He looked at Cranston. "Am I right?"

Cranston smacked his blackjack into his palm.

"You guys murdered Sunshine and Misty," I said. "You've got a big secret to protect."

"A secret, eh?" said McKibben. "What exactly is this alleged secret?"

"I don't know."

"Why in the world would you think we'd murder anybody?"

I shrugged. "They learned your secret."

"He doesn't know anything," said Cranston.

"I know you've got something to hide," I said. "Something you think is worth murdering for."

"Albert's right," said McKibben. "You don't know anything." He turned to Cranston. "What do you think, Albert? Should we let Mr. Coyne go home?"

Cranston shook his head. "I don't see how we can do that."

McKibben sighed. "I suppose you're right," he said. "We can't risk anything interfering with our work."

"Your work?" I said.

He smiled.

"What's your work?"

"Don't worry about it, Mr. Coyne," he said. "Albert will take care of you."

"Horowitz knows I'm up here," I said. "Detective Mendoza, too. She and Horowitz. Both of them. They'll have the police come looking for me, I guarantee."

"Maybe so," said Cranston. "But not for a few days. Not until they decide that something happened to you. And where do you suppose they'll look? Let's see. They'll begin here in Churchill. That's the last place they knew you were. They'll ask around, trying to track you down. They'll probably start at the motel where you spent the night. Joanne Sweeney will tell them you paid your bill and said you were heading home. No doubt she saw you drive out of her lot and turn south on the highway. Nick will tell them you stopped there for breakfast. You told her you were heading home, too. After you ate, sure enough, you continued south. You stopped at the Exxon station to fill your tank, and you told Francis that you were heading back to Boston. Then you pulled onto the highway, still heading south. So the place to start looking for you would be somewhere alongside the road south of here." Cranston was smiling. "It's another snowy night out there. The roads are slippery. Terrible visibility. There are dozens of places in the mountains south of here where someone unfamiliar with the area might take a wrong turn, and if he was driving a city car like a BMW, he could go skidding off the road and tumbling down into a rocky ravine, and if nobody saw it happen — if it happened late on a Sunday night, say, and if the snow kept falling — the car might not be found until springtime."

As Albert Cranston spun out his scenario for my death, I tried to spot the holes in his logic.

I didn't notice any. It would be easy enough to crack my skull with that damned blackjack, strap me in my seat belt behind the wheel of my car — which I assumed they'd spotted at Don's Auto Body — and push it off the road on some mountainside. If the fractured skull didn't kill me first, I'd freeze to death, and unless they made a blatant mistake, it would be impossible to tell that it wasn't some late-night winter automobile accident. A deer or a moose in the road would make you stomp on the brakes and go into a spin. You could hit an icy patch. It would be the obvious explanation, and easy to believe.

"You guys've got it all figured out," I said. "Except for the fact that the police know the reason I came up here was to get the goods on you. They'll be all over you."

McKibben was nodding. "I expect you're right about that, Mr. Coyne. Thank you. Forewarned is forearmed, as they say. But one thing at a time." He pushed himself to his feet. "We'll be back in a little while. Try to make yourself comfortable. You won't have to wait too long."

Cranston suddenly snapped his blackjack down on my shin.

I screamed.

Then both of them walked out of my stall. The door closed and I heard the bolt slide into place.

Their footsteps scuffled away on the dirt floor and faded into the distance.

A minute later, the lights went out, and I was left there in the cold stable in absolute darkness, wrapped in duct tape, with my knee and shin and shoulder and head shoot-

ing off darts of dull throbbing pain with
every beat of my pulse.

# Twenty-Four

I didn't have the luxury of wallowing in pain and self pity, even though wallowing was an attractive option.

I had to get away from there, and I didn't think I had much time. When McKibben and Cranston came back, if I was still there, they'd kill me.

I had to find a way to get the duct tape off my wrists and free my hands. If I freed my hands I could unwrap the rest of the tape. If I could get the tape off my arms and legs, I could climb and crawl and run, and if I could climb and crawl and run, I could find a way out of the stable.

If I could get out of the stable, I'd run like hell and they'd never find me.

I was sitting on the damp dirt floor with my taped-up legs sticking straight out in front of me. Faint gray light glowed from the small mesh-covered window high on the outside wall, but it wasn't enough to enable me to see more than shades of black in the dark stall. My wrists were bound behind me, and my shoulders were leaning back against the wall. I found I could bend my knees a little. The one that Albert whacked with his blackjack shot hot darts of pain up my leg when I flexed it. Nothing I could do about that. By pulling up my knees and then pushing against my feet, I found I could slide my back up the wall. It was an inch-by-inch process, but after a minute or two I levered myself into a standing position supported by the wall.

As I stood there I felt the blood suddenly begin to recirculate through my numb legs, and with the blood came the intense pain of reawakening nerve endings. I gritted my teeth and endured it for what seemed like hours, although it was probably no more than a couple of minutes.

As the pain subsided, feeling and balance returned to my legs. I was standing on my feet. I could wiggle my toes. If I could get the tape off, I could walk.

I inched my way along the wall in the darkness, shuffling my feet, which were bound at the ankles, using my shoulderblades and elbows to keep my balance. I was feeling for something sharp — a nail head would've been perfect. If I came to nothing as I slid along the wall, I remembered the latch on the inside of the stable door. I assumed Cranston and McKibben had made sure that lifting the inside latch would not open the door. I had noticed the large metal rods that served as deadbolts on the outside of all the stable doors.

But the latch was about the right height to hook my taped wrists under, and if there were any jagged edges on it, I might get a tear started. That was all I needed. A small tear in the tape.

So I emptied my mind of everything else and focused on finding a way to start that little tear in the tape on my wrists. I knew that my life depended on it.

I inched my way along the wall, working toward the front corner of the stall, teetering uncertainly on my bound-together feet, feeling for a nail head, or anything hard and sharp. A couple times wooden splinters dug into my shoulders.

Then I lost my balance and fell on the same shoulder that Cranston had smacked with his blackjack. Pain once again throbbed through my body. I was drenched with sweat. I was dead tired. Dehydrated. Nauseated.

I lay there. I didn't have any energy left. My whole body hurt. The hell with it. It was futile. I was getting nowhere. Soon Cranston and McKibben would come back to kill me. The easiest thing would be to accept that, to lie there and wait for it.

The easiest thing.

Since when did I settle for the easiest thing?

After a while — one minute? half an hour? — I gritted my teeth, took a deep breath, and pushed myself up the wall into a standing position again.

I resumed inching my way toward the front of the stall.

Then I thought I heard something. I stopped. A minute later I heard it again. It was a soft sibilant sound, a quick movement of air, so faint that I wondered if what I'd heard was my own breathing, or my pulse pounding in my ears.

I stopped, held my breath, kept my body still.

And I heard it again. It was closer. The quick exhalation of a small breath. Somebody — or some thing, some animal, maybe — was out there in the darkness. A dog. A barn cat. A rat.

Then a whisper. "Mr. Coyne?"

I said nothing.

Again: "Hey, Mr. Coyne. Where are you?"

It was a woman's voice, soft, not quite a whisper.

I cleared my throat. It was dry. It hurt to swallow. "Here," I rasped. "I'm in here."

"Can you tap on the wall? I can't tell what stall you're in."

I made fists behind me and rapped my knuckles against the wall planks.

A minute later I heard the clank of the latch on my stall door. Then the door creaked open. "You in here?"

"Right here," I said.

Suddenly there was a beam of light. She had a flashlight. It swept around the stall and stopped on me. She shined it in my face, and I clenched my eyes shut.

"Sorry," she said.

I squinted at her. "Kayla?" I said. "Is that you?"

"Yes. It's me."

"What are you —"

"Shh," she hissed. "We gotta move. I've got a knife. Let's get that tape off you."

She shined the flashlight over my body, then tucked it into her armpit. She went to work on the tape that bound my ankles together and soon had it off. I turned around and she freed my wrists, then cut through the tape that held my arms against my sides.

I rubbed feeling back into my arms and legs. It felt glorious to lift and bend my elbows, to rotate my wrists, to flex my ankles. I took a few experimental steps. I was a little shaky, but I could do it. I could walk.

Kayla was watching me. "How you doing?" she said. "You gonna be okay?"

"I'm good," I said.

"You're limping."

"I'm fine. Don't worry about it."

"Okay. Good." She grabbed my arm. "Let's go. We gotta get outa here. Follow me. I'm gonna turn off the flashlight. They might be able to see it from the house."

The light went off and it was all dark shapes and shadows.

Kayla slid her hand down my arm, found my hand, held it tight, and tugged me along behind her. She led me out of my stall and then we shuffled down the wide aisle, staying close to the inside wall. There were more windows there in the open part of the stable, and in the gray light up ahead the shape of the Lincoln SUV materialized.

When we got to it, Kayla squeezed my hand, a signal to stop. She put her mouth close to my ear. "The other truck's right outside," she whispered. "Albert always leaves the keys in the ignition. Do you think you can move quickly?"

"You bet," I said.

She opened the door to the Lincoln, and the dome light suddenly lit the area. She reached in, snatched the keys from the ignition, shoved them into her pocket, then eased the car door shut.

"What're you doing?" I said.

"We don't want Albert following us. We'll take the van." She looked at me. "Ready?"

"Let's do it."

We went out through the side door. The area outside the stable was illuminated by outdoor floodlights. The panel truck with the bear logo on its side was parked there on the other side of the garage door.

"I'll drive," she said. "Get in."

I went to the passenger side, slipped inside, and latched the door shut without slamming it.

Kayla got behind the wheel. "Ready?" she said.

"Ready."

She turned the key in the ignition. The engine started with a roar. Without turning on the headlights, she put it in gear and headed down the driveway, which wound around the barn and alongside the house, then curved down a long slope through the woods.

When we got to the end of the driveway, Kayla turned on the headlights.

And then we were moving. It was snowing hard, and the road hadn't been plowed in a while.

She glanced sideways at me. "You don't have a coat. I'm sorry. I should've brought a coat for you."

"I'll be all right when the heater kicks in."

"They took your boots, too?"

"Yep."

"Well," she said, "let's hope we don't have to walk in the woods."

Kayla drove fast, and it was immediately apparent that the panel truck did not have four-wheel drive.

"You better take it easy," I said. "If we go off the road we're screwed."

"I just want to get away from here," she muttered.

She leaned forward, tense and alert, gripping the steering wheel with both hands. The snow in the headlights was blinding.

"So what's going on?" I said. "What're McKibben and Cranston up to?"

"It's a long story," she said. "I don't understand all of it. They bring girls . . . girls like me . . . up here. Street girls, I mean. Runaways. Girls with no families, no friends. Nobody who'll miss them. Albert finds them in Boston. He's got somebody down there who scouts around, helps him identify likely prospects. He promises the girls money, a warm bed, good food. It's a chance to do some good, he says. To make a contribution. It's for science. It gives meaning to our lives. He's very convincing."

"Does it?"

She turned her head. "Huh?"

"Does it give meaning to your life?"

She blew out a quick, cynical laugh.

"You don't buy it?" I said.

"Me?" She shook her head. "I mean, I did at first. It sounded good. But I don't now."

"Why not?"

She shrugged. "Lot of reasons."

"You said someone in Boston helps Cranston find girls."

"A couple of the other girls mentioned it," she said. "I don't know who it is. A doctor, I think. A friend of Dr. McKibben."

"Dr. Rossi?" I said. "Does that ring a bell?"

"I know her," said Kayla. "She's nice." She hesitated. "I guess it could be her. I just went with Albert. He talked to me, made it sound good. Maybe Dr. Rossi told him about me and he tracked me down. Maybe that's how it works. I don't know."

We came to a stop sign. Another narrow

two-lane road intersected the one we were on. Kayla turned left onto it.

"Where does this go?" I said.

"I don't know," she said. "South, I think. I don't know where the hell I am. This road looks like it was plowed recently, that's all. We can move faster. We've got to get away from here and ditch this van."

This new road may have been plowed, but we were still driving through a blizzard on a layer of hard-packed snow.

"Dana Wetherbee was pregnant," I said. "She came up here, she got pregnant, she ran away, and then she died. Can you explain that?"

"Everybody who comes up here gets pregnant," said Kayla. "As far as I can see, that's the whole point. That girl Dana wasn't the only one who died."

"You mean these men —"

"It's nothing like that," she said. "It's not about sex. They get us pregnant in the laboratory."

"What laboratory?"

"In the basement of the house. It's got all kinds of equipment and instruments and stuff."

"Why? What are they trying to prove?"

She shook her head. "They don't explain it to us."

"Are you pregnant?"

"Me?" She laughed quickly. "Not yet. I've only been here since last Tuesday. They do a lot of tests first. They take your blood, take your urine, check your blood pressure and heart and everything. They were gonna do it to me next week, I think."

We were rounding a curve. Kayla downshifted. I felt the rear end of the truck begin to slip, but she pulled us out of it.

"You came here voluntarily?" I said.

"Yes."

"So why are you leaving?"

"Escaping is the word," she said. "You come here voluntarily, but you can't just leave. They give you drugs. Downers. Tranquilizers. You lose your will to do anything. I faked it, didn't take them. I know how they work. I would never have tried this — what we're doing — if I was swallowing their pills."

"I don't understand why you came up here in the first place," I said.

"I came here," said Kayla, "because I wanted to do something good for once in my life. Albert makes it sound good. Important. Misty and Zooey, they tried to talk me out of it. Misty kept saying it was wrong. She said it was evil, but I didn't think she knew what she was talking about. I figured it was just Misty being selfish, wanting us to stay together. We were a good team, me and Misty and Zooey, you know what I mean?"

"Friends," I said.

"Best friends."

"Okay," I said. "So you came here voluntarily. But now you want to leave. What happened?"

She was silent for a minute. Then she said, "I snooped. I always snoop. I'm a nosy person. They don't watch you very closely, and they're not careful about what they say in front of you. They think we're all dumb robots because of the drugs they give us. So it wasn't hard, snooping, eavesdropping. I overheard things they were saying. Albert and Jeanette and the doctor. The girls all die. I heard them talking about it. They say it's for science. When they're done with you, you die — they give you drugs that kill you — and they bury you out back. That girl Dana got away, but it didn't matter. She died anyway. And Albert, I heard he killed some homeless woman because she knew something. They'll kill anybody." Kayla hesitated. "I think they wanted to kill Misty."

"They did," I said. "Misty was murdered."

She turned to look at me. "It's true?"

I nodded. "I'm sorry."

She pounded the steering wheel with the heel of her hand. "Son of a bitch. I'm gonna — oh, shit."

We were rounding a bend, and headlights suddenly appeared ahead of us, coming in our direction. The vehicle seemed to be driving right down the middle of the narrow road. Its high beams were blinding.

Kayla hit the brakes. Too hard. We skidded, spun, and the rear end of the truck slammed into the snowbank.

About then a blue light began flashing on the roof of the oncoming vehicle. It was a police cruiser, and it was coming toward us.

Our engine had stalled. Kayla muttered, "Shit . . . damn it." After a minute, she got the engine started. She stomped on the accelerator, and the wheels spun. But we were stuck.

"Fuck, fuck, fuck," she muttered. "I'm sorry."

The police car stopped beside us. Chief Nate Harrigan stepped out from the passenger side, and a uniformed officer got out from behind the wheel. They were pointing flashlights and pistols at us.

The officer yanked my door open. "Get out," he said.

I started to slide out. Not fast enough, apparently. The cop grabbed my arm and yanked me. I staggered, lost my balance, and sprawled on the snowy road.

He was on me instantly. He pushed my face into the snow and wrestled my arms behind me. I felt handcuffs click on my wrists.

"Take it easy, Howard," said Harrigan. He came over and squatted down beside me. "You all right?"

"No."

He grabbed my arm and helped me onto my feet.

"Thanks," I said.

He shrugged. "Brady Coyne," he said, "you're under arrest for attempted kidnapping." He started to recite my Miranda rights.

"Hey, asshole," said Kayla. "He wasn't kidnapping anybody."

"Watch your mouth, sweetie," said the uniformed cop.

Harrigan repeated the Miranda for me. "You understand?"

"Gotcha," I said. "Nice job."

The other cop said, "Hey, Nate. That guy don't have any boots on."

"There you go," said Kayla. "He's kidnapping me with no boots or coat. What's the matter with you?"

"Where's your boots?" said Harrigan to me.

"Albert Cranston took them," I said.

"Cranston and McKibben," said Kayla. "They had Mr. Coyne tied up. They hurt him."

Harrigan cocked his head and looked at me. "That right?"

"Yes," I said. "Cranston hit me with a blackjack."

Harrigan's eyes crinkled in a smile. "That's some story," he said. He opened the back door of the cruiser. "Get in, please."

I bent to get in. He guided me with his hand on the top of my head.

The other cop led Kayla over and pushed her in beside me. Then Harrigan got in front and the other cop got behind the wheel.

Harrigan pecked out a number on the cruiser's car phone. "Yeah, it's Nate," he said. "Sorry about the hour on a Sunday night, but we got a vehicle in the snowbank on Dawson Road, couple miles south of the Dry Run intersection. . . . Yeah, bring the wrecker. It's Dr. McKibben's. . . . Yeah, a Chevy panel truck. I don't know if it's running. You might as well just tow it to his house. Keys're in the ignition."

"Where are you taking us?" said Kayla.

"I'm bringing you back to your uncle," said Harrigan.

"My *uncle?* What're you, stupid? Why won't you listen to anyone?"

The uniformed officer — Harrigan had called him Howard — turned and looked at us through the wire mesh that separated the front from the back. "I told you, young lady," he said. "You better watch the way you talk to a police officer."

"You guys should open your eyes," she said. "You're supposed to be cops? Mr. Coyne isn't the criminal here. It's them. They're a bunch of lunatics. McKibben and Cranston. They're conducting experiments on human beings. They're killing girls, for Christ sake."

"The doctor said she was paranoid," said Howard to Harrigan. "She's on medication."

"Oh, bullshit," said Kayla. "They were torturing Mr. Coyne. They were going to kill him. Right?" she said to me. "Tell them."

"They don't want to hear it," I said.

Harrigan turned in his seat and looked at me through the mesh that separated us. He started to say something, then shook his head and turned back.

A minute later we turned onto the curving driveway that led up to McKibben's house and stopped at the front door.

Both cops got out. Howard opened the door on Kayla's side. "Come on," he said to her. "You're home now."

"This isn't my home," she said. "Will you please listen to me?"

"Let's go," said Howard. He gripped Kayla's upper arm and led her up the steps onto the front porch.

Harrigan opened my door. "Let's go," he said.

"I thought I was under arrest."

He nodded. "You are. Come on." He reached in, took my arm, and helped me slide out.

"I don't have boots or a coat," I said, "and in case you didn't notice, it's winter."

"Sorry." He steered me in the direction of McKibben's porch.

"If you don't listen to me," I said, "you're going to be extremely embarrassed."

He put his hand on my arm to stop me. Howard and Kayla were several yards ahead of us, heading for McKibben's front door. "You should've listened to me," Harrigan said quietly. "You should've gone home when you had the chance. It would've been better for everybody."

"These people are conducting medical experiments on human subjects," I said.

"Some of them have died. What they're doing is illegal. They've murdered at least two women who figured out what was going on."

Harrigan looked at me. I couldn't read his expression behind his bushy mustache.

"They were going to kill me, too," I said. "Kayla helped me get away. That's why I don't have any boots. They took my boots and my coat when they captured me. Not to mention my car keys and my good German binoculars and my brand new digital camera and —"

Harrigan shook his head. "I've known Jud McKibben my whole life," he said. "He's no murderer. He's a doctor. He saves lives."

"If McKibben isn't a killer," I said, "then Cranston is. He's a sadist, I can vouch for that. Check my knee or shoulder or shin. You'll see the bruises his blackjack made. Feel the bump on top of my head." I tapped where the bump was.

Harrigan surprised me by touching the bump on my head. "You could've got that a million different ways." Then he narrowed his eyes at me. "What did you mean by experiments? What kind of experiments?"

I shook my head. "I don't know."

He put his hand on my shoulder. "Let's go."

"I thought you arrested me," I said.

"Aren't you going to take me to your jail?"

"Not yet," he said.

About the time we got to the top of the steps, the front door opened and Dr. Judson McKibben himself was standing there.

He went to Kayla and embraced her. "I was worried about you, dear girl," he said. "I'm so relieved that you're safe." He looked over her shoulder and nodded to Harrigan. "Excellent work, Chief. Bring your prisoner inside, now, please."

# TWENTY-FIVE

McKibben put his arm around Kayla's shoulders and led her into the house. Harrigan held on to my elbow and steered me along behind them, and Howard followed. We entered a wide hallway and turned into a big square living room in the front corner of the house. A fire was blazing in the fieldstone fireplace, and Albert Cranston was sitting on the sofa holding a wineglass and gazing into the flames. When we entered the room, he looked up, smiled, put his glass on the coffee table, and stood.

Jeanette came in from a different room and waited there inside the doorway with her hands clasped in front of her and a frown on her face.

Kayla was hunching her shoulders and darting her eyes around. I guessed she was wondering what kind of punishment awaited her. I stared at her until she caught my eye. I gave my head a small shake and pursed my lips, a silent Shh. I figured, for her sake, the less she said the better.

She gave me a tiny nod, then looked away.

McKibben lifted his chin at Jeanette. "Poor Kayla is exhausted," he said to her. "Take her to her room, give her her medication, and help her get ready for bed, please."

Jeanette nodded. "Of course." She went over to Kayla, put her arm around her shoulders, murmured something into her ear, and herded her toward the doorway.

"Hang on there a minute," said Harrigan.

Jeanette stopped, turned, and arched her eyebrows at McKibben.

McKibben frowned at Harrigan, then turned and waved the back of his hand at Jeanette. "No, no. Go ahead. It's all right."

Jeanette shrugged and started to lead Kayla away.

"I asked you to wait, Miss," said Harrigan.

She stopped again and looked from Harrigan to McKibben and back to Harrigan.

"Please sit for a minute," Harrigan said to Jeanette and Kayla. "I need to ask you both a few questions."

Kayla sat on the sofa.

Jeanette hesitated, then sat beside Kayla.

McKibben turned and arched his eyebrows at Harrigan. "What are you doing?"

"I just have a couple questions."

"Of course." McKibben nodded. "You have your job to do. Which reminds me. I need you to fetch Mr. Coyne's automobile from Don's." He reached into his pocket, pulled out a set of keys, and tossed them to Harrigan.

The Chief snatched them out of the air and looked at them. Then he showed them to me. "These yours?"

"Yes," I said.

He turned to McKibben. "Where did you get these keys?"

McKibben frowned. "I beg your pardon?"

"I asked you where you got this set of car keys."

"I heard what you said," said McKibben. "I'm just not quite believing the insolence I thought I detected in your tone. Who do you think you're talking to?"

Harrigan looked at Jeanette. "Would you get Mr. Coyne's boots, please?"

Jeanette turned to McKibben with her eyebrows arched.

He nodded. "Get the boots. Then the Chief can take his prisoner to jail."

"I have a few questions," said Harrigan.

"Questions for whom?" said McKibben.

"For you."

"Really?"

Harrigan looked at me. "A friend of yours called me from Boston this morning."

"Horowitz, I hope," I said.

He nodded. "We had a long talk." He reached over and ran his hand over the top of my head. When he touched the bump where Cranston had whacked me with his sap, I winced.

"That hurt?" said Harrigan.

"Yes."

"There's a big bump there," he said. "How did you get it?"

"Albert Cranston hit me with a blackjack."

Harrigan pointed at Cranston. "Him?"

"Yes," I said.

Cranston smiled and shook his head.

Harrigan turned to Howard. "Take those cuffs off Mr. Coyne."

I turned my back to Howard, and he reached down and unlocked my handcuffs.

Then Harrigan pointed at Albert Cranston and McKibben and said, "Howard, handcuff those men."

Howard stepped forward. "Give me your right arm," he said to Cranston.

Cranston hesitated, then held out his right arm.

Howard snapped one cuff on Cranston's wrist. Then he looked at McKibben. "Give me your right arm."

"I beg your pardon?" said McKibben.

"Do it," said Harrigan.

Howard grabbed McKibben's right arm and snapped the other cuff onto it so that Cranston and McKibben's right wrists were attached to each other. That way, the two men had to stand beside each other facing in opposite directions. Clever. If one of them tried to run forward, the other would have to run backward to keep up.

Chief Harrigan smiled. "Judson McKibben and Albert Cranston," he said, "you are both under arrest for kidnapping, assault, and battery. We'll come up with some more charges pretty soon, I'm sure, but those will hold you for now." He recited their Miranda rights to McKibben and Cranston.

Jeanette came into the room carrying one of my boots in each hand. She stopped at the entryway and frowned.

Harrigan nodded to her. "Give Mr. Coyne his boots, then come over here."

I took my boots, went over to a chair, sat down, and wrestled them on over my wet socks. The effort exhausted me. All the adrenaline had drained out of me, and suddenly all I wanted to do was go to sleep.

Kayla came over and knelt in front of me. "Let me," she said. She laced up my boots and tied them for me, while I slumped back in the chair.

Harrigan was talking with Jeanette. Howard was holding his gun on McKibben and Cranston, who were standing awkwardly in the middle of the room.

When Kayla finished with my boots, she looked up at me and smiled. "How's that?"

"Wonderful," I said. "Thank you."

"Mr. Coyne," said Chief Harrigan. "I'd like you to come with us."

"Where?"

"Jeanette here has agreed to show us around. I want you to be able to verify that it's all voluntary." He turned to Howard. "Give the state cops a call, tell them they better come pick up some prisoners. Young lady," he said to Kayla, "you stay here, keep Howard company."

She shrugged. "Sure. Okay."

Harrigan and I followed Jeanette out into another room, through the kitchen, out the back door, across the driveway, and into the stable. Jeanette flicked on the lights and led us down the long packed-dirt aisle past the stalls, including the one where I'd been imprisoned.

At the far end of the stable, Jeanette stopped and pointed at one of the stalls. "In there," she said.

A strange orange flickered against the walls inside.

"Please open it," said Harrigan.

Jeanette unlatched the door and stepped back.

Harrigan went to the doorway and looked inside. "Have a look at this, Mr. Coyne."

I went over and stood beside him.

The stall glowed in the candlelight. The walls were painted pink. A life-sized oil painting of a girl — it was Ursula, Mc-Kibben's dead daughter, sitting on a horse wearing her formal riding outfit — hung in the center of the wall. The high window was hung with frilly white-and-pink polka-dot curtains. A flowery carpet covered the dirt floor. Against the walls there were little tables and bookcases covered with dozens of candles. Their flames wavered in the air currents, and they gave off a scent that reminded me of funeral parlors.

And in the center of the room were seven shiny wooden boxes laid out side by side on a lilac-colored cloth. It looked like satin. The boxes were about the size of shoe boxes. Cherry wood, I guessed. They had brass hinges and latches. An ivory cross was inlaid on the top of each box. Under each cross was a brass plate.

I stepped forward and bent to read the

inscription etched on one of the plates.

"Ursula," it read.

All of the other brass plates said "Ursula," too.

There were seven Ursula boxes in the stall. Caskets.

I turned to Jeanette. "Fetuses?"

She nodded. "Dead fetuses, yes." She turned to Harrigan. "You want to see the other?"

He nodded. "Yes."

At the end of the stable was a heavy wooden door. Jeanette took a key from her pocket, unlocked the big padlock, swung the door open, and we stepped outside.

A tin roof extended over the rear outside wall of the stable like a kind of lean-to. It appeared to be an area where hay bales once had been stacked and kept dry from rain and snow, but now it was bare ground covered with straw.

Three wooden crosses stuck up through the straw.

"Graves," said Harrigan.

Jeanette nodded. "Surrogates."

Harrigan bent over and pulled the straw away from one of the graves. The earth was mounded up a little. Otherwise, it was just bare dirt.

He straightened up, looked at me, and

shook his head. "Jesus," he said.

"Amen," I said.

We went back inside. McKibben and Cranston, their right wrists cuffed together, now sat side by side on a hassock, McKibben facing one way and Cranston facing the other. Howard and Kayla were sitting on the sofa watching them. Howard was holding his revolver in his lap.

Harrigan looked at Kayla. "Miss," he said, "how many other young women are here? Besides yourself, I mean?"

"Four others," she said.

"Would they all be asleep now?"

"What time is it?" she said.

He looked at his watch. "Almost midnight."

"They're asleep. All drugged up and out for the night."

"Can they be awakened?"

Kayla nodded. "Sure. They'll be groggy, but you could talk to them."

"Would you mind waking them up and asking them to get some clothes on and come down here, then?"

"Absolutely," she said.

She left the room.

Harrigan turned to Howard and said, "You doing okay?"

"All set," said Howard. "We're getting

along fine. State cops should be here pretty soon."

"Good," said Harrigan. He looked at Jeanette and me. "Let's go in the other room."

We went into an adjacent room. It was the same cozy room where I'd talked with McKibben the previous evening. Jeanette sat in the upholstered chair beside the fireplace. I sat on the sofa. Harrigan picked up a straight-backed wooden chair, took it to where Jeanette was sitting, and sat in front of her.

She looked up at him.

He put his hands on his thighs and leaned toward her. "Let's talk about what's been going on here. Okay?"

She nodded.

"I'm going to record what you have to say."

"Are you going to arrest me?"

"Maybe," he said. "It depends."

"If I talk to you? . . ."

"It is to your advantage to talk to me," he said. "Whether or not I have to arrest you. Okay?"

She nodded. "I want to tell you."

Harrigan took a small tape recorder from his coat pocket. He spoke into it and played it back. It was working. He stated his name and the date, time and place, said he was interviewing Jeanette Perkins, then put the recorder on the coffee table between himself and Jeanette.

I understood that my job was to witness the process, to verify that Harrigan had not coerced Jeanette's statement, and to be prepared to testify to that if necessary.

Harrigan recited her rights to Jeanette. She said she understood them.

Harrigan blew out a breath. "Okay, then. Let's start with you. You work here, right?"

"Against my will," she said. "I'm not —"

"Please start at the beginning," said Harrigan.

She nodded. "I'm a nurse," she said. "An RN. I met Judson McKibben when he was in medical school. I knew Greta — that was his wife — and I knew Ursula, their daughter, when she was little. I was married in those days, and we sometimes socialized with the McKibbens. That was in Cambridge. I liked them. Admired him, the work he was doing. He was a pioneer in stem-cell research in those days. Anyway, after I got divorced, I took a job in Chicago and pretty much lost touch with the McKibbens. I heard about Greta's death, and a while later I heard about what happened to Ursula. I wrote Jud cards each time, sent flowers.

When he called me and asked me if I'd join him here, share his work with him, it happened to come at a time when I was looking for something different. I'd worked in big impersonal institutions for too long. I was sick of doing everything by the book, of worrying about getting sued, of measuring a patient's life by a cost-benefit analysis. I was ready for something new and exciting and important."

"What did he say your work would be?" said Harrigan.

"He was setting up a laboratory," she said. "He intended to conduct some experiments." She hesitated. "He was interested in cloning."

Harrigan blinked. "Cloning?" He glanced at me. "Human cloning?"

"Therapeutic cloning," said Jeanette. She looked at me, then back at Harrigan. "Therapeutic cloning is a way to get stem cells. You clone an embryo, let its cells multiply for fourteen days, then harvest the stem cells. Dr. McKibben said he was very frustrated with the intrusion of politics and religion and general ignorance into the scientific laboratory, and all the people who wanted to believe that a two-week-old cloned embryo was a human life. Most of the medical people I know have the same frustrations. But Dr. McKibben said he wanted to do something about it. It's very exciting. You can do amazing things with stem cells. He told me he had private funding, so he didn't have to worry about all the regulations and restrictions that come with government grants and programs and agencies. There are no federal laws against therapeutic cloning, and no state laws in New Hampshire, either, although there's plenty of prejudice. Anyway, what he described was perfectly legal. He said he needed me to harvest eggs from volunteers, to collect and measure data, and to help him and Albert Cranston run the laboratory."

"Cranston," said Harrigan. "What was his job?"

"He's a biologist," she said. "He does the science."

"The eggs," said Harrigan, "they have to be fertilized, right?"

She nodded. "It's kind of technical. The nucleus is removed from the egg. Without its own genetic materials, it's called an ovacyte. Then cells from somebody else — they could be regular body cells, like skin or hair, or they could be stem cells, and they could be from a man or a woman, it wouldn't matter — they're inserted into the ovacyte. The ovacyte is kept alive for no more than fourteen days, and then its stem cells are harvested."

Harrigan was frowning. "Women volunteer to donate their eggs, is that right? That's all you need them for?"

"To do therapeutic cloning, yes."

"So why did you have these young women living here?"

Jeanette blew out a breath. "Because," she said, "it turned out that Dr. McKibben wasn't really interested in therapeutic cloning."

"He wasn't?"

She shook her head. "It's what he told me he wanted to do. It's how he described his work. It's what convinced me to come here to work with him. It's what I was interested in." She looked at Harrigan, then at me. "But it's not what he's doing."

"Reproductive cloning," I said. "Cloned human babies. All those Ursulas in their miniature caskets."

She nodded. "Yes. It turned out, that's all Dr. McKibben was interested in from the beginning. He wanted to create another Ursula."

"Clone his daughter?" said Harrigan.

Jeanette shrugged. "Yes."

"That's nuts."

407

"Of course it is," she said. "It's crazy and it's evil. But, if you think only about the science of it, it's very exciting. It hasn't been accomplished yet. But Dr. McKibben has pretty much proved it could be done."

"Except people die," said Harrigan.

She nodded. "Yes."

"Those graves out back," he said.

Jeanette nodded. "It's the embryos he cares about. We experimented with various drugs and therapies to keep the embryo healthy in utero until it could survive independently."

"Clomiphene," I said.

Both Harrigan and Jeanette turned and looked at me.

"That was one of the drugs, right?"

Jeanette nodded. "It's a common fertility drug. It's one of many that Dr. McKibben experimented with, in various combinations."

"They all didn't work, then," said Harrigan.

Jeanette shrugged. "Let me explain how he thinks, okay? Jud McKibben is a scientist. The human part of him died with his daughter. All that's left is the scientist. So as a scientist, he'll tell you, he sets up controlled situations, tries different things, and observes and measures the results.

That's what science is. Testing hypotheses in a laboratory. You experiment, and keep records, and process the data. As long as you are faithful to your protocols, there's no such thing as a failure. Whatever happens gives you information. When a subject dies? That's interesting, he says. He wants to know why. He'd study it and try to learn from it." She looked at Harrigan. "Do you understand?"

"Understand?" He shook his head. "I understand what you're saying. I guess I don't understand how anybody could take science to this extreme."

She shrugged. "He does. We found, for example, that cloned embryos tend to grow faster than natural embryos, and sometimes the surrogate's system — the girl's, I mean — it can't keep up with that rate of growth."

"Then," I said, "she dies."

"Yes," said Jeanette. "Sometimes they die."

Harrigan cleared his throat. "Did any of the, um, surrogates . . . those that didn't die, I mean . . . were they allowed to leave?"

"You mean," she said, "just leave us, go back to where they came from?"

He nodded.

"Oh, no," she said. "Dr. McKibben couldn't allow that."

Harrigan glanced at me. Then he said to

Jeanette, "These girls — your surrogates — where did they come from?"

"As far as I know," she said, "Albert Cranston recruited them. They were lost children, homeless girls, girls who were wasting their lives. They came here. We cleaned them up, fed them, made them healthy. The doctor said we were giving purpose and meaning to their lives."

"You gave them drugs to keep them in line," said Harrigan.

She nodded.

"Can I ask a couple questions?" I said to Harrigan.

"About what?"

"About Dana Wetherbee."

He nodded. "Go ahead." For the benefit of the tape, he said, "Brady Coyne is going to ask some questions."

I turned to Jeanette. "Was a girl by the name of Dana Wetherbee here?"

"Yes." She smiled. "Dana got away."

"How did she manage that?"

"I helped her," said Jeanette. "It's the one decent thing I've done since I've been here."

"You helped her?" I said.

"She was pregnant." Jeanette smiled. "She was starting to think of herself as a mother. She was becoming emotionally involved with her — her embryo. She wanted to have

410

her baby. I— it was risky. If the doctor finds out I helped her . . ."

"It won't matter," said Harrigan. "He can't do anything to you."

She shook her head. "I'm not sure I'll ever believe that. That he has no control over me."

"Tell us about how Dana escaped."

"She kept talking about having her baby. She was a very sweet girl. So I sneaked her into the truck one day when I was going out for groceries. I drove her to the bus stop in Hardwick — that's the next town south of here — and gave her some money. She said she knew somebody in Boston who could help her."

"That was Evie," I said to Harrigan. "My girlfriend."

He nodded.

"Dana found her way to my house one snowy night a couple weeks ago," I said to Jeanette. "She bled to death in the snow in my backyard."

Her eyes brimmed with tears. "I was hoping . . ."

"Did you mail a Christmas card for Dana?"

She nodded.

"McKibben doesn't know about this?" I said.

"If he knew," she said, "he'd kill me."

"So you don't approve of what he was doing here," I said.

She looked at me and smiled quickly. "Approve? Hardly. I'm a nurse. I believe in life."

"Why did you stay, then?"

"I had no choice."

"He would've killed you?" I said.

She nodded. "Without any qualms. For science. He'd kill anybody who threatened what he was doing."

"We'll talk some more," said Harrigan. He shut off the tape recorder. "Let's go, join the others. Jeanette do you know where Mr. Coyne's coat and other belongings are?"

"I'll get them," she said.

Harrigan and I went into the living room. Howard was still sitting there watching his prisoners. McKibben and Cranston sat stoically, cuffed at the wrists, staring in opposite directions.

"Everything okay?" said Harrigan.

"Dandy," said Howard.

Jeanette came into the room. She had my parka draped over her arms. "Here's your coat," she said.

I took it from her. And then I saw the gun. My gun. She was holding my Smith & Wesson .38 Chiefs Special.

She went over to where Judson McKibben

412

was sitting. "You turned me into a monster," she said. "I'll never forgive you."

He smiled up at her. "I turned you into a good scientist," he said. "You should thank me."

"I'll curse you forever." She raised the gun, gripped it in both hands, and aimed it at McKibben's face.

"Jeanette," said Harrigan quietly. "Please."

She was glaring at McKibben. Her hands were trembling.

After a moment — it was probably just a few seconds, but it seemed like a long time — she lowered the gun and let it fall to the floor.

Howard went over and picked it up.

Harrigan put his arm around Jeanette's shoulders. "That would have been a very stupid thing to do."

She shook her head. "I expect I'll forever regret not pulling the trigger."

Right then a siren sounded outside, very close. A moment later two uniformed state troopers came bursting in, followed by a man in a suit who I assumed was a detective.

Harrigan talked with the detective for a few minutes. Then the state cops uncuffed McKibben and Cranston, recuffed them separately, and marched them out of the house.

The detective pulled out his cell phone and wandered into an adjoining room.

A minute later, Kayla came into the room. Four other young women shambled along behind her. They were rubbing their eyes and yawning and whispering to each other.

Harrigan swept his arm around the room, taking in the furniture and the girls. "Please sit down," he said. "All of you. Sorry to bother your sleep. Kayla, you want to make some coffee? It looks like we're going to be up for a while here. We've got to talk with all of you."

"Sure," she said. She left the room. One of the other girls went with her. The other three found seats in the living room. They sat there primly, their knees pressed together, staring down at the floor. They showed no interest in me or Jeanette or Nate Harrigan or Howard.

It was going to be a long night.

"You mind if I make a call?" I said to Harrigan.

He shrugged. "Go ahead."

I found a phone in the hallway. Evie answered on the first ring, and when I said, "Hi, honey," she said, "Jesus Christ, Brady. Are you all right? What the hell is going on?

You're such a bastard. I expected you to be home hours ago, and you didn't call, and all I could think. . . ." And then she sobbed, and I realized she'd been crying from the beginning.

"I'm fine," I said. "I'm sorry you were worried. Everything's all right. It's a long story. I'll tell you when I get home."

I heard her blow out a quick, hard breath. "I imagined you driving off the side of a mountain in a blizzard," she said. "It was very vivid. They didn't find you until springtime."

"I imagined that, too," I said. "But it didn't happen."

"Where are you?"

"I'm still in Churchill."

"You haven't even left yet?"

"I got kind of tied up here."

"I admit," she said, "I'm very angry with you. Before I was worried. Now I'm totally pissed. I know it's irrational. I can't help it. If you don't like it, tough."

"I found out all about Dana Wetherbee," I said.

"Tell me when you get home."

"Okay."

"When will that be?"

"Tomorrow," I said. "I can't leave quite yet. But I'll be home tomorrow."

"Do you promise?"

"I promise."

"I intend to stay angry at least until you get here."

"I understand."

"Were you in danger?"

"A little," I said.

"Did you get hurt?"

"I picked up a few bruises."

"I knew it," she said. "You almost died, right?"

"Let's not be dramatic about it."

"Hereafter," she said, "you've got to promise me you'll just take care of your clients and go fly fishing and stop snooping around and getting in trouble and nearly dying. Okay? Promise?"

"I don't know," I said.

"Meaning no . . . right?"

"That's a hard promise to make, babe."

"You could humor me, you know."

"I respect you too much to try to humor you," I said.

Evie didn't say anything.

"You planning to be angry for a while?" I said.

"Bet your ass."

"Until I get home, huh?"

"At least."

"Then you'll probably want to make love with me."

"Yeah," she said. "Probably."

# ABOUT THE AUTHOR

**William G. Tapply** is the author of more than twenty books of crime fiction, most recently *Nervous Water* and the forthcoming *Gray Ghost,* as well as numerous books on fishing and wildlife. The writer-in-residence at Clark University, Tapply lives with his wife, novelist Vicki Stiefel, in Hancock, New Hampshire. Visit the author's Web site at www.williamgtapply.com.